THE SPACE
BETWEEN

THE SPACE BETWEEN

Brenna Yovanoff

razOr
bill

AN IMPRINT OF PENGUIN GROUP (USA) INC

The Space Between

RAZORBILL

Published by the Penguin Group
Penguin Young Readers Group
345 Hudson Street, New York, New York 10014, U.S.A.
Penguin Group (USA) Inc., 375 Hudson Street, New York, New York 10014, U.S.A.
Penguin Group (Canada), 90 Eglinton Avenue East, Suite 700, Toronto, Ontario,
Canada M4P 2Y3 (a division of Pearson Penguin Canada Inc.)
Penguin Books Ltd, 80 Strand, London WC2R 0RL, England
Penguin Ireland, 25 St Stephen's Green, Dublin 2, Ireland (a division of Penguin Books Ltd)
Penguin Group (Australia), 250 Camberwell Road, Camberwell, Victoria 3124,
Australia (a division of Pearson Australia Group Pty Ltd)
Penguin Books India Pvt Ltd, 11 Community Centre,
Panchsheel Park, New Delhi – 110 017, India
Penguin Group (NZ), 67 Apollo Drive, Rosedale, Auckland 0632, New Zealand
(a division of Pearson New Zealand Ltd)
Penguin Books (South Africa) (Pty) Ltd, 24 Sturdee Avenue, Rosebank,
Johannesburg 2196, South Africa

Penguin Books Ltd, Registered Offices: 80 Strand, London WC2R 0RL, England

10 9 8 7 6 5 4 3 2 1

First published in hardcover by Razorbill 2011
Published in this edition 2012

Copyright © 2011 Brenna Yovanoff

ISBN 978-1-59514-483-6

Printed in the United States of America

ALWAYS LEARNING

PEARSON

THIS BOOK IS FOR MY FAMILY—
each and every one of you.

PART ONE

HELL

PROLOGUE

Once, my mother told a whole host of angels that she'd rather die than go back to a man she didn't love.

This was a long time ago, before famine or war or the combustion engine. Before my father fell from grace and killed a thousand divine messengers on the way down. Back then, my mother was young and wild. She had another life.

❋ ❋ ❋

God made Adam out of dirt, complete with a soul, and a heart in his chest, and that was the first man. There was a garden filled with beasts, where Adam lived alone.

Then, because it wasn't good for man to be alone, God made Lilith. And that was the first mistake. She came to Adam across a meadow delirious with flowers and he was in love.

She didn't love him back.

He didn't see the darkness in her. He was young and thought that she could change. My father says that's just what happens when you're young, but I still think Adam should have known. He should have seen it in her eyes, seen the truth in her jagged fingernails. He should have known you can't change a girl with iron teeth.

They lived together in the Garden, and Adam was happy. Lilith, though, was meant for fiercer places. When Adam tried to tame her, she fought him. She wasn't made to be told how to behave or what to do. When she left, she did it calmly. She simply stood up and walked away. She belonged in the wilds, outside the Garden, and so she stayed, night after night, hovering on a black beach beside a sea like polished glass.

There was no reason to go back to Adam. She didn't miss him. She thought she could leave behind their entire life together, and that was her mistake.

My brother was born on a bed of black stones, under a blood-red moon. Our mother named him Ohbrin, a name of mysteries, in a language only she knew. He was like her in almost every way, with her sleek black hair and gray eyes, but he laughed sometimes and smiled up at her. She knew she wasn't meant to raise a child, and she took him back to show Adam a son whose smile was so like his own.

But in the Garden, things had changed. Adam sat beneath a strange, spreading tree and there was a strange woman beside him, heavy and round, made from a piece of Adam's own body, so she could never stand up and wander away.

When Lilith showed him the baby in her arms, he took one look and turned away. He said he didn't want him. Didn't want his own child.

Before, when Lilith left, she'd been stony and remote.

Now, she trembled, outraged that a man could refuse his son. She spit in Adam's face and cursed the day she ever saw him. It was the day she'd been born.

Then she took Obie and left, pelting away through the dark.

✳   ✳   ✳

In the dark is where she met my father.

THE GARDEN
CHAPTER ONE

I'm watching *North by Northwest* when the picture goes out on the TV. It's at the part where Thornhill is being chased by the airplane and the scene is very tense. Then the sound cuts off abruptly and Cary Grant dissolves into a sea of tiny dots.

My mother's silhouette appears in the glass, dim and faceless. When she speaks, her voice comes from far away, distorted by the hiss of static. "I need you to come up here."

She vanishes again before I can answer and the picture doesn't come back. I know I should go up and see what she wants, but just for now, I don't move.

✳   ✳   ✳

In Hell, we tell our stories on the surface of things. The histories are forged a piece at a time, hammered on posts and pillars, pounded into the tiled streets. The Spire building, where I've lived my whole life, is a celebration of the deeds of my family.

The stairs to the roof are polished to a high shine, carved with engravings of the fallen army. At the top, I push open the little gate and step into the courtyard. Lilith's garden is a squirming mass of silver flowers and metal vines. My father built it for her. Every leaf and branch is handmade.

She's sitting with her back to me, on a filigree bench beside a man who isn't Lucifer. Her hair has slipped loose from its combs, spilling in a black curtain over her shoulders. Her dress is long, red as embers, and open all the way down the back. Her skin is blinding white.

"Come in," she calls without looking in my direction. "Don't hover."

Her companion glances at me and gets to his feet. The heels of his boots are heavy, carved with twin crocodiles, and they clang like bells on the tile roof.

"Look who it is," he says, smiling broadly, showing gray teeth filed to points. I can tell he doesn't know my name.

"Daphne," my mother says, sighing like the word has unbearable weight. Like two syllables can contain a whole tragedy. Then she turns to her latest admirer. She doesn't even say anything, just lifts a hand and he knows it's time to go.

When we're alone, she motions me to sit down. The bench is small and we sit side by side, uncomfortably close.

"I think you should start spending more time with your sisters," she tells me in a cool, offhand voice, like she's telling me that smoke rises.

It isn't what I expected and I don't answer right away.

She says *sisters*, but really, she's talking about the Lilim. She says *more*, which implies that I spend any time with them at all. They might look like me, but their fathers are all minor demons like the one my mother just dismissed.

7

"Why?" I say, trying to sound just as indifferent as she does. "I'm nothing like them."

"Of course you are," she says without looking at me.

She stares out at the shining garden. Her eyes are silver-gray, flat and pale. Our faces bear more than a passing resemblance, but my eyes are dark like my father's.

I don't point out all the things that set me apart from my sisters and would be obvious if she ever really looked. Like my smooth, translucent fingernails and that fact that I can talk about something besides what it's like to prowl around on Earth, tricking men into offering themselves up for nothing.

"How do you know what I'm like?"

"Smile for me," she says, like it will prove something.

I don't smile. My teeth are my most striking feature, but my mother won't see it. My whole mouth is full of enamel, white like my father's, but she's only interested in the flaws—the twin metal points of my dogteeth, which prove, more than my colorless skin or my black hair, that I'm hers.

"Bad blood will out," she says, as though I've illustrated her point. The look she gives me is triumphant. It says that bad blood is the only kind of blood worth mentioning.

What my parents have is nothing like the crumbling marriages in movies. There are no thrown dishes, no tears or arguments, just Lilith's endless supply of lovers, and all the ways that she can slash at my father without even leaving the rooftop garden. If I start tagging around after the Lilim, then I'm just another one of those ways. He might not care what her other children do, but he's less cavalier about his own daughters.

"I'm not going to go do something common so you can gloat about it," I tell her. "If you're mad at him, that's got nothing to do with me."

Lilith acts like she hasn't heard. She crouches on the bench, staring down at a huge silver sundial set into the roof at her feet, intent on something I can't see.

My father gave her six daughters before me and all of them are gifted with some kind of sight. They were all born a long time ago, and maybe that's why. The world was new and raw, still full of magic. Or maybe it's just that I was born after my parents stopped loving each other.

The face of the sundial is as smooth as a mirror, and Lilith watches it the same way I'd watch the television. She sees the world in flashes, tiny scenes in every reflective surface. After the Fall and the temptation in the Garden, she and my father were punished, exiled to Pandemonium, and now this is the only way she can even pretend to visit Earth.

She holds perfectly still, ignoring the vines that writhe up from the flower beds, creeping over the bench, winding themselves around her ankles and her wrists.

The murals on the roof are all about the war for Heaven and the Fall. Lucifer, the vengeful outcast and fallen revolutionary—villain of the deepest dye. Lilith, standing alone on the black stone beach. She was pale and remote, the beautiful demoness. He was proud but wounded and saw himself in her.

Now, she's sitting in a metal garden, in a place she can never leave, and my father is somewhere in a gleaming skyscraper, wearing a tailored suit and overseeing an empire. She blames him for everything.

Below us, the city shines silver, as highly polished as a wish. The streets sprawl out in complicated spirals, winding between glossy buildings. Far out at the center, the Pit glows red with the heat of the furnace.

"I'm not going," I say.

Lilith smiles into the face of the sundial. "Don't be ridiculous. You love Earth."

For a moment, I just look at her. I like paper flowers and Cary Grant movies. I like the stories my brother Obie tells when he comes home after one of his jobs. I can't say that I like Earth, because I've never been there.

Life outside of Pandemonium is for girls like the Lilim, girls who crave things, while I'd like to think my own interest in the world is merely scholarly. A fascination for things rather than people. I keep hoping for some piece of undeniable proof that I'm nothing like my sisters.

If I had the gift of sight, even a little—the power to see the future or divine people's secrets in a sheet of polished metal—it would show I was meant for something else. But sometimes, especially when the phonograph is playing love songs or James Dean is on TV, I feel strangely hollow, gripped by a want that seems to sit inside my bones, and then I suspect I'm just like the rest of them. Made for preying.

"Are you afraid of Earth?" Lilith says, like it's a challenge. "Don't be afraid. You might have weak, worthless teeth like your father, but you have my blood."

Demon blood is powerful, but hard to predict. On Earth, it can burst into flames or eat through the floor like acid. Some demons find that they can escape through tiny cracks or vanish in a flurry of shadows, and others have skin that can't be cut and bones that can't be broken. They eat glass and jump from buildings and climb straight up the walls.

In Pandemonium though, those things don't matter. Down in the Pit, the damned might shriek and suffer, but we can't feel a thing. The blood only matters on Earth, because it gives us an advantage against Azrael.

He's there on the wall with the rest of the archangels, looking righteous, but not beautiful. His features are ruined by a thin, ugly mouth, eyes gouged so deep they look black. They seem to bore into me and I prefer the engraving of the angel Michael. Even with his spear leveled at my father's chest, he seems noble. Azrael looks like he wants to burn down everyone.

"You don't have to worry about *him*," my mother says, turning to follow my gaze. "He doesn't waste his time on girls like you, as long as they don't make trouble or stay too long on Earth."

I'm not studying him though but the engraving of his monstrous beast, Dark Dreadful. She looks like a woman, but sharp-clawed, gaunt, and towering. She does his killing for him because demons are notoriously difficult to destroy. The stories say she'll tear you open and drink your blood to take away your power, then peel away your skin and string your bones to make garlands.

11

"He won't bother you, as long as you don't stay," Lilith says again, like the thing I'm scared of is a monster carved on a wall and not the thought of becoming my sisters. "Azrael might do everything he can to keep us from infesting Earth, but he can't be bothered with the occasional visitor."

In his portrait, he looks proud and cruel. Behind him, Dark Dreadful towers above a heap of bodies. Her dress is ragged, covered in bones and strands of teeth, braided hanks of hair.

I've seen the picture so many times before, but now it bothers me and I sit looking up at it, looking up at Dark Dreadful, and the vengeful face of Azrael. Like something is getting closer and I just don't see it yet.

OBIE
CHAPTER TWO

My mother finally dismisses me, and I go back my room. The artisans in the Pit have closed the doors to the furnace to let their newest batch of sheet metal cool and the sky is a deep, smoky gray.

Now, with the city dark, I can take out all my pictures and my books and charms and tiny glass figurines—all my things from Earth—and they won't melt or burn up like they would if the furnace was at full blaze. My favorite artifacts are delicate and bright—paper streamers and tiny dolls with satin dresses and plastic wings. In the twilight, my whole room is cluttered with trinkets.

I'm sitting on the couch with my feet pulled up, playing with a little snow globe that Obie got in Prague. Inside is a figure of a dancer, standing under a leafless tree. When I shake it, white flakes swirl down around her. The only light is flickering from my television, making everything waver.

It's hard to know what to do about my mother. The fact is, even when I'm so sure she's wrong, her voice has the ring of authority. I want to think I'm good for more than creeping around Earth like my sisters do. I want *her* to think that. Mostly, I just want to be good for something.

I see the shadow behind me reflected in the globe before I hear Obie's footsteps. When I look around, my brother is standing just inside the doorway.

He's dressed like the medical staff at a hospital, in elastic-waisted pants and a short-sleeved smock with no buttons. The whole outfit is pale green and looks like pajamas.

"Hey," he says. "Do you have a minute?"

I nod, cradling the snow globe in both hands.

It's a strange question—an Earth question, because there, a minute means something. There are no minutes here and time is a vast, looping thing.

"I brought you a bus schedule," he says, tossing a folded paper booklet onto the couch beside me. "It's only for a local line, but I thought you might like the colors."

Against the backdrop of my room, filled with wind chimes and mechanical toys, he is Easter-egg green, like he belongs here. Under the scrubs though, he's as colorless as I am, all black hair and white skin.

"Thanks," I say, thumbing through the pages so they riffle one way, then the other. Each route is marked in a different shade.

Like most of the demon men, Obie works in various cities all across the world, but he doesn't trade in suffering like they do. When it became clear that he wasn't suited for Collections, my father took pity on him and now Obie is the sole employee of the Department of Good Works. It's a better job than collecting, although most of the men would disagree. When faced with a choice, most of them would rather reap than save.

There's a dark smudge on the front of Obie's shirt, high up, near the sleeve. It's small—asymmetrical—and I want to ask where it came from, if someone was bleeding. It would be a silly question, though. In Obie's line of work, someone is always bleeding.

The people he's assigned to help are the half-human children of fallen angels. They're called Lost Ones, and most of them earn the title. I can't remember an assignment Obie's had that hasn't involved a hospital or a prison or an institution. Lost Ones are always in the process of self-destructing.

He picks his way toward me, stepping around a brass floor lamp and a stack of children's picture books. He drops onto the footstool, facing me with his hands clasped between his knees.

I watch him through the dome of the snow globe. It warps him, but I can still pick out individual features. Mouth like mine. Chin and cheekbones and hair like mine. Eyes, not.

"I'm leaving," he says suddenly. He says it like he expects me to argue, but the announcement isn't really worth remarking on. He leaves all the time.

"If you're going to be anywhere near Malta, can you get me a piece of Gozitan lace?"

Obie plucks at one of the braided tassels on the footstool. Then he shakes his head. "Leaving," he says again. "Daphne, I'm not coming back."

And for a moment I just sit, letting the snow globe dangle in my hand. "What are you talking about?"

He looks away and bows his head. "I can't stay here anymore. I'm just . . . it's too hard, living here. Pretending like I belong."

And for a moment, I think I understand what it is that makes him so convinced he shouldn't be here. His father was an actual man, real flesh, real blood, with a soul and a heart. Virtuous. Mine used to be a star, before he became the Devil.

Then Obie glances up and I wonder how I could have doubted his place in Pandemonium. His eyes are pale gray. He looks incredibly like our mother.

"It's not pretend," I say. "This is home."

He nods, but his gaze is unfocused, like he's thinking of something else. "Sometimes things change."

But the fundamental law of Pandemonium is stasis. Nothing changes. "*How*?" I say. "How is that possible?"

"I'm in love," he tells me, so calmly and so simply that at first, I don't grasp the meaning. "Her name's Elizabeth and she's smart and beautiful, and she understands me. She's one of the Lost Ones, and she knows exactly what it's like to be half-human."

Love is deceitful. It's mysterious and impossible. Just watching Lilith should have been enough to make us fully aware that it will never happen to us.

"Did you talk to Mom about this?"

He shakes his head, staring down at the carpet. "I'm not going to tell her."

I sit on the couch, looking at Obie, who is the only brother I have—my mother's miracle, and the one solitary reason she ever went back to the Garden at all. Leaving.

My voice comes out in a whisper. "She's going to be so mad at you."

"Look," he says, and for the first time, he sounds truly sad. "Do you think I *want* to hurt her? I don't want to leave this way, but I don't really have a choice. She's not going to understand."

"She'll find out." The idea of doing anything in secret is hopeless where Lilith is concerned. This is the consequence of having a mother who sees through mirrors. She finds out everything.

"I know. But at least this way, I can leave without causing a scene—without her trying to stop me. You wouldn't understand. You're so *good*, Daphne. I can't be what she wants me to be."

Demons go to Earth. I know this. They go to Earth, but not to live. Not to stay there. Because although they might be perfectly happy to work and play and feed there, no one just decides to trade the spectacle and the glory of Pandemonium for the danger of a place where an avenging angel wants to kill you just for existing.

"What's it like there?" I ask, knowing he won't tell me the truth. *What's it like there*, when what I really want to know is, *why are you leaving?*

He turns so I can't see his face. "It's nice. When I'm there, I don't feel like there's something wrong with me all

17

the time. It's easier to be myself there. It's easier not to be noticed."

But he's not even that remarkable. His father may have been a mortal man, human to the core, but down in the crowded streets of Pandemonium, Obie looks just like everybody else.

"It's not pretend," I say again. "It's not like you just got here by accident. You belong with us."

Obie's head is still down. His expression is pensive and he's staring at the snow globe in my hands. "I don't think anyone belongs here."

He tells me this like he knows it for sure, knows so much more than I do. I've never left the city. How can I argue? My carpet is so silver in the low light that it looks like a lake of metal.

He leans toward me, reaching for the snow globe, and I let him take it. When he shakes it, fake snow powders down. The dancer only stands there, motionless under her tree. "Daphne," he says. "This is something I have to do."

"Don't you even care that it's *dangerous*? What about Azrael?"

Obie smiles and it's soft and faraway. "Sometimes the danger doesn't matter. I'm leaving a place I can't stand, for a life I want more than anything. I'm in love," he says again, like he's pleading with me to understand.

But my brother is an expert at loving everything—even the broken things. I'm not even sure I know what love is.

He sighs and gets to his feet, offering me the snow globe.

"You can have it," I tell him. It comes out sounding small and uncertain, like I'm asking a question.

I want him to have something to take with him, but the snow globe isn't even a sentimental representation of myself. He's the one who gave it to me. So maybe it's just something to remind him that once, when he lived in Pandemonium, he had a sister he cared about.

He drops the globe into the pocket of his scrubs.

"I'll see you again," he says and at first I think he means this isn't permanent, that he'll come back. But as he starts for the door, he turns back and adds, "I still have to get some stuff together before I go."

I nod.

Out my window, the spires of the high-rises look like giant fingers, reaching. My brother is walking out of the room, and I want so badly to keep him here.

I hug my knees and stare straight ahead. The room is as dim as it ever gets and my collection of paper flowers and glass chimes doesn't seem so beautiful anymore. I rest my forehead on my arms and close my eyes. Maybe I don't know about love or belonging, but I'm terribly sure that if I don't find a way to stop him from leaving, Obie will die.

THE MUSEUM
CHAPTER THREE

In all of Hell, there's only one person my mother hates more than she hates my father.

A long time ago, Beelzebub was a lieutenant in the army of the fallen, and even after millennia, he's still my father's closest friend. Now he's in charge of the Collections Department, which handles the reaping of souls. He knows more about Earth than anyone else in Pandemonium.

Someone needs to talk Obie out of what he's about to do, and Beelzebub is the only person I can think of who might be able to.

I push the television into its insulated cupboard. After a few mishaps, I've learned to be careful.

Down in the street, the city doesn't look so clean. The roads are paved with sheets of steel, seamed and bolted, while from the roof, they look like one unbroken stream of silver, flowing off in all directions.

The museum is situated on a craggy little hill of brimstone, above one of the many plazas. It's huge and windowless, built entirely from the same heat-resistant material as my insulated drawers.

At the entrance, I press my hand to the pass panel. The entrance to the museum will only open during twilight, when the furnace is cold. I say *"musca domestica"* and wait for the door to unseal.

Inside, the main gallery is immense, filled with a fleet of shelves that seems to go on for acres. Some of them are made of glass or wood, brought in from Earth when the furnace was closed, but most of them were made here, forged in the Pit. They're crowded with relics from past assignments, an item for every soul that's ever passed through Collections. It's the source of all my best toys, aside from the pamphlets and souvenirs that Obie sometimes brings me.

There's a whole aisle devoted to elaborate bottles of perfume and tiny vials of cologne and aromatic oils. The museum is the only place in the city where we can feel the jab of a pin or smell the delicate fragrance of Chanel or *eau de fleurs*. The scents are faint, and Beelzebub says that on Earth, sensations like smell and touch are a thousand times stronger, but this is as close as the artisans could come to creating an environment that mimics the quality of the atmosphere there.

His office is at the back and to reach it, I have to make my way through rows filled with leather-bound books, delicate table lamps with ceramic bases and painted silk shades—all these things that aren't native to Pandemonium. Usually, I'd take the time to admire the artifacts, but now I just cut straight through the gallery without stopping.

When I step into the office, Beelzebub is at his desk, hunched over the blotter. He's sorting through a box of small, shiny toys, oblivious to the cloud of flies that whine around his head.

"Daphne," he says with his back to me. It's just a parlor trick, but I can never figure out how he always knows it's me. "Did you let something else burn up? If you wrecked the TV, you're out of luck. I'm not giving you another one."

With a flourish, he swings around in his chair, turning his hands palm up. In them is a small mechanical bird, wings beating rapidly. When he flicks the bird with a forefinger, it rises above us in a flurry of clockwork to perch somewhere in the upper shelves.

I suspect one of the reasons my mother hates him is because he looks how an angel is supposed to look. Under his cloud of flies, his hair is a dark golden blond and his eyes are pale, but not the silvery-pale of demons. Here, the color is nearly transparent, but in sunlight I think it might look blue.

The cloud of flies is less angelic. When Collections was first conceived, Beelzebub was the only employee and he reaped the casualties of entire armies by himself. He spent centuries wading across battlefields, gathering up the dead, and the flies came too. Now they swarm around his head, circling him like a halo.

In Pandemonium, everything has a kind of permanence. I've seen demons come in through the terminal with steel spikes driven through their skin or covered in blood, and those spikes or that blood becomes their condition. Even little things—the state of your hair, the clothes you happen to be wearing—can become an intrinsic part of you if the circumstances surrounding them are powerful enough. Beelzebub's flies are a constant reminder of who he is and where he comes from.

He pushes back his chair and goes across to the wardrobe, and I stand in the doorway, watching. "I need to talk to you about something."

Running his fingers along a row of black suit coats, he selects one that looks like twenty he just ignored and tosses it over the back of his chair. "I'm just on my way out," he says, gesturing apologetically toward the coat. "Do you want to tell me about it while I get ready?"

I nod, even though I'm still thinking how to divulge what's worrying me. "Where are you going?"

"Belgrade. Could you hand me the nine millimeter?"

On the far side of the office is Beelzebub's private arsenal. Most of the collections agents carry weapons, but they get their gear standard-issue from the arms depot. All of Beelzebub's guns are custom-made.

I open the munitions cabinet and lift the nine from its place between the Mauser and the .45. Along the barrel are stamped the words, JUDGE NOT, LEST YE BE JUDGED. Beelzebub is sitting at the desk, feeding cartridges into a magazine. When I pass the gun to him, it looks like it belongs in his hand.

I point to the inscription on the barrel. "Isn't that hypocritical?"

That makes him smile. "No, it's ironic. I have been judged, and I've been found lacking." He holds up the gun and slides the magazine into the well. "And now, I'm going forth to do some judging of my own."

I pull up a heavy leather chair and sit down across from him, leaning my elbows on the desk. "If a demon decided to stay on Earth, what would happen?" I say, attempting to sound casual.

He scratches his temple with the barrel of the nine. "They would probably burn down a holy monument or two, demand a few sacrifices, terrorize some nuns, maybe find a nice house in the suburbs, and after awhile, they would get very bored. Why, are you thinking of making the move?"

He raises his eyebrows like he expects me to laugh, then looks mildly confused when I don't.

"Can you tell me anything about Azrael?"

That makes him smile. "You know all those old horror stories already—probably better than I do. Personally, I like the one where he makes a magic carpet out of the skins of seven highly unfortunate smoke demons and flies away into the night like a giant bat."

"I don't mean the fables," I say. "I need to hear the real stuff."

Beelzebub gives me a questioning look. Then he checks the nine and snaps it into his shoulder holster. "I knew him, you know—back when we were just kids. Difficult to get along with, but honest. He likes mandates and rules, big on keeping his word. Why the sudden fascination?"

For just a moment, I feel lost, unsure of how to proceed. I won't be able to explain Obie's choice the way he could. It will sound worse when I say it. But maybe I want it to sound worse. I want it to sound worth preventing. Beelzebub has abandoned his box of ammunition and is watching me with interest. If anyone will know what to do, it will be him.

"I'm worried about my brother," I say. "He's about to do something really reckless—you need to talk to him."

With great deliberation, Beelzebub takes a windup dog from the pile of toys, twisting the key between his fingers. "Is it one of those reckless things that's just bound to happen once in a while, or is it the kind of reckless thing I should probably hear more about?"

"He's leaving Pandemonium to live on Earth. He says he's in love."

I expect this revelation to be at least a little shocking, but Beelzebub only leans back in his chair, fidgeting with the toy dog. "Well, I can't pretend I haven't been there a few times. It's not the wisest thing—love—but when it happens, there's not a lot you can do to stop it. Sometimes you just have to soldier on through."

His smile is nostalgic and far away, but I can't quite believe it. The idea of Beelzebub breaking rules out of love for a human woman is ridiculous. He's too clean, and much too reasonable.

"That's not even the most reckless part, though," I say, trying to convey the gravity of the situation. "I think he wants to be human. He's leaving now, as soon as possible, not even telling Lilith or anything. You need to talk him out of it."

Beelzebub doesn't answer right away. He sets the dog

loose, letting it trundle around the desktop. The tiny buzzing of its motor doesn't quite drown out the buzzing of his flies. "And you're sure he's made up his mind?"

"All I know is that he told me he wasn't coming back. He sounded like he meant it."

Beelzebub bows his head, considering his folded hands. Then he looks up. "I could talk to him, but I don't think it would make a difference."

"Why not, though? You're in charge of the whole department—everything that happens on Earth is approved by *you*. He has to listen to you."

That makes him laugh, shaking his head. "You give me far too much credit as a dictator." Then his expression turns solemn. "It would be different if we were talking about new weapons regulations or who gets what job, but you can't just sit down and talk someone out of being in love."

I sit in silence, watching as the little toy dog buzzes on the desk between us.

"You have to let him go," Beelzebub says, and he says it with something like tenderness. "What you have to understand is that this is his life, and he's the one who has to live it. People make decisions, and maybe you don't always agree, but those choices are still their own."

"He doesn't belong there, though. He even *looks* just like the rest of us."

Beelzebub looks down at me, leaning his elbows on the blotter. "He *acts* human, Daphne. He can yearn for Earth and be in love and do the job he does because he *feels* human, and that's what you have to understand. You're never going to talk someone out of how they feel."

Beelzebub has a knack for seeing things as they are, without the complications of bias or attachment. All my life, I've trusted him to know the answers. But right now, I'm so scared that he's wrong.

WATER
CHAPTER FOUR

When I leave the museum, the plaza is empty. The center of the square is tiled in the shape of a huge snake, coiling around itself in a spiral. In the Pit, they've just closed the furnace. The sky is still orange, but cooling rapidly, and the sound of hammering tapers off. Everything is silent.

Then Obie calls my name and I turn, following his voice to the road above the plaza. He's holding a metal suitcase, and it looks too small to be the only property of someone leaving home for the last time. He's still wearing the green scrubs.

He comes over to the top of the little flight of steps. "Hey, it's time for me to go."

"So soon?" I ask, not ready to face the thing that wasn't supposed to happen. I'd just assumed Beelzebub would be the one to stop him, and now that he won't, I don't know what to do.

"Come on, walk me to the terminal." Obie gives the suitcase a little shake and smiles. "I've still got your snow globe."

When he offers me his hand, I climb the steps to stand beside him.

We follow the main road, making our way through the city, toward the terminal. I have so many things to say, but I don't speak and neither does he. I'm trying to remember everything about this moment—the soft, billowing sky and the way the smoke looks, hanging low over the Pit. I keep glancing at his profile, knowing that this might be the last time I ever see him.

At the Pit, we walk along the edge until we come to the bridge, then start across. The bridge is as wide as a river and black with soot, arching over the forges. The artisans work below, in the red glare of the foundry, where the heat makes the air look like water.

As we cross the bridge, I lean close to the railing and look down. The Hoard is down there, filling the outer edge of the Pit, all the souls knocking together with their slack faces and their dead eyes. They come into the city thrashing and shrieking, but it doesn't last long. After the pain demons have gotten their fill, the Hoard goes blank and silent. From so high up, I can only see the tops of their heads, gray with the soot. They seem to go on forever.

We leave the bridge behind and continue along the street that leads to the terminal. Ahead of us, the entrance is more crowded than usual, bodies packed shoulder to shoulder. Everyone is talking in low, excited voices.

Obie shoves through the mob, fighting his way through the doors, and I stay close behind him, curious to see what the disturbance is.

The terminal is a long, high-ceilinged building with big,

open skylights and a row of turnstiles running along each wall. At the far end, a crowd has gathered around something on the ground and Obie makes his way over to them. Then he stops. So do I.

A boy is sitting in the center of one of the inlaid murals. He's barefoot and soaking wet, hair plastered to his forehead. My cousin Moloch is standing over him, arms folded like he owns the boy and the growing puddle around him.

Obie stares down at him, then turns to Moloch. "What do you think you're doing? That's one of mine."

Moloch lowers his chin and smiles, showing a mouthful of gray, crowded teeth. When he passes his tongue over them, they gleam like the lowest, most common metal. "Well then, it looks like you missed one, doesn't it? We don't ask questions, cousin. We just collect the bodies."

Moloch is younger than most of the other collections agents—the bone men, they're called in less respectful circles. He's tall, with hard, narrow eyes and flat cheekbones. He keeps his hair shaved close on the sides, but wears the middle like a spiky rooster's crest. The stripe that's left is dyed a deep, brutal red.

I edge closer, trying to get a better look. I don't know what I'm expecting—someone proud or glorious, with a radiance fitting the misbegotten son of an angel. But the boy on the ground is very human-looking. I'm captivated by his wheat-blond hair, his lightly freckled arms. I can't stop staring at the way his shirt sticks to his shoulders. The fabric is half-pink with watered-down blood, but I can't see where it's coming from.

Obie catches Moloch by the arm and when he speaks, his voice is furious. "Tell me all about it. Did you rough him up first? Did you have some *fun*?" He says *fun* like it's an obscenity. *Fun*, like *gangrene*.

Across the walkway, a cluster of the Lilim are laughing, heads tipped back like jackals. They giggle and shriek, tossing their hair like movie stars, darting furtive looks in our direction. Their teeth are sharp and metallic, and all of them are terribly alike.

"I could show him something fun," I hear someone whisper before they dissolve into laughter.

Moloch raises his eyebrows and removes his arm from Obie's grasp. "Maybe you didn't get a good look, but that walking calamity didn't need anyone else to put the damage on him. He's managed quite well on his own, thank you."

Moloch is thinner than Obie, but taller, and there's an insolent bulge where the tip of his tongue presses into his cheek. The toes of his boots are nearly touching Obie's sneakers and he smiles. It's a huge, avid smile—the kind that makes me think of crocodiles or sharks. It is the exact opposite of warm.

At their feet, the mural is of the temptation in the Garden and the apples are all done in pulsing, molten red. The boy sits bloody and soaking in the middle of it, covering his head with his hands.

There's a fluttering feeling that starts in my chest and feathers out, tingling down my arms, humming in my fingertips. I want to touch his hair, his dripping face, to feel

31

the thing that makes him special. He's nothing like one of Obie's half-demons. They come into the city joyful, so glad to finally be home. This boy just turns his face against his shoulder like he understands that Pandemonium is the worst possible place for him to be.

Around us, the pain demons are already gathering—the Butchers and the Eaters. I wonder if they sensed the boy's divinity even before they saw him—a smell or a sound that told them he was here.

In front of me, he seems to be getting smaller, curling in on himself. Water is running off his elbows, pooling around his bare feet. I have a feeling that if I touched him, he could make me a better person, and maybe that's why Moloch doesn't want to give him up. Maybe that's why my sisters are creeping closer, licking their lips. They sense his goodness and it draws them. They want it for themselves.

I kneel beside him, studying the shape of his hands. They're bony, pink with watered-down blood. It coats his skin like the wash of color when light shines through stained glass.

Carefully, I reach out, letting my fingers graze the contour of his cheekbone. At my touch, he looks up. His skin is marked by a smattering of freckles, and his eyes are a clear, arctic blue, so bright and icy that I flinch and drop my hands.

"Where am I?" he whispers, sounding dazed.

From the heart of the city, there's a deep, resonating crash as the furnace door slams open. The sound makes him recoil. His eyes are so wide, so painfully blue. All at once, he's fumbling for my hand, finding it, catching hold. His touch is shocking, too unexpected and too actual to contemplate, and instead of jerking back, I just hold on.

"Where am I?" he says again, and his voice is hoarse but louder, echoing in the terminal.

I shake my head and the air around us shimmers. It only takes the furnace a few scorching increments to reach full blaze. Then the hammering starts and anything that wasn't built here or brought in on the shelter of someone's body is going up in smoke.

Around us, the puddle shrinks rapidly. It vanishes in a rush of steam, only to be replaced by the water that won't stop pouring down his arms, and if he stays, it will soak his bloody shirt forever, like Beelzebub's flies. Like a story that never gets past the first sentence. It will be what defines him.

My sister Myra breaks from the crowd of Lilim. She comes picking her way across the thoroughfare with her eyes bright and hungry, her hands outstretched. Her fingers look like claws.

"No fair," she says, pouting decadently. "If Daphne gets to play with him, I want to play too."

"Get *back*." Obie's voice is sharp. It sounds like a whip cracking, and Myra retreats, skipping back with her fingers pressed to her mouth like a naughty child. The others squeal and duck away, laughing, but the damage has been done.

The pain demons are stirring now, moving closer. One of the Eaters creeps up beside me with a wild, gleeful look. Her hair is tangled, matted with someone else's blood, and when she reaches toward the boy on the ground, he grips my hand so tight I think he'll never let go.

"Lost Ones make the best toys," she whispers, stroking his face. "Just enough angel in the blood to keep them lively."

Her teeth are long and jagged. She looks ravenous, like she's never wanted anything more, and in that eager, hungry expression, I see an eternity of suffering.

No matter how animated the common damned are when they come in, they all go dark eventually. Usually sooner, rather than later. An angel-boy is a different matter altogether. The simple fact is, he's half-eternal and if this Eater or any of the other leering creatures on the walkway goes to work on him, he won't break or burn out or go silent. They can make him scream forever.

Suddenly, I'm sure that in another instant, they'll start on him right here in the terminal, on the carved panel of temptation. They'll brutalize and maim him and they'll go on doing it. The Eater smiles a wide, festering smile and I hold on tighter, bracing myself for the scream.

Then, without warning, the crowd shifts. There's a rustle, a stepping-back, and the whole atmosphere changes.

"What's all this?" says a voice from the walkway and I glance up, nearly shaking with relief.

Beelzebub is here, striding through the terminal in his polished wingtips and his work suit, surrounded by flies. His expression is mild, but Obie and Moloch both drop their eyes and stand at attention, and the Eater slinks back toward her cluster of friends, still casting hungry glances at the boy on the ground.

"So," Beelzebub says, clapping Obie on the shoulder. "Mind telling me what the fuss is about? Are we having a party?"

"That kid on the floor," Obie says, gesturing. His voice sounds hoarse. "That's a Lost One, and these cannibals know it—they all know he might as well be one of us. He shouldn't *be* here."

Beelzebub studies the two of us, crouched in front of him. I stare up, trying to communicate using my eyes, but his expression is inscrutable.

Please, I say without words. *Please, this is too awful. Don't let it happen.*

His gaze is intent, sweeping over my upturned face, the boy's bent head. For a strange moment, I think he's going to reach down and pull us apart, but he only sets his weapons case on the portrait of Leviathan and straightens his tie.

"Take him back," he says. It's directed at Obie, but he's still looking at me. "Take him home."

His tone is loud and definite and for the first time, everyone in the terminal stops talking. The only sound is the low, repetitive strike of the hammers, a long way off.

Beelzebub turns to face the crowd and they all stare back, but no one says anything.

"Are you still here?" he asks with a sharp, derisive smile.

"There's nothing here for you. Go on, go find something else to amuse yourselves."

The Eaters on the walkway scowl, but no one argues. None of them would dare question Beelzebub when he makes his wishes known, even now, when the decree is something unheard of.

The look Obie gives him is grateful, but I can't help thinking that Beelzebub is doing this for me and not my brother. That if it were Obie sitting on the ground with a bleeding boy, reluctant to hand him over to the Eaters, Beelzebub would shake his head and smile regretfully, or maybe lecture him on jurisdiction, remind him that once a job comes into the city, they all belong here—no exceptions. He wouldn't, under any circumstances, send the boy home.

Moloch looks away. "Do what you want—I'm just the errand boy—but don't go thinking you're his savior. Trust me, he'll be back here again in six months. A year at the outside."

"Sorry," the boy whispers and his voice is almost too soft to hear. "I'm sorry."

The word sounds choked and I don't know what he's apologizing for. His hand is slick and solid in mine, and I adjust my grip but don't pull away.

Obie gestures for the boy to stand up, but he doesn't move. He stays crouched next to me, until I struggle up from the floor and help him to his feet. Obie takes him by the elbow and starts for the gates, but the boy hesitates. His fingers are tangled with mine, his grip obstinate.

Obie tugs harder. "Daphne, let go."

"I'm not holding on."

Obie tries again to steer him back toward the row of turnstiles, but the boy just clutches me tighter.

"Stop it," I tell him, struggling to pull away. "You can't stay here."

I have to peel his fingers off me one by one before he will loosen his grip. Even as we slide apart, the boy won't drop his gaze. His eyes are pale as ice chips, boring into mine, and I think he can see my deepest wishes and my secrets, see all the way inside of me. I need him to stop looking.

"Quite the trousseau," Beelzebub says, raising his eyebrows at Obie's suitcase, which is lying on the floor. "Packing light for someone who's leaving for good."

Obie doesn't answer. He takes me by the arm and pulls me away from the crowd, looking down into my face. His eyes are wide and hurt. Betrayed.

"This is the most important thing in my life," he says in a low voice. "Do you understand that? I *need* this. How could you just run out and tell everybody?"

I gaze up at him, mute as he searches my face. I don't tell him that it wasn't everybody, that it was only Beelzebub.

"I had to tell someone," I whisper, shaking my head. "I'm scared you're going to die."

Obie's hand is resting on my arm and the way he looks at me is pleading. "Don't—don't make it harder. I *know* what could happen. Don't you think I'd stay if I could?"

37

And I see in his eyes that he's telling the truth. He can't be happy here. He needs to leave, and needing that means nothing will stop him.

"I understand," I say, with my hands clasped tight together. "Just please, be careful."

Obie nods. His eyes are the interminable silver of our mother's, but gentle and liquid. "I love you," he says, so softly I think I've misheard it.

"You what?"

"Love you," he says again, louder.

And I've only ever heard that word coming from the television. Not from someone's actual mouth, not talking about me.

With an expression so tender it makes something spasm in my throat, he leans down and kisses me on the forehead. Then he lets me go. He picks up the suitcase and rests a hand on the boy's shoulder, turning him toward the gates, and all at once, I know that he's leaving—really, and for good. That in another instant, my brother will be gone and I'll still be here.

He presses his hand against the pass panel beside the gate, leaning in to speak the word that will let them leave. There's a stifled hiss as the gate unlocks and he pushes it open.

The boy stumbles once, lurching through the turnstile. As he does, something slips from his hand and lands with a clatter. Then they're through the gate and gone, and I'm alone, standing in the spot where they stood. My hand feels numb, like it's lost connection to my body.

I bend down, reaching for the thing the boy dropped. It is an onyx-handled straight razor. I hold it away from myself, my hand dripping with slick, pink water.

The red sky is already fading to gray again, leaving the terminal hazy with smoke. The razor feels light and graceful in my hand. I slip it into my pocket, then turn to face the crowd. Beelzebub might have been wrong when he said there was nothing here for them, but I can't help thinking that just now, for me, it feels true. I know it's not right or rational, but suddenly I'm overcome by loneliness, remembering all the endearing, baffling things about my brother. Everything I'm losing. Remembering how easy it was to wait for him when I always knew he'd come back.

For the first time in my life, it feels like there's nothing keeping me anchored.

SISTERS
CHAPTER FIVE

Twilight has settled in, leaving the city dark. I walk out of the terminal with my head high and my hands at my sides and it takes all my will to do it slowly.

Then I'm outside, away from the building, and in the next instant, I'm running—darting through the crowded streets, winding my way between open cooling vents. The smoke rises in columns around me, pouring out of the grates, making everything gray.

Obie is gone. He's chosen to take his chances with Earth and Azrael, and I don't know what to do now, so I run faster. Away from dropped razors, bloody water. Away from the dripping boy with his fierce, tragic eyes, the way it felt when I let him go. My feet are numb with the impact, pounding up the spiral stairs of the Spire building, up to my room, where I'll sit alone on the couch and figure out a way to fix this.

But I open the door to find my sister Petra standing on the end table, hanging an assortment of rainbow-colored streamers. My collection of glass apothecary bottles has been set out in perfect order, each one positioned according to size.

Petra unfurls a streamer and holds it above her head, tying

the end neatly to a ceiling hook. She's dressed like the Pit girls, in a shift that hangs on her shoulders like a shroud, gray with soot. Her feet are bare and her hair is dense and stringy. She's humming, lips pressed tight over gray teeth, arranging the streamers so they hang down like paper vines, green and blue and purple. In the riot of color, she looks strangely monochromatic.

"I thought you might like it if I did decorations," she says, pivoting carefully on the tabletop.

For a moment, I just stand in the doorway with my mouth open and my hair a tangled nest around me. When I speak, it's in a flat, dull voice. "It looks nice."

My hands feel weightless. I have to lace my fingers together and squeeze, just to prove they're still connected to me.

Petra steps down from the table. "Is everything okay? You seem upset."

I nod. The floor seems to shift under me and I can't catch my balance.

"Here, sit down. I know something to cheer you up."

Taking me by the hand, she leads me over to the vanity where she situates me on the little stool and opens the makeup box. She sorts through my collection of cosmetics and selects a tube of dark lipstick. I tell myself that this is right. It's familiar, and now my life will go back to normal. It doesn't work. I'm already considering the next step, the next possible move.

Petra applies the lipstick deftly, careful to follow the precise shape of my mouth. My reflection stares back at me with blank features and hard, blazing eyes. Petra just tucks her hair behind her ears and keeps her own face turned away from the mirror.

Her father is one of Lilith's Pit demons and it shows in the shape of her thin lips, the grayness of her complexion. If she were vain like some of the others, she might lie. She might at least say she was the daughter of Belial, who built the foundry and the forges back when the city was nothing but a few crooked shacks above a pit of molten rock. He's gray-faced, but angelic under his layer of soot. People might even believe the story if she told it often enough.

She doesn't lie though. Instead, she shuffles and looks at the floor and everyone knows that she belongs to some gaunt, shambling artisan. She doesn't belong in the Spire, but she's here anyway, because she's Lilith's daughter.

Our other sisters mock her sometimes, call her Ash-Girl or Maid of the Metal-Workers, but I don't mind her iron fingernails or her huge, heavy-lidded eyes. Better to be ugly and sure of what you are than to spend your time like I do, staring into the mirror, wondering if I'll turn out to be just another one of the Lilim.

Petra begins to line my eyes with a burgundy eye pencil and I let her, fighting the urge to stand up, to pace between the window and the door because if I'm moving, then I can at least pretend I'm doing something, instead of just thinking about how to proceed.

"This is to make you seem flushed," she says, steadying my chin and sweeping pink shimmer over my cheeks. "So you look warm and friendly. Like a regular girl."

I fold my hands in my lap and don't say anything. She likes to make me up in fresh, soft colors my sisters would never wear and usually, I like to let her do it. Now though, all I can think is that Obie is gone, and even with my face powdered pink, accented with burgundy and taupe, I feel colorless.

Petra reaches for the eye pencil again. Holding it like a calligraphy pen, she studies my face and then begins to draw lightly on the top of the vanity, smearing the makeup with the tip of her finger. The chin and mouth of a girl materialize, followed by dark eyes, the suggestion of a nose, a scribble of shadow to mean ear, jaw, neck. The drawings are always temporary. They burn off as soon as the furnace is open.

Suddenly, from out in the hall comes the sound of heels on the stairs.

Footsteps echo around us like the crisp tinkling of bells and Petra drops the pencil. "Your sisters are coming."

"It's all right," I say. "They can't do anything to you." I don't point out that they're her sisters too.

She doesn't answer, only crosses the room and slips into the closet as Myra and Deirdre sweep in together, arms linked. They stop in front of me, looking eerily similar—two dolls in elaborate outfits.

The Lilim deal in seduction. When one of them holds a man, he feels the heat of her body like it's flooding him. She soothes him with the warmth of her breath, but really she's robbing him of his dreams and his memories, everything that makes him who he is.

There's a story that says my mother has a magic kiss, and

43

that's why my sisters turned out how they did. When Lilith met my father, he was broken, and when she kissed him, she drew his grief from him like poison from a wound. She took away his hopelessness, gave him back his valor and his strength. The common version is that she did it because she loved him, but there's nothing loving about what the Lilim do.

They call it the fix, like something in them is actually broken, but feeding on misery and desire doesn't cure them. Every time they do it, they just crave more. It's all they talk about.

"You awful little hypocrite." Deirdre's voice is like mercury, thick and quick and silver. She has on a black strapless dress, fine as smoke, held together by thin chains and pulsing with embers. She's smiling like she's never enjoyed anything more than the idea of my being a hypocrite.

"Daphne, Daphne," Myra croons, wagging her finger at me. "You *bad* girl. Why didn't you tell us you had a yearning for broken boys?" Her lips are the wet, red color of blood and candy. Her dress is silver, showing devastating curves, the body I do not have. Fastened to her back are a pair of wings, fashioned out of wire. They dance and jitter as she comes closer, flashing wildly.

"I don't," I say, not knowing how to explain the fragile line of the boy's bowed shoulders. Not wanting to share the feeling of his fingers tangled with mine.

Deirdre picks up a framed photograph of Marilyn Monroe, smiling down at it contemptuously.

I snatch the picture back and set it on the table. "Don't touch that."

Marilyn looks kind behind the glass, hopelessly soft. Surrounded by tangles of streamers and silk ribbons, Deirdre looks like a molten-lipped monster.

Myra slides her arms around my neck. "You can't lie to us, Daphne." Her voice is a trembling band of silver, her mouth soft against my ear. "I know you want the fix as much as we do. It's only a matter of time."

She lets me go, twirling away to poke through drawers and cupboards, running her fingers over my collection of padlocks. Her enameled nails hiss and ping against the steel. The sound fills my room like steam escaping.

Deirdre sighs and smiles, backing me into the corner by the vanity. She touches my face, smoothing her thumb against my cheek. "You're so lucky your father was an angel. Your teeth are almost perfect."

When she brushes my lips with the tip of her finger, I shrug her off and retreat behind the sofa. "Leave me alone."

She grimaces at the red smear on her hand, then wipes her fingers on her dress. "Are you wearing lipstick? Honestly, Daphne. We have to get you some *real* makeup."

Her own face is expertly made up in the colors of the Lilim, red embers and white ashes. Her mouth is hot with melted brimstone and soot is smeared black in the hollows of her eyes. I shake my head, staring off over her head. I know that if I don't respond—if I just wait—they'll get bored and leave.

"Oh, come on, don't you want to play with the boys? Don't you want to know what it's like? They go crazy for us on Earth." Creeping around the sofa, she leans in like she's about to kiss my cheek. "They *worship* us."

I stand with my palms pressed flat against the wall, but she only snaps her teeth beside my ear and dances back, eyes glittering wickedly. For a moment, I consider it—consider the possibility that I could go to Earth with them and instead of looking for someone to prey on, I could look for Obie. But it's too impractical going with the Lilim. They won't be any help.

Deirdre gives me one last sly smile and turns away. Then she and Myra link arms again, smooth, practiced, like there's never been a time when they weren't holding onto each other. When they slink out the door, it's with a laugh and a wave, without looking back.

"You can come out now," I say, watching the shape of Petra sway in the shadows.

She creeps from the closet to stand next to me. With the palm of my hand, I scrub the lipstick off my mouth.

Petra hunches her shoulders and turns toward the window. Outside, the sky is gray like ash. "Will you go hunting for the fix like your sisters do?"

I think of the boy in the terminal, even though it's not my right to want him. His arms were wet and I want to believe that the flutter in my chest is only astonishment at how the water ran down his skin in perfect drops, wonder at the miracle of surface tension. My hands feel numb and sticky, and his blood will burn off soon enough, nothing left to prove he ever existed.

"No," I say, trying not to let my face change. "No, that's low. It's common."

I sound utterly certain, like it's the truth. But really, I don't know the answer. There is only the memory of myself, standing over the boy. The feeling of being unable to move or look away, and I know my sisters' hunger is in me, too. It's sleeping deep somewhere, murmuring in my blood, and that knowledge scares me more than I can say.

ABSENCE
CHAPTER SIX

The strange fluttering I felt in the terminal is gone, and in its place, there's another feeling that's just as hard to name. It beats in my chest like a war drum. With no way to reckon time, it feels like only a moment since Obie left, and also like forever.

I'm lying on the floor of my room, picking apart the fuses on a string of Black Cat firecrackers and lighting them off one by one. Every explosion makes a sharp popping sound and I lie on my back, tossing the lit crackers into the air. They burst above me in a shower of noise and blackened paper.

On Earth, a person could be badly burned, but here, the flash of sulfur and charcoal doesn't matter. Nothing leaves a mark. I keep hoping the noise will jar something loose in my head, but it's hard to know how to spring into action when I've never had to do anything before. The palms of my hands are black from all the times I let the crackers explode too soon.

I light another one, then set it on my chest and wait. There's a brief impact that shudders through my ribs when it goes off, but that's all. The muted *bang* of the explosion is the only sound in the whole world.

Until my mother starts screaming.

The sound is shrill, reverberating in the stairwells, and I lie perfectly still. I've never even heard her raise her voice.

Then she screams again, raw and anguished, ringing down through the tower of empty rooms. I can feel it in my teeth.

I scramble to my feet and bolt up the stairs to the roof, slamming through the gate and out into the courtyard. She's standing alone in the middle of the garden, staring down into the reflective surface of the sundial. Her back is straight and her hand is pressed against her mouth.

Around her, the vines are growing out of control, squirming up from the beds, crawling in a silver network over the roof.

I fight my way through the tangle and then stop, because it's occurred to me that if I keep moving forward, eventually I'll reach her and then we'll be standing side by side and I don't know what to do. I'm used to her dreamy and distant, cold and cruel. The sight of her standing perfectly still in front of the sundial is all wrong, and it is terrifying.

"Mom," I say, and my voice sounds so tiny that it barely exists. When she doesn't react, I say it again. Then I shout it, trying to make myself heard. To make her see me. "Mom! What's wrong? What happened?"

"He isn't there," she whispers. It comes out sounding thick and choked. She points to her own reflection. Her eyes stare up at me from the sundial, storm-gray and fathomless.

I stand with my hands held out, but not touching her, never touching. "What do you mean? Who—who isn't?"

"Obie." She leans closer to the sundial, staring into its flat, sliver face.

We're motionless and silent, standing five feet apart in the middle of the garden.

"What are you talking about?" I say, more impatiently than I mean. "What did you see?"

She turns to face me and her eyes are so wide and glassy they look like polished steel. "Darkness, a flutter of shadows. Daphne," she whispers. "There was blood."

The roof is a flat expanse of engraved tile, full of stories and poems, but the vines are growing over it now. At my feet, they've covered words like *love* and *sea* and *war*. There's just the shining tangle, leaves as sharp as thorns.

"Shouldn't his blood have protected him?" I say. "Didn't it turn to acid, or burn or *something*?"

Lilith's face is impassive, half-turned away. "It didn't do anything."

"He can't have just disappeared," I say, talking fast and breathless. "How did it happen? Did you see who hurt him?"

But she doesn't have to tell me what she saw. I know the answer, the penalty for demons who choose a life on Earth.

"Is he dead?" I say the word with precision, even though it feels like a solid object in my throat.

My mother stares down at me, showing her teeth, which are small and straight and very gray. When she clutches at her hair, she looks like an animal.

"Mom, is he dead? Did you see what *happened*?"

She shakes her head, a short, quick little shake. "It was very sudden. He was walking through a park, past a frozen fountain. Then there was a spray of blood on snow, and like that, he was gone."

I fight the temptation to stroke my mother's hair. I'm reluctant to touch her at the best of times, but especially now when her eyes have gone flat and empty. She looks combustible.

I wonder if I was wrong to ask Beelzebub to be the one to talk to Obie. Maybe if I'd come to Lilith instead, told her about Obie's plans to leave, she could have dissuaded him. He'd be safe now. But it's always felt unnatural to go to Lilith for anything, and even now, the idea seems foreign. I never even thought to ask her for help.

"He's my son," she whispers, crossing her arms over her chest and digging her fingers into her bare shoulders like she's trying to make me understand something vital.

I've always known that she preferred him to the rest of us, that she valued and praised him, when her general state has been to tolerate me and despise the Lilim. But if I ever resented the way she liked him best, seeing her now would have cured me of it. Her fear is real. It's as if something has finally cracked inside her, letting the true, unguarded core of her show through. It's shocking and for just a moment, I catch myself wondering what it would take to make her care for me like that.

"Don't worry." My voice sounds quiet, but steady, and that's reassuring. "We'll find him."

Lilith only stares into the sundial. Her garden is awake now, rustling all around us. I shake myself free from the tangle of vines growing over my feet, then clamber up onto one of the benches. The line of her profile is straight and proud, the very image of the woman on the wall, but her eyes have a wild, hunted look. From the safety of the bench, I study her face like I'm seeing her for the first time. Her long, narrow eyebrows and her pale mouth. Her throat is smooth. The little hollow at the base of it looks delicate enough to tear like paper, and I don't understand how I ever could have believed that she was indestructible.

"I'd track him down myself," she says, gazing down into the sundial. "If I had any way to leave the city, I'd raze Earth to find him."

She stands amid the rustling leaves. After a moment, she lifts her head and her vines fall still. She's never talked about leaving. About how deeply she's been punished for her disobedience and for standing beside my father. She's never before talked about being trapped.

For the first time, it occurs to me to wonder if the reason she's constantly pushing me to be more like my sisters is because it eats at her to see me sitting quietly when she would run if she could. I've never been fierce or brave, though. I've never been impulsive. It's always been in my nature to consider things carefully and then decide upon the best solution. Except, sometimes the circumstances change. Sometimes things get so complicated and so bad that your nature just doesn't matter anymore.

"I can't leave the city," Lilith says again, turning to stare into my face. And then she smiles. Her eyes look desperate.

I clasp my hands in front of me and look up at her. "But I can."

❋   ❋   ❋

In the museum, Beelzebub is counting out a stack of Russian banknotes and tossing them onto the desk in groups of twenty. I don't have to ask him what the money's for to know that he's already on his way out again. The nine millimeter handgun is lying out and the desk is covered with combat knives and loose papers.

When he looks up, I can tell there's something wrong with my expression, because he stops counting and gets to his feet. "Everything all right?"

I cross the little office and stand in front of him. "We have to help Obie. My mother saw something in the mirror—she saw blood, and all I can think is that Azrael's found him. You said it would be okay! You said it was *safe*."

Beelzebub waits for me to finish. Then he holds up his hand and gestures for me to sit. "Slow down. Is it possible your mother's confused, or under some sort of misapprehension? These things do happen from time to time."

Time. The great, elemental force of Pandemonium is time, the cessation of time, the freezing of it. I know this like I know epic poems and algorithms—information to collect and memorize. But I don't know it the way people do on Earth, born into it and bound by it. There, parents become grandparents and widows and corpses. Children grow up.

Here, it's like there's no time at all, only distance, sprawling on and on forever, and every moment we spend deliberating could be an hour on Earth.

"We can't *wait*," I say, dismayed at the way my voice spikes up without my control. "He's still alive, but we don't know for how long or what's happening to him!"

Beelzebub begins to tidy up the desktop, keeping his eyes on my face. "I know you're worried, but we're not going to benefit from haste. We can't just assume that Azrael has your brother."

I turn away, trying to control the panic racing in my chest. Trying to close my mouth. My mother might be unpredictable, but she doesn't make mistakes. If she can't see Obie, then he's gone someplace her sight can't reach.

"Please," I say, trying to sound persuasive without sounding like I'm begging. "You don't even have to help me. I can go myself."

"What are you talking about?"

"My mother said we could find him. She said if I went looking for him, she'd help me. She's not sure what happened or why she can't see him, but if she has me there to search for clues, maybe we can save him."

Beelzebub has frozen with his hand on the stack of uncounted money. When he raises his head to look at me, he does it with utter composure. "Let me see if I have this straight. Your mother is convinced that something violent and untoward has happened to your brother and her grand *solution* is to send you in after him?" He stares out over the gallery and his jaw is hard. "She is absolutely unbelievable!"

"But what if she's right? She can't go out to find him and I *can*. I'll be careful, I'll—"

He throws the remainder of his Russian banknotes into the desk and slams the drawer. "No. Under no circumstances. I hate to be the one to say it, but in case you hadn't noticed, your mother has some of the most truly terrible judgment I have ever encountered. You are not obligated to act as her little deputy, and you're not to leave this city. She isn't thinking straight."

"But I can't just sit here and do *nothing*. He's my brother!"

"I appreciate the sentiment Daphne, but right now, I've got a Siberian prison teetering on revolt, and I can't just drop everything because your brother decided to break every law in the book."

I'm running my fingers over the stack of papers on the desk. I know I should stop, but can't seem to control my hands. The feeling of unraveling is getting worse and I pluck restlessly at the pages in front of me. Then a tab on one of the folders catches my eye. OBIE is printed in Beelzebub's unmistakable script. Inside is a stack of forms, each stamped with red ink to indicate closure. Pages and pages of red stamps, all RESOLVED, FINAL, THE END. There are margin notes everywhere, mostly in Beelzebub's careless hieratic, a jumble of slashes and curving lines. Hieratic is difficult. I always confuse the symbol for *praise* with the one for *strike*.

I touch the last form, white and unstamped. "Who's Truman Connor Flynn?"

Beelzebub has put away the knives and is now recounting the banknotes. "Sorry, what?"

"He's the last entry in Obie's file. The case is still open."

Beelzebub wrinkles his forehead, still counting. "That's your friend from the terminal—the boy with the razor. With the water."

The boy who reached for my hand.

"Well, what about *him*?" I say, unable to keep a note of hope out of my voice. "He might not know what happened, but he could still help. Maybe he even knows who Obie's friends are or where he was staying."

Beelzebub sighs. Then he sits down across from me, pocketing his Russian money and his gun. He's looking into my face and his eyes are almost like a real person's—pale, but not transparent anymore. He would pass for human on the street.

"I'm not trying to be a beast," he says. "But we have no idea what kind of a situation we're dealing with, and until we do, the best course of action is to sit tight and exercise some caution. I don't want you getting hurt. There will be a time for you to go to Earth, but now is not the time. Do you understand what I'm saying?"

I nod. My face feels stiff and I can't think of anything to say.

He reaches for his weapons case and stands up. "I have to go," he says. "But the minute I'm done, we'll get this all taken care of—I promise."

He starts out of the office, then turns back like he's about to say something else. He looks so righteous and so good, even crawling with flies. He raises his hand, a kind, helpless gesture, before turning to make his way through the gallery and out of the museum.

Then I'm alone, sitting at Beelzebub's desk. The room is still. Still enough to think. And what I think is that my mother never would have accepted this stillness. She made her own fate when she was younger than me. She defied God and angels, even if it meant being banished, then chose my father, even when that choice confined her to a jagged, brimstone world. And maybe it's not what she dreamed of, but she did it anyway.

I've never chosen my mother over Beelzebub. I've never trusted her judgment more than I trust his, but this is different. Somewhere on Earth, Obie is bleeding, and I don't have a choice.

I get out an atlas of North America and take it back to the desk. Then I open the folder again and pull out the paperwork on Truman Flynn. His home address is in Cicero, Illinois. The street is named Sebastian, like the saint.

I flip through the pages, but there's nothing in the file that tells me about Obie. Just Truman's name and the address in Cicero, which the atlas informs me is a township outside Chicago.

Leaving isn't hard, there's no trick to it. I've watched Beelzebub get ready hundreds of times.

I deal with the money first—bills and plastic, a stack of paper transit cards for the subway, and a handful of coins for good luck. After that, I gather up every map I can find for

Chicago and the surrounding area. Then I search the museum for clothing.

The gallery is huge and organized by a complex cataloging system that only Beelzebub understands. The first stash of girl's clothing I find is in a big steamer trunk with a piece of masking tape on the lid labeled GREAT DEPRESSION TO WWII. A lot of the dresses are bloody or torn, but at the bottom, I find a few that look rumpled but clean. They all have short, cuffed sleeves and Peter Pan collars. I pull them out and take them back to the desk.

In the back of a wardrobe marked PROHIBITION, I find a black women's coat and a pair of patent leather gloves shoved inside a hatbox. I pile everything into a black bag with twin handles and silver buckles.

Then I rifle through the gallery looking for shoes. Finally, on a shelf above the guitars, I come across a battered cardboard box labeled ALTAMONT, 1969. Inside are an assortment of leather jackets and paper flyers, some clasp knives, and a pair of motorcycle boots, which are a dull, scraped black.

With unsteady hands, I open the bottom drawer of the desk and pull out the directory for the terminal. It's nearly four inches thick, and I sit in Beelzebub's chair with the directory spread open on the blotter, figuring out my itinerary. I memorize the gates first, and then the complex network of hallways beyond. The door itself will be marked, and I should come out right in Cicero. From there, it's only a matter of blocks to the Sebastian Street address. The route seems simple enough, and if I lose track of my position, I'll look it up.

"Can you do this?" I ask myself aloud, staring down at the heap of clothes and supplies piled haphazardly into the bag.

"Yes," I reply, knowing that there is no other answer.

❊   ❊   ❊

Entering the terminal, I might as well be invisible. I have a long black coat, a pair of boots with ankle buckles. A plaid dress and a striped sweater. I have a black bag full of money and information. I have two ideas of how to behave, one for demons, one for angels. I run my tongue over a pair of metal teeth and don't know what I am.

At the turnstile, I press my hand to the pass panel and say "Truman Flynn." There's a soft click as I speak it and the door unseals.

When I step through, the corridor lies empty before me, a series of twists and turns. In the hall leading to eastern Illinois and Chicago, I search through rows of mismatched doors until I come to a small wooden one marked CICERO. At my touch, it hisses open like a secret, and I'm gone.

PART TWO

EARTH

MARCH 7
4 DAYS 0 HOURS 3 MINUTES

Truman Flynn woke up.

His head felt heavy, and he had a bad, metallic taste in his mouth. For a second, he didn't know where he was or if he was still dreaming. Then a car horn sounded outside and he sat up, relieved to find himself in his own bed.

His heart was hammering in his chest. When he pressed his palms against his eyelids, he saw squirming red shapes, afterimages of his dream.

It wasn't one of the bad ones—not a bloody bathtub or a hospital room. It was not a dark, decrepit church. Not a funeral full of crows. This time, he'd dreamed about the girl.

She wasn't anyone he knew from work or school, but more like a fantasy—the kind of girl who only existed when you closed your eyes and wished for some magic genie, some storybook princess to sweep in and save you from your life. Her hair was black, and her face was very pale. Behind her, there was nothing but a huge, gleaming expanse of polished metal.

In his dreams, she never talked. Even when he pleaded with her, desperate to hear her voice, she only sat next to him and held his hand.

This time had been different, though. When their eyes met, she had smiled, a wide, dazzling smile. She'd said his name, but nothing else.

Truman untangled himself from the covers and swung his feet over the edge of the bed, leaning forward with his elbows propped on his knees. He thought it was Friday. Wasn't sure. School was out for the Easter break, and without the routine of late bells and missing homework, the days had begun to bleed into each other. His ears were ringing and he felt pretty catastrophically hungover. He started to stand up, but the room did a slow half-turn and he sat back down.

The voice spoke from the corner of the room then, low and patient. Pleasant, except for the fact that it was coming from his open closet. "Come here. I need to show you something."

Truman froze. The window in his room faced east and the shade was up, flooding the worn-out carpet with weak sunlight, but over in the corner, the closet was a rectangle of darkness.

"Let's not waste time," the voice said. "I have something to show you and it's important."

Truman crossed his arms over his chest, already knowing that he didn't want to see it.

"Get up out of that bed and come over here *right now*. I need you to see this."

Truman pressed his back flat against the wall, shaking his head. He already knew what the man in the shadows wanted to show him. In the dream, his mother would still be in her hospital bed, surrounded by tubes and monitors. The room would be too small and too cold, just like it had when she'd lain dying in the ICU at Mount Sinai. He could almost smell the antiseptic and the sour, acrid smell of disease. He could picture her face—horribly, painfully thin—and he knew that when she opened her eyes, the corneas would be a sick, faded yellow.

He pulled his knees up and ground the heels of his hands hard against his eyelids. "I'm already awake," he said aloud. "I'm not dreaming, so get out of my room."

"Are you sure about that?"

"I'm *sure*." Truman's voice sounded hoarse, and as soon as he said it, he began to doubt himself.

The man just laughed a low, ugly laugh. It rose and faded, then disappeared altogether as the closet door swung shut. The room was quiet.

Then a truck rumbled by outside and Truman came suddenly, violently awake. He flailed up from the mattress, kicking at the sheets, trying to untangle himself.

His hands were shaking and every time he blinked, he could see the black-haired girl, flashing that silver smile, whispering his name, but it was all mixed up with the voice from the closet and he needed more than anything to drown out that slow laughter.

He rolled out of the bed and crossed the room to the desk, where he dug through the drawers until he found an unopened can of High Frequency. It was room temperature and tasted like cough syrup, but it had more active ingredients than any other energy drink at the Stop-N-Go.

In the last year, he'd gotten pretty good at not sleeping. There were cold showers, cigarettes, caffeine pills, and black coffee. At school, he lived on nicotine and adrenaline, pounding energy shots at his locker or smoking behind the dumpsters between classes. It only lasted so long, though. Eventually, you *had* to sleep.

He drank the High Frequency, wincing at the taste. Then he got dressed. He started a load of laundry so his stepdad, Charlie, wouldn't have to. He made the bed and brushed his teeth and combed his hair—all the little things a person did when they weren't crazy. He didn't go near the closet.

In the kitchen, Truman found Charlie sitting at the table in his undershirt and eating cold pasta out of a plastic container. He'd peeled his coverall down to his waist and was reading the newspaper. Truman squeezed past his chair and they nodded at each other. Charlie worked the graveyard shift at Spofford Metals, and didn't usually get home until eight or nine in the morning, and by then, Truman had usually left for school. Their lives ran more or less adjacent, but rarely intersected.

"Hey now," Charlie said, setting down his paper without looking up. "Shouldn't you be at school? I thought we talked about this."

"It's spring break." Truman dropped a fresh filter in the coffee maker. "It's been spring break for like five days."

"Huh." Charlie nodded vaguely, hunching over his pasta. "Any big plans?"

"Not really. Maybe I'll hit the library later—got a project for biology."

They both knew it was a lie, but neither of them said anything. It was the kind of lie that just made life much easier for both of them.

Truman drank his coffee and ate a handful of dry cereal, telling himself he didn't care about the way that he and Charlie ignored each other. By the time Charlie had finished his dinner and left Truman sitting alone in the kitchen, he almost believed it.

He poured another cup of coffee and drank it, even though he was starting to feel uncomfortably wired. Then he left the apartment.

Out in the stairwell, he stood with his back against the wall, trying to decide what to do. He could be responsible for once and actually go to the library, but that might be a bad idea. It was quiet there, and warm, and if he sat down at one of the study tables he was going to fall asleep. He pressed his cheek against the wall. The cement was freezing and the jolt of cold helped to clear his head. He was so tired that the whole world was starting to feel surreal.

When his neighbor Alexa pushed through the outside door into the stairwell, he jumped a little. She was carrying a paper grocery bag in each arm, and her hair had spilled out of her plastic barrettes, falling sloppily in her eyes. She was too young to be grocery shopping on her own—twelve, maybe thirteen—but the kids in the Avalon Apartments were all like that, running household errands and raising themselves or their siblings.

"Hey, Lexi," Truman said, stepping away from the wall. He reached to take one of her bags. "What's happening?"

She shrugged and looked away, letting him have the groceries. "I hate when you call me Lexi." But she was grinning at the floor, cheeks pink, eyes downcast.

He reached out with his free hand and tweaked her nose. "I'm just being a dick. Seriously, has your break been good?"

Alexa nodded, still looking somewhere else, over his shoulder maybe, or above his head. She seemed on the verge of floating off, only anchored down by the bag of groceries she held against her chest.

When Truman started for the stairs, she followed him and they went up side by side, not talking.

On the fourth-floor landing, he held the stairwell door for her. She slipped past him, then turned and looked up into his face. Her expression was serious. "Were you drunk last night?"

The question surprised him and he didn't answer right away, just started down the hall to her apartment, wondering what he should say. Alexa was a weird kid, but sharp. She noticed things. She hung around the stairwell or the lobby pretty much all the time, but she didn't pester him or tag along, and he could always count on her not to say anything to Charlie or her mother.

"No," he said finally. "I mean, I might have gotten a little buzzed after I got off work, but not *drunk*. Why?"

They were at Alexa's door now, and she was fumbling the keys out of her coat pocket. "I was out in the parking lot," she said, not looking at him. "I thought I saw you come in."

"Nah," he said, feeling tired and guilty.

Not guilty enough to stop doing it, though. Drunk was good. It was necessary, because when he was drunk, he didn't dream. Only lately, it took a lot of alcohol to get him there and even a blackout usually wore off by dawn, making for bad scenes like the one this morning.

He leaned against the wall, looking down at her. "It could have been one of the guys up on the fifth floor or something. Anyway, what were you doing out so late?"

"Nothing." She worked the toe of her sneaker on the carpet. "Looking for you. I just thought—it's stupid, but I thought something had happened to you."

Suddenly, Truman's throat felt very tight and he laughed uncomfortably. "Me? I'm fine."

She didn't answer, simply looked. He tried to imagine what she must see and it wasn't good. The shadows around his eyes were so dark it looked like someone had been hitting him.

"I'm fine," he said again, and this time her face cleared and she smiled.

"Yeah, sure. I was just being stupid."

But there was a look in her eyes that reminded him of last winter, of red water soaking into the hall carpet. A memory that he spent every minute of every day trying to forget.

CICERO
CHAPTER SEVEN

When I step through the little wooden door, everything is so bright that, for a moment, I can't even make out shapes. Then the blindness clears and the world shimmers into focus.

I'm standing under a bridge. The sky above me is blue, but it's much paler than I had expected sky to be. At my feet, the pavement is littered with empty bottles and the stubs of cigarettes. I can feel the air on my face, uncomfortable and strange. This is cold. And I like it.

I stoop to touch the ground and my palms come away gritty and smeared with something black. A new and hungry part of me wants to stand under the bridge forever, breathing the air, feeling the cold on my face. But time exists now. I don't think I have very much of it.

I take out my map, opening it against one of the cement pylons supporting the bridge, and run my finger along lines meant to represent roads, trying to find Cicero. I trace the streets, their almost-regular intersections. The sheer vastness of the world is thrilling.

I'm scanning the map for Sebastian Street when there's a stealthy footfall behind me.

"Hey," says someone from quite close by. "What are you doing down here?"

When I look around, a man of indeterminate age is standing in the shadow of one of the pylons. His clothes are grimy and his beard is heavy and matted. "You lost?" he asks.

"Perhaps." I turn to face him, rattling the map closed. "Can you tell me how to get to Cicero from here?"

He comes closer, parting his lips to reveal crooked yellow teeth. The movies can't convey how everything on Earth has a smell. He is an unpleasant array of things I don't know the words for, all of them tight and sharp and high-pitched.

"I'll do you one better," he says. "I can show you."

He motions me back into the shadow of the bridge and when I follow, he takes something from his pocket. It's black, as long as my hand from wrist to fingertips, and decorated with pictures of the same red flower over and over, linked together by a tangle of vines.

"What is it?" I ask, leaning closer.

His wrist twitches and suddenly the thing opens with a click and I see that it's a knife. He holds it out to me.

"It's beautiful," I say.

Then he brings the blade up level with my chin, not offering it after all. "Give me your money."

I watch the knife tremble, red flowers swarming over

the handle. They wriggle and squirm as his hand shakes, making it hard to identify the genus.

"Are you deaf?" His voice is taut now, panicked. "Give me your fucking money."

"No," I say, stepping closer, reaching out.

At first, I'm not sure what I'm about to do, only that he's standing much too close and my hands are tingling. Then he lunges for me and as he does, I reach out, pressing the tips of my fingers against his throat.

The instant I touch him, red light blooms behind my eyelids and I smell a strange smell, heady and sweet. It's the smell of burning flesh.

His cry is short and shocked. Then it cuts off and he wrenches away, my fingerprints smoking along the side of his neck. The knife falls from his hand, clanging on the pavement, and I bend to pick it up. When I straighten, he's gone, the sound of his feet still echoing under the bridge.

Petra warned me about the dangers of Earth—traffic accidents and fairy tales. But those things only seem to happen to people who aren't being careful, and I just burned a man by touching him. Above me, the bridge begins to shake, making a noise so loud I feel it in the ground. It shudders through the soles of my boots, and in a parking lot across the street, the cars burst into a cacophony of loud, rhythmic honking, each with its own tempo and pitch.

A train rumbles overhead, rattling and clattering along its track, and for the first time, I understand that I'm the most dangerous thing here.

⚹ ⚹ ⚹

There are a lot of streets in Cicero, which is confusing, but not impossible. The map shows them laid out in uniform squares—nothing like the chaotic spirals of Pandemonium.

I'm six blocks from Sebastian Street when I first notice the ache in my chest. It echoes in my ribcage, making me breathe too fast. I think it started under the bridge, right after my encounter with the thief. The farther I go, the worse it seems to get.

On the steps of a public building, three skinny boys are passing a cigarette back and forth. The smoke looks like home, and I have a strange, unbidden idea that I want to put it in my mouth. The ache in my chest is terrible now, and with it there's the ghost of something else, something like emptiness. I find myself clenching my teeth and wonder if this is what people mean when they talk about feeling hungry.

I walk faster, searching the storefronts for a place that serves food. Halfway down the block I find a small shop with a neon sign in the shape of a sandwich. When I pull the door open, a bell rings, far off and tinkling. Inside, the shop is warm. It smells sublime and after a few deep breaths, the ache isn't as bad anymore.

The boy behind the counter has dark, golden-hued skin and is wearing transparent plastic gloves on both hands. I think they must be to keep him clean from the world.

I approach and he smiles. His teeth are very white.

"I'd like the best thing you have to eat, please," I say.

He smiles wider, and the wideness makes dimples at the corner of his mouth. "Best? Isn't that different for everybody?"

I shrug. "I don't know. What do you like best?"

"On a sandwich? I like something with capicola and salami, peppers, mozzarella, maybe vinegar, salt and pepper. Some flavor, you know."

His accent is different from mine, dusky and lilting, and at first I think he's saying Salome, who once asked her father for the head of John the Baptist on a platter. I repeat the word, trying to pronounce like he does. "Salami, what's it like?"

He passes a small piece of marbled-looking meat over the glass countertop, holding it between his plastic-gloved fingers. "Try it and see."

When I reach to take it though, he stops and pulls his hand back. "*Whoa*—you need to go wash your hands." He grins wide, shaking his head. "They're *filthy*!"

I study my palms, which are black, greasy from touching the pavement.

"Go," he says again, waving me past the counter and down a short hall to the bathroom.

Inside, the floor is tile, smeared with footprints. There are a pair of cubicles with toilets against one wall and two chipped porcelain sinks with a long mirror above them along the other.

I regard my reflection with interest, trying to see the girl I am on Earth. The girl someone thought it would be a good idea to rob. Of course he did—of course he thought it would be so easy to take something from me. I still look like the silly princess at her vanity, hair long, face pristine. Hands, dirty.

I run them under the faucet, soaping and scrubbing until the grime sloughs off down the drain. Then I open my bag.

The razor is on top, nestled in with the maps and the clothes. I pick it up and unfold the blade. I don't cut myself, even though I keep thinking about it, how it might be good to know what my blood will do. How maybe I should have let the man under the bridge try it, because then at least I'd know what my protection is. I examine the edge of the blade and consider finding out.

But I'm here in the bathroom of a restaurant and some of the protections are dramatic enough to damage the floor, or possibly destroy whole buildings. The boy outside seems friendly and I don't want to do anything that might vandalize his shop.

Instead, I adjust my grip and grab a handful of my hair. Standing on top of my bag, I lean over the sink until my nose almost touches the glass. My reflection saws at her hair, and in my hands, I feel it drop away. The cut ends tickle and scratch against my neck and already I feel wild and a little frightening, the kind of girl no one would ever think to steal from.

When my mother speaks, it's in a fierce whisper and directly into my ear. "Daphne."

Her reflection stares out at me from just over my shoulder and the sight of her startles me so badly that I almost lose my footing on the bag.

The razor slips from my hand, landing in the sink, but when I whirl around to face her, no one's behind me. I turn back to her reflection, feeling breathless. "What are you doing here?"

It's a stupid question, though. I should have been expecting her to find me—it's what she does. I've just never seen it from this side of the glass.

"Have you learned anything yet?" she says, staring out at me with ringing gray eyes. "Do you know what happened to your brother?"

I shake my head, forcing myself to hold her gaze. "Not yet—I only just got here, but I'm about to go talk to someone who knew him. Have you seen anything in the sundial?"

"Nothing but a silly girl ruining her hair. You need to hurry."

"I will, but I have to eat first," I whisper, feeling guilty for the way my breath comes faster when I remember the scrap of salami still waiting for me out in the shop, held in the boy's plastic-covered hand. "I'm on my way, I just have to get a sandwich."

Lilith smiles, but it's chilly and tightlipped. "You can feed yourself on salt and bread and meat. It still won't be enough. You'd be better served looking for a fix."

And then, without any warning, she's gone. I'm alone in a bathroom, standing in front of a smudged mirror. The sink is full of my hair.

I brush the loose cuttings off the razor and drop it back in the bag, staring past myself to the place where Lilith appeared, then vanished. It's strange to hear her talk about the fix the way my sisters do, like it's necessary. I don't quite believe it.

Out on the street, I was nearly desperate, but now the ache has settled down to more of a dull throb and I feel almost calm. Simply breathing the air inside the shop made the hunger recede—at least a little—so there have to be other ways to cure it. If I go back out into the restaurant and buy myself a sandwich, maybe that will be enough to fill the hollow in my chest.

When I leave the bathroom, the boy is waiting at the counter, still holding my scrap of salami. "What'd you do to your hair?" he asks, eyeing me doubtfully. "You had a whole lot more a minute ago."

"Yes, but now my hands are clean." I reach for the salami and he lets me have it.

The meat feels greasy, flecked with white, and when I put it in my mouth, it's full of flavors—sharp, oily, tingling.

I buy a sandwich with extra salt and some of everything. As he makes it, the boy tells me about meats, the difference between dry-cured and hickory-smoked. Sausages and ham, and how cheese gets made by squeezing water out of milk in a cloth. When I ask him about the gloves, he just laughs and says they're for hygiene.

"To keep you clean?"

"No, to keep all this clean from me." He wraps my sandwich in white paper and passes it across the counter to me.

"You're very kind," I tell him. "How did you become so kind?"

He smiles an honest smile for the first time, and the difference is hard to describe but easy to recognize. "It's my job, you know. Just a job."

The way he says it makes me think of Obie, always so preoccupied with his job, but talking about it never made him smile. I can't say for certain, but I don't think I'd mind a position in the Department of Good Works. At least it would mean knowing that I wasn't going to turn out like my sisters.

Now, I take my sandwich, counting out dollars for the boy behind the counter. "You do your job well," I tell him because it seems like something people ought to hear, and I don't remember anyone ever telling Obie that, even though it's true.

"Nah," the boy says, shaking his head, grinning like I'm the strangest thing he's ever seen. "You ain't from here." It's not a question.

"No," I tell him, handing him my money. "I'm not."

SEBASTIAN STREET
CHAPTER EIGHT

In my bag, I have a folder containing the address of Truman Connor Flynn. I have a memory of him—his fierce, anguished eyes, his hand fumbling for mine. How wholly shocking it was when he touched me, and how real. The memory is bright, but strangely transparent, like it's already starting to fade. I wonder if I'll even know him when I see him again.

I go four more blocks before I come to a dingy brick building with a sign out front reading THE AVALON APARTMENTS. A boy is bouncing a hard rubber ball against the wall, his breath like smoke in the cold air. When I approach the double doors, the sidewalk feels uneven beneath my boots.

Beside the entrance is a panel of buttons, lettered and numbered, but if there's a password, I don't know it. I push numbers randomly, but nothing happens. After a moment, the boy stops bouncing the ball to watch.

"It's broke," he tells me. "You don't got to buzz in—just open it."

When I pull the handle, the door swings wide, squealing against my weight. It opens into a stairwell with a large number 1 painted on the wall. According to Obie's file, Truman lives in apartment 403, and so I begin to climb. The stairwell smells damp and is nearly as cold as the air outside. The sound of my boots is almost deafening.

When I step out onto the fourth-floor landing, three girls are sitting on the floor. All of them are wearing tennis sneakers and extremely short skirts. They look away when I approach and pull their feet up to let me pass.

Apartment 403 is at the far end of the hall. I knock crisply and when no one comes, I knock louder. When I press my ear to the door, I can hear muffled noises inside, but it takes several minutes of bumping and rustling before a short, stocky man answers, blinking hard in the light from the hall.

"Is Truman Flynn available, please?"

The man's eyes are squinted to slits and his hair seems slightly on end. "He's not here."

With my hands clasped in front of me, I smile without showing my teeth. "Can you tell me when you expect him back?"

"Sweetheart," he says, closing his eyes and sighing deeply before he answers, "I've got *no* idea."

I thank him for his time and leave the building, trying to conceal my disappointment, trying to think what do to next. I'm outside, almost to the sidewalk, when one of the skinny girls in bare legs and tennis sneakers comes running out after me.

"Hey," she calls. "Hey!"

Her hair is limp and stringy, flopping against her shoulders as she jumps down the front steps. I stop and wait until she catches up. She has on a jersey athletic shirt with a zip-front and is pulling it tightly around her shoulders. She comes to a stop in front of me, looking skittish and out of breath.

"Who are you?" she says, staring hard. "Did one of the Macklin brothers tell you to come here? I mean, you don't know Victor or any of those guys, do you?"

"No," I say. "Should I?"

The girl only steps closer, staring up into my face. "What's your name?"

"Daphne. What's yours?"

"Alexa." She waves a hand dismissively at herself, still pinning me with her muddy eyes. "How do you know Tru? You a friend of his or something?"

"I don't even know him."

This makes Alexa raise her eyebrows and she stares up at me with deep distrust. "What do you want him for, then?"

"I'm looking for my brother. I think Truman may have seen him."

"Oh." She bends forward, picking at a scab on her knee. Then she sighs and straightens. "Okay, look—I bet you I know where he went, but you can't tell Charlie."

"Charlie?"

"Yeah, his dad. Stepdad. It's not a big deal, but Charlie doesn't like him going so far."

"How far did he go?"

Alexa shrugs, looking apologetic. "When I saw him this morning, he was saying he might go to Dio's later."

Her face is so clean that it seems reflective. I can see a soft, whirling affection in her eyes when she talks about him. It's sweet and steady, a world away from the feverish desires of Myra and Deirdre. This must be what they mean in movies when they say "crush."

"Might?" I say, trying to discern how this is useful. *Might* is uncertain. *Might* is no good to me.

Alexa sighs again, raising her hands and letting them flop back down. "He meant *would*, would go to Dio's. *Desmond*, I mean."

"What's Desmond?"

"A person, a guy. Desmond Wan. He lived here a long time. Him and Tru are sort of best friends." She's talking faster now, like the words are in danger of bursting inside her chest. She has to get them out before they detonate. "Then Dio got into college though—Northwestern—I mean, it's *crazy*. They gave him this huge scholarship and everything. So now we don't really see him except when he comes home to visit his grandma. Tru just goes there a lot. They still, like, party together and—"

I can only decipher half of what she's telling me and I hold up a hand to make her stop. "Thank you. Could you tell me where to go?"

"Can't you just come back later?"

"I have to talk to him now, as soon as possible."

Alexa is watching me shrewdly, her gaze traveling over my black bag and my boots, studying my face. "Is your brother in a lot of trouble?"

"I think so."

She nods, and now her eyes are shining in the sunlight, clear and glittering. "Boys," she whispers, looking at the ground. "They're just so dumb sometimes." Then she reaches into the pocket of her sweatshirt and pulls out a battered cell phone, clattering with plastic charms. "Do you have anything to write with?"

When I offer her a subway map and a ballpoint pen, she takes them. Pen in hand, she leans forward, copying something out of the cell phone, scribbling against the top of her thigh.

"Dio's," she says, handing the map back to me. A street address is printed in the margin and she's drawn a sloppy circle around a pair of cross streets. "It's pretty far. But I guess that's kind of the point. To be far, I mean, to just . . . get *out*."

She trails off, waving the phone halfheartedly, watching as I study the map. Her expression is complicated and something about the sweetness and the sadness of it makes me think of Petra.

And I hold out my hand because she shouldn't be here. She's so much cleaner than this place. "You could come with me."

She looks up at me like she might be considering it, eyes fixed on my face. Then she reaches out and carefully takes my hand.

"I can't," she says. Her touch is light and warm and she digs her fingers into my palm. "It doesn't work like that."

I understand what she means. I might be a long way from

Pandemonium, but home is still with me, a pair of eyes that follows along, measuring my progress, waiting to see if I'll fail. I nod and let Alexa go, even though it feels like the wrong thing to do.

I turn back in the direction of the train, studying the address on the map, but as I start to walk away, she catches me by the sleeve. "Hey, if you see Tru, tell him—just tell him to be careful."

"I will," I say.

I'm almost across the street when she calls after me again.

"Hey," she yells, standing forlornly on the front steps of the Avalon Apartments. "Hey, I hope you find your brother."

I raise a hand to show I've heard and that I thank her for her concern.

That I hope I find him too.

MARCH 7
3 DAYS 7 HOURS 53 MINUTES

Dio's kitchen was small but bright, with green formica countertops and brand new linoleum. It was refreshingly far from Cicero and the Avalon apartment complex.

Truman was at the table. He was drinking Dio's bad, cheap bourbon, and had been for awhile. His head felt numb and heavy. Most of the party was out in the living room.

Across from him, Johnny Atwell sang along with the stereo, drumming his hands on the tabletop. "On course to get wrecked, or what?"

Truman nodded, but he was thinking of the voice from the closet, thinking that he'd settle for feeling like he wasn't losing his mind. Somewhere behind him, a girl was laughing, a high, taut sound. It made his skin hurt.

Johnny poured him another shot and Truman drank it, closing his eyes as the familiar heat bloomed in his throat. Everything seemed to be rushing toward him, the whole world converging on the point where he sat, leaning his elbows on Dio's table. He blinked slowly and stopped holding his breath.

The shot was just starting to kick in when Dio burst into the kitchen, small and kinetic. He banged Johnny hard between his shoulder blades, smiling a little too widely. "Hey, it's big John! What's happening, my man?"

To Truman, he said in a savage whisper, "Dude, I thought I asked you to stop bringing your friends around."

He meant Johnny, of course, but also Claire Weaver, who was Truman's sometimes-girlfriend. Or maybe Victor Macklin, although Victor was scary-unpredictable and had recently promised to kick Truman's ass over a misunderstanding involving a bottle of shoplifted vodka and twenty-five dollars. Dio meant all of them, any of the tragic losers who drank with Truman or skipped class with him or scored him alcohol.

And Truman got that—he did. He could see his life as Dio saw it, watch the train wreck from the outside. He knew what it looked like, but Dio was wrong about Claire and Johnny. They weren't his friends. They were just messed up enough to hang out with him, and Dio was the only real friend he'd ever had.

The two of them looked at each other, not speaking. Dio's hair was long, past his shoulders, and his eyes were the narrow almond shape of a stone god's in a history book. His expression was angry and helpless.

Truman missed him suddenly, even though they were in the same room. Loud, fast-moving Dio, two floors down. They'd spent years, maybe their entire lives, smoking on the sidewalk and now Dio was gone. Going somewhere. Everything was wrong. He felt his jaw tighten and made himself stop clenching his teeth.

"Forget it," Dio said, shaking his head and reaching for Truman's shoulder. "Just go easy, okay? Don't do that *thing*."

Truman pushed Dio's hand away and stood up, fighting a surge of anger, and under that, shame. "Don't do what thing?"

"That thing where you drink like a madman, then pass out. Not tonight, okay?"

Intellectually, Truman knew that Dio was only talking to him this way because he was worried. But something about Dio's concern just made him feel worse.

Even in a house packed with college kids and alcohol and noise, he was completely alone. There was no place in Dio's world for anyone from the old neighborhood. Especially not a kid who was still in high school and who was never going to aspire to anything as ambitious as college, let alone pre-law.

At the table, Johnny was offering him another shot. Truman didn't really want it, but he reached for it anyway.

He smiled, holding Dio's gaze. "Hey, don't get worked up. I'm fine." He felt the familiar mixture of loneliness and overwhelming relief as Dio's face relaxed. "I'll be fine."

His own voice sounded warm and easy, and that made everything worse. *Fine* was the biggest lie of all.

He turned away from Dio, then froze, before letting his breath out in a strangled sigh. "Shit."

Claire had come into the kitchen and was standing against the counter, wearing a bright pink shirt. Her fingers were laced together in a way that made it look like she was about to start begging.

He watched her from across the kitchen and she stared back. He knew that she expected him to kiss her, but his head was spinning now and the times they'd had together had not been good. Suddenly, Truman wanted to tell her he was sorry, but it wouldn't make a difference. It was the one thing that she would never believe.

She moved away from the counter and started toward him, her footsteps sharp on the linoleum. In his altered vision, she moved like stop-motion, flashing closer. Then she was right in front of him, her hands plucking at his sweater, slipping under. When her fingers skittered over his stomach, he flinched.

It was painful, being so close to someone. He could see her too clearly, eyes caked with makeup, lips slightly parted. She was thin and hungry-looking, with Clorox-colored hair and too much perfume. She pushed herself up on tiptoe, and her kiss tasted sugary and like wax. When he pulled away, she didn't hold on.

Dio was watching from the doorway. He wore a tense, pitying expression that Truman couldn't stand. It was a look that said, *Truman Flynn, you are so fucking tragic.*

Truman grabbed the bottle and slopped liquor into his glass. Everything had stopped moving except him. Claire still stood exactly where he'd left her, arms at her sides. Her mouth was working and he hoped she wasn't going to cry. He could picture it already, smeared eye makeup and snot and pitiful hitching sobs. But she didn't cry. She just looked at him, her lower lip glossy and trembling. He drank off the shot and poured another.

"Tru," Dio said in a low, anxious voice, "Go *easy*. You're crazy, man."

And Truman laughed because it was the truth and because

Dio had said it out loud. For a second, it made him feel lonely, and then he pounded the shot and didn't feel anything at all. The refrigerator kicked on, humming to the ebb and flow of his pulse.

The night was long, stretching out, washing over Truman like dirty water. He smoked one cigarette after another and the filter in his mouth kept his teeth from grinding.

When Johnny slid him another shot, he tipped it back, coughed, but couldn't actually feel the drink in his throat. Johnny was laughing, muttering something out of the corner of his mouth. Then he leaned forward expectantly. Truman couldn't decipher the question, so he shrugged. He realized his hands were shaking and dropped his cigarette into the bottom of his shot glass.

Johnny studied him, leaning closer. "Hey Tru, you look like you're about to puke."

Truman took a deep breath and tried to answer, to say he'd be all right, but his voice got caught in his throat. He closed his mouth.

"Christ," said Johnny, shaking his head. "Go in the fucking *bath*room."

And that sounded fine, that sounded good. He couldn't stop shaking.

Then Claire was right next to him, tugging at his elbow. "Tru," she said. "Tru, are you okay? You want me to come with you?" Her voice was too shrill to be kind and she was plucking at his sleeve in a frantic, needy way. It revolted him.

He pushed himself away from the counter, out of Claire's grasp. Away from the kitchen, the linoleum, the bright light.

He made it through one doorway and then another. In the living room, the music was a jarring mess of bass and screaming. Bodies thumped, jostling each other, knocking into him. He had to shove his way through, but no one seemed to care. He stumbled into the back hall and pressed his face against the wall, breathing hard. Johnny was right. The bathroom. He felt sick now and too hot. Under his sweater, his T-shirt was sticking to his back.

The hallway was dark and full of doors. He covered his face with one hand and tried to think. He was dizzy and the stereo was much too loud. The carpet was soaked with beer.

There in the hall, standing across from him, was a chubby girl with butterscotch hair and a bored expression. She was leaning against the wall by the bathroom door, which was closed.

"Are you waiting?" he asked thickly, trying to keep the words from running together. He reached for the wall and fell against it harder than he'd meant to.

The girl looked up at him. "Hey," she said. "Hey, are you all right?"

He shook his head and rubbed one hand clumsily over his eyes.

"Look, do you want to go in front?"

He nodded and tried to thank her. He could feel himself choking and covered his mouth.

When the door swung open, he didn't wait, but slipped quickly past the girl coming out. Fumbling behind him for the knob, he locked the door and leaned against it. He was sweating through his shirt, hot and shivering.

In the yellow light he could see his reflection above the sink, gauntly shocked. A used-up-looking boy with a shining face and desperate, starry eyes. In the mirror, he didn't look like himself anymore. He didn't look like anyone. The fluorescent tube in the ceiling dimmed. He felt his head hit the floor, but it didn't hurt at all.

THE PARTY
CHAPTER NINE

The address Alexa has given me is on a street to the far, far north and it takes me a while to decipher the timetable for the train. I have to take the Blue Line and then switch to the Red Line, which travels along a high track overlooking all of Chicago. Out the window, the city looms like five or ten Pandemoniums, but without the glossy splendor of home. Everything is caked in grime.

My stop is in a clean, quiet neighborhood with trees, much nicer than Truman's. The air coming off the lake is murky and cold. It smells like minerals.

On the front steps of Dio Wan's house, I pause and touch my mouth, testing the shape of my smile. It feels wrong under my fingers—too wide, too hard. Clearly, I'll need more practice.

The house itself is narrow, with a short flight of concrete steps leading up to the door. No one answers when I knock. Inside, voices rise and overlap and when I knock again and no one comes, I turn the knob and let myself in.

The entryway is full of smoke and people. To get through the crowd, I have to touch them. I can't help it. Their shoulders and chests and backs press against me, but no one pulls away when I get close. No one seems remotely disturbed by my presence. They could knock me down and still barely notice I'm here.

"Hey," yells a girl over the steady thrumming of the music. She is wearing outrageously green pants and a wide plastic headband. "Hey, I like your boots! Are those vintage? Those are vintage, right? Where'd you get them?"

"Altamont," I say, trying to keep things simple.

A girl with a pink blouse and plastic fingernails pushes through the crowd and shoulders her way in next to us. "Morgan," she yells. "I've been looking everywhere for you." Her hair looks white in the light shining from the end of the hall.

"Hello," I say, turning to face her. "Do you know a boy named Truman Flynn?"

She just looks at me without saying anything. Her eyes are pale and frosty.

"What?" shouts the girl with the plastic headband.

I ask again, yelling the question this time, and it feels strange to be so loud.

She cups her hand to her mouth, leaning to my ear. "You mean Tru? He's kind of tall?"

"Yes, I think so. Do you know him?"

"*Every*one knows Tru," the girl with the white hair says in a tight, cold voice.

"Do you know where I could find him then?" I try my smile, but it feels wrong and it must look wrong because now they both pull back like they want to flatten against the wall.

"Oh wow," says the white-haired girl. "Where'd you get your teeth capped? Those must have been really expensive."

I look back at her, trying to decipher the question. "What does capped mean?"

"Ew, are you telling me they're *permanent*? I'm sorry, but that's completely disgusting." She doesn't sound sorry though. She sounds scandalized and a little bit pleased. She sounds satisfied. "And what do you even want Truman for, anyway? I mean, maybe no one told you, but you're not really his *type*."

I put my hand to my mouth to make sure my teeth aren't showing. "Why? Type of what?"

She twitches her shoulders, looking past me. "He's just not into the whole Goth scene."

"Visigoths?"

"How are you so *weird*?"

The girl with the headband steps between us. "Claire, just quit, okay?" Then she turns and addresses me in a tone that suggests she's taking pity on me. "Hey, I saw him like twenty minutes ago, but he was looking pretty rough. Not good, you know."

I want to tell her that his appearance might not be worth remarking on. That he didn't look good the last time I saw him either. "Please, I need to talk to him."

"Good luck. I'd check the bathroom. He's really drunk."

I nod and make my way farther into the crowd. When I glance back at the white-haired girl, she smiles tightly. Her smile doesn't look any more real than mine. I wonder if she has to practice too.

Truman Flynn is a piece of paper in my coat pocket. He is a memory of water and of loss, his hand sliding free from mine, no way to hold on.

It's strange to be in the house with him now. To know that he's here, somewhere in this sprawl of dark rooms and noise. I wish he were a star. Then he might shine through the spaces in the walls, gleaming between boards and under doors. If he were a star, I could follow the light. But there's nothing. Time, which did not exist before, is rushing past me like a long gust of wind. And Obie is somewhere in the world. Missing.

The house seems to go on forever. Over in one corner of a large, noisy room, a boy with a shaved head and buckles all over his jacket is pressing the dark shape of a girl against the wall, running his mouth all over her throat.

"Excuse me." I tap him on the shoulder. "Hello, I was wondering if you could help me."

He turns and there is a moment—I see it clearly—when annoyance turns to simple confusion.

"Can you tell me where the bathroom is?"

He jerks his head toward a doorway on the far side of the room, but says nothing. Then he turns away from me and fills his mouth full of the girl.

This is the world, I tell myself as he begins to feel her breast right there by the television table. This is the real world.

I step into a dim hallway. There are beer cans on the floor, scattered across the carpet, and a closed door and standing beside it, a girl. She looks pleasant and solid, like a nice toy.

Her hair is braided into two short plaits, bright yellow, and she's standing with her arms folded, almost expectant.

I point to the closed door. "Is this the bathroom?"

When she nods, I pound on the wood with the flat of my hand, but there's no answer. "Do you know who's in there?"

The girl shakes her head and shrugs. "Some guy. I was waiting, but he looked kind of sick, so I let him go ahead. He's been in there awhile, five-ten minutes maybe."

I want to ask why it doesn't bother her that no one answers. Her mouth is wide and honest. Maybe this isn't the kind of thing that worries people.

I knock again, harder. "Do you think he's all right?"

"He's fine. Just sick, is all. I'm about ready to go down the street to the Marathon if he doesn't come out, though."

"Marathon?" I think of Greeks, barefoot or in leather sandals, racing away along an arid coast, a blue sea glittering in the distance.

As though she can see into my dream, the girl smiles. "You know, the Marathon. The gas station. You wanna come with?"

"Thank you, but I'll wait."

She shrugs, and I watch her step through the doorway into the living room, disappearing into the crowd.

As soon as she's gone I try the door, only to find that it's locked. The knob moves loosely for a second, then stops and won't go farther.

I examine it, but find no real keyhole, only a small round

opening. In the movies, hairpins open doors when you don't have a key, so I rummage in my bag for a pin. I stick it into the doorknob and turn it back and forth, but nothing happens and I don't quite know how to proceed.

The knob is metal, though. Metal can melt, and this afternoon, I burned a man standing under a bridge simply because it was what my hands knew how to do.

I close my eyes until everything gets red—red as the light that shimmers and drips above the Pit. There's sound in my head like the roar of the furnace, air rasping in and out. There is a pin in my hand. Anything can get very hot. A thin coil of smoke rises out of the knob as the tumblers begin to soften. When I turn the handle again, the door swings open slowly.

THE BOY IN THE BATHROOM
CHAPTER TEN

He's thinner than I remember, shoulder blades showing through his worn-out sweater like wings. He's lying sideways on the bathroom floor.

"Truman Flynn?" When he doesn't move, I get down on my knees beside him and touch his shoulder. "Truman, wake up."

Light glows from a buzzing tube above the sink. Everything else stays quiet.

The skin around his eyes looks purple, like all the blood has drained out of the rest of him and settled beneath his eyelids in dark, poisonous bruises. Out in the hall, the party is thumping away like a heartbeat.

I grab him by the front of his sweater and drag him up off the floor. Obie said he was going to take care of Truman, but he looks worse than the last time I saw him. The waxy pallor of his face is scaring me. His mouth looks delicate, but too blue and too raw. It's strange, but seeing something broken is somehow worse when you can tell that it used to be beautiful.

"Truman, listen to me. You have to wake up."

His hands are moving on the linoleum, opening and closing in weak spasms. He pulls away from me and tries to sit up, then slides sideways.

I catch him, but only sort of.

The top of his head hits my chin and I yelp without meaning to, letting him go to cup my hand over my mouth, but I'm not bleeding.

"Daphne." The voice is clear and sudden, shattering into the bathroom from everywhere. Lilith is reflected in the mirror above the sink, staring down at me with brilliant eyes. "You're wasting time. That boy is completely insensible."

"He's just sick," I tell her. "He isn't himself right now."

"Then never mind him. I want you to visit the apartment where your brother was living. You need to go here." Her reflection fades, replaced by the image of a door with dark, scalloped trim, and after that an oblong yellow sign that simply reads ESTELLA.

I stare up at the mirror, trying to understand what I'm looking at. "I don't know where that is."

"Neither do I," Lilith says, reappearing above me. "That's why I need you to find it." She says it with finality, like the world is not entirely full of doors.

"I can't find a place if I don't know where to look for it. Truman might be unconscious, but at least he isn't completely hypothetical. He's here right now, he knew Obie, and it's likely that he knows the city. He's got to be able to tell me something."

"Well, wake him up then and make him tell you."

"*How*?" My voice sounds uncharacteristically shrill and my throat feels tight with frustration. Truman is slumped on the floor, partway in my lap, and the throbbing of my chin is already fainter. "How can I help him? He can't even lift his head."

In the mirror, Lilith's smile looks brutal. Her eyes are fixed on my face, so intent that I'm not even sure she sees me. "If you ponder that one long enough, I'm sure you'll figure it out. But I don't think you'll like the answer."

I turn my back on her and when I look again, she's gone and I'm breathing too fast. I pull a battered hand towel down from a bar beside the sink and wipe Truman's face. His eyes are half-open, a strange, pale blue that is almost like no color at all.

"Oh, God," he whispers as I scrub his face with the towel. His voice is low, catching in his throat, and his chest hitches and jerks.

I touch his cheek, his damp hair, trying to find the way that people touch each other on Earth. Tears are dripping down his face in clear, perfect rivers, landing in the palms of my hands. "You're crying," I whisper, and my voice sounds awed. "Why are you crying?"

But he doesn't answer.

Then, from out in the hall, there is the sound of footsteps growing louder, sharp and purposeful even through the music. The bathroom door swings open and Moloch stands over us, raking a hand through bright, unruly hair.

He tucks his thumbs under his suspenders and sighs. "You have *got* to be kidding me."

"What are you doing here?" I ask, holding Truman tighter.

Moloch steps inside and closes the door behind him. "I might ask you the same thing. I just had a bit of a holdup in the terminal, because *apparently* someone had already gone through using the name for my job. Now, I'm here to collect."

"But he's not dead."

"In point of fact, he was supposed to be dead twenty minutes ago. What have you done?"

"Nothing, I just told him to wake up. That's all."

The look he gives me is scathing. Then he reaches into his coat pocket and takes out a length of wire. "Fortunately, this can be resolved in no time."

I grab Truman, sprawling over him. "No! What are you doing?"

Moloch loops each end of the wire carefully around a hand. "Someone is about to die of asphyxiation."

I hold Truman close, clutching at his sweater and staring up at Moloch. "You can't take him!" My tone is so shrill I'm nearly begging. The feeling isn't one I'm accustomed to.

Moloch laughs, shaking his head. "I assure you, I can. Look, I won't even cut him, I promise. What I'm going to do is, I'm just going to choke him a little bit—just very gently— and then it will be all over." He takes Truman by the shoulder and begins implacably to pull him out of my arms. "What do you want this joker for anyway? The guy's not even capable of looking after himself."

"I don't need him to look after himself, I *need* him to help me find Obie." My voice echoes in the tiny bathroom,

99

ricocheting off the tile, and Moloch stares down at me like I've sprouted wings.

Then he tucks the wire back into his pocket and sits down with his back against the wall. We face each other in silence.

Finally, he rakes a hand through his hair and says, "Do you mind telling me what in the holy hell is going on? As in, what's all this noise about Obie, why are you here, why is *he* not dead?"

"Something's happened to my brother," I say, hating how dismal I sound. "I need to find him, but I don't know where to go, and now you're here to collect the only person who might know where he is."

"And see, here I thought I was just stopping by to collect an abject loser I was supposed to bring in a year ago. Daphne, the guy's a wash. I hate to break it to you, but his primary state is facedown on the floor, and he *still* couldn't help you find gravity."

"You don't know that."

Moloch sighs and reaches into his boot, producing a small silver knife. Then, before I can stop him, he leans across me and presses the point to the ball of Truman's thumb. Blood wells up in a fat, glossy drop. Moloch catches the drop on his knife, then raises the blade to his mouth.

"What are you doing? Are you drinking his blood?"

Moloch pauses with the knife an inch from his tongue. "I'm not drinking it, I'm tasting it. Now sit tight and let me have my moment of I-told-you-so."

I watch as Moloch licks the blood off the knife, closing

his eyes and tipping his head to one side like he's listening for something.

"Can you taste what's in it?"

He shakes his head. "Not what's *in* it, exactly. More like the history—where it's been, what it's touched. Everything carries its past, even blood." He smiles down at the knife. "Not a very macho talent, is it? Bet you thought a bone man would at least melt flesh or torture saints, right?"

He looks so abashed that I shake my head, even though at home, the talent of psychometry is considered unimpressive at best. "Did you learn anything?"

"He's been drinking a lot lately—no surprise there. No drugs, though. He's got a love affair with caffeine, doesn't eat too well, and about a year ago, he lost a lot of blood, but we already knew that." Moloch touches the blade to his tongue again. His expression is dispassionate. "He's a mess, Daphne. Just let me take him."

I don't answer, but squeeze Truman's hand, shaking my head.

"Perhaps we aren't understanding each other," Moloch says, holding up the knife. "You think you're doing him a favor, but he would beg for this. If he were well enough to tell you, he would *beg*."

"Liar," I say. "People like to stay alive." In movies, they outrun crazed killers, outer-space monsters, tidal waves, and volcanoes just to survive for when the credits start to spill up the screen.

Truman's lips look bluish. He will not run anywhere.

When Moloch speaks, his voice is strangely desolate. "Look, this isn't a one-time thing. It's not like a car accident or a shooting or a fire. Do you see how unhappy he is? That doesn't happen in one night. He is *always* almost dying."

I touch Truman's cheek, which feels warm under my hand. "But he's not dead yet."

Moloch leans closer, staring into my face. "It's no good, you saving his life. If you do it tonight, you'll have to keep saving it again and again."

"Is it hard to do that—save lives?"

He smiles, but it's small and morose. "I wouldn't know. Look, you're not cut out for the savior bit. And this kid, he's not good for much of anything either. Are you sure there's no one else who can help you?"

I shake my head. There's the image of Estella and the door, but I don't know what it means. My mother can see clearly and she can see far, but she doesn't understand about maps or distances. Even if she could tell me how to find the door, it might not be enough, and Truman was actually *with* Obie when he left Pandemonium.

I look back at Moloch, feeling something like inevitability. "It has to be him."

Moloch sighs and slides the knife back into his boot. "Fine, then. But be advised, this isn't over. I'm just the hatchet man. He's the one who's obsessed with killing himself." He gets to his feet then, shoving his hands in his pockets. He leaves the bathroom without looking back.

At the sink, I run the faucet as cold as it will go and wet

the hand towel. Then I crouch over Truman and say, "It's time to wake up."

When I ring the towel out over his face, nothing happens for a moment, and then he sucks in his breath in a huge, hoarse gasp, his eyes opening wide as the water runs down his neck and his temples, into his ears.

"Don't," he mutters, looking up, blinking against the water. "Leave me alone."

I stare into his eyes, which are impossibly transparent, but blue, blue all the same. "I can't leave you."

"You can. Just go home."

"I can't go home," I say, knowing that it's true. There's nothing for me there.

The city was never enough, even before Obie left. I just didn't know it yet. And now my brother's lost, the world is huge, and I have no idea how to begin looking for him. I want to say a swear like they do on TV, but suddenly I can't think of any except *Goddamn* and that doesn't seem adequate.

I grab the front of Truman's sweater and pull. "I know you don't feel well, but I need you to stand up."

At first, he doesn't move. Then I tug harder and he rolls over and pushes himself onto his hands and knees. "Stand up," I say.

He makes a low whimpering noise and shivers in a convulsive jerk.

My legs ache from kneeling. "Stand up," I say again.

And even though it takes him a long time, and even though his whole body is trembling, this time he does it.

MARCH 8
3 DAYS 6 HOURS 2 MINUTES

The bathroom seemed to feather out from the center of Truman's vision. He tried to get his balance and stumbled sideways, grabbing for the edge of the sink.

"Good," said the girl from somewhere near his shoulder. "That's good. Now let's go."

For a second, Truman was sure that he was only dreaming her, and dreaming the way the room seemed to waver and smear. After all, he'd dreamed her plenty of times before.

When he let go of the sink and looked down at her, it was hard to focus on anything but the dark flash of her eyes. She peered out at him from under the black fringe of her hair and reached for his arm. Her touch was electrifying.

It had to be a dream, because the light coming from the florescent tube above the sink was too blue and he couldn't feel his hands and girls this pretty and this pale might exist in some sort of altered reality but they did not appear in Dio's bathroom in real life.

Then she yanked hard on his wrist and he lurched forward and considered the possibility that she might exist after all.

She led him out of the bathroom and toward the front of the house. In the living room, the crowd was thicker, swarming around him. The air felt sweaty and there was too much noise.

Suddenly Claire was right next to him, clutching at his arm. "Truman!"

Her voice sounded broken, full of fractures and echoes, and he turned clumsily. She was a pink blur, winking around the edges, and he was dizzy with the sound of his own pulse.

Someone's shoulder hit him in the chest, knocking the breath out of him. For one second, everything looked bright pink, and then nothing did.

Claire pulled hard on his arm, yanking him away from the black-haired girl. "Where are you going?" she cried, sounding angry and far away.

He tried to answer, but his throat was too dry and the words got lost in the noise of the crowd. He closed his eyes, and it felt good to just shut everything out. He wanted to stand like this, here in the dark—the house and the party and the whole world gone—but he was so dizzy. Everything seemed to tip and he staggered and opened his eyes again.

He was in the front hall now. Claire was gone and the crowd seemed to press in on him. Then the black-haired girl had him by the arm again, dragging him toward the door.

"Come on," she said. "We're going now."

On the front stoop, he tripped and almost fell. His blood felt slow and thick in his veins.

"Careful." The girl squeezed his hand, looking back over her shoulder at him. Her eyes were huge and dark and strange. "There's a step."

The wind was freezing. It caught and tore at his clothes, whipping his hair. He made a low noise in his throat, but the girl was smiling. When her lips parted, something flashed silver, blinding under the streetlight. The cold made it hard to breathe and he reached for her arm to keep from falling. He was leaning forward, trying to catch his balance, and when his legs turned rubbery and buckled, he landed hard on the sidewalk.

"Get up," she said.

Her voice was clear and insistent, not a request, not a suggestion. He felt his muscles tensing, his body straightening even when he was sure he would never be able to stand by himself. He was trembling, shivering, unsteady.

He was on his feet again.

SNOW
CHAPTER ELEVEN

The Red Line roars up to the platform, accompanied by a vast wind. Paper is blowing everywhere, grimy with the dirt of the city. When the train comes to a stop, the doors gasp open and people file out in twos and threes.

Truman is sitting slumped against the wall of the L-train shelter with his head tipped back, mouth open a little. His eyes are closed, but I can see that he's still breathing.

"This is our train," I tell him, looking down into his face. His eyes are half-closed and the lids are still a bad bruised color. "It's here, so you have to stand up now."

When he doesn't respond, I grab the front of his sweater and pull until he stands. He has to use the wall to do it, keeping his back against the shelter. Every part of him looks like it hurts.

With my hand on his arm, he steps through the open doors and sinks into the nearest empty seat.

I settle myself beside him and try to make sense of the nighttime train-riders. There are boys and girls with haircuts so jagged and bright that their heads look like the plumage of tropical birds. On the other side of Truman is a man with a dark, wrinkled complexion and a light blue coverall. His hands are cracked at the knuckles and there's something black beneath his fingernails. Even when I watch him for minutes at a time, he will not look in my direction.

At Jackson Street, we transfer to the Blue Line. In the seat next to me, Truman shivers, holding his elbows. I can't think of anything to help him. He's rocking, making a low noise in his throat, and I reach for his hand.

"We need to get off the train," he says in a thick, hoarse voice. "The next stop, I need to get off."

"No, our stop isn't here yet. Two more platforms."

He shakes his head, his eyes barely open, pulls his hand away. "I have to get off right now."

"I read the timetable. It had a map. Your stop isn't for two more platforms."

"I have to get off the train." He's leaning forward, his elbows propped on his knees and his head hanging down. "I feel really sick."

I touch him and feel the bones in his back, the way his spine juts through the sweater.

"Please," he says again, looking up. His lips are a cold blue-gray color.

As the train slows into the next station, I try to help him, but he's already on his feet, stumbling toward the sliding doors.

I smile politely at the girl who steps out of Truman's way to let him off, and at the other people in the car. The smile feels false, but no one comments on my teeth this time. When

I step out onto the platform, it's a relief to be away from their stares. The doors wheeze shut behind me and I go to retrieve Truman Flynn.

I find him in the dark, beside the little station shelter. The lights above him have all blown out, leaving shards that crunch under my boots and glitter with the reflected glow of the street. He's on his feet, but barely, hands braced against the shelter wall, head hanging down. I stand with my bag propped against my shins and my hands in the pockets of my coat, and wait for him to finish being sick.

I'd make a face to show disdain or disgust, something that Moloch would do, but I don't know the way to shape my mouth. Everything feels wrong and I don't know how to act like I'm above it. The train is roaring away, the platform shaking roughly, the shelter rattling. There is broken glass everywhere.

"You can help him," my mother says at my feet in a hundred bright, clear voices. She echoes from the shards under my boots, reverberates in the jagged reflections of herself. "All you have to do is take away tonight. He'll feel better and you need the fix."

"I can't just take a whole night from someone. This is *his*."

The horde of tiny Liliths smile up at me maliciously. "And clearly an experience worth cherishing. He doesn't need it and you do. Don't tell me you've got no appetite."

She's right. The hollow feeling in my chest is there, not unbearable, but growing. I look away, shaking my head. "I'm not doing that."

"Your sisters were never this squeamish," she says, twinkling in the scattered glass, already disappearing. "Take him home then and let him sleep. In the morning, make him tell you what he knows."

I step into the shadow under the broken lights, where Truman is still slumped with his palms braced against the shelter. I touch him, resting my hand on his back, and he leans his forehead against the wall.

"Who are you?" he mutters, mouth close to the cement. "Why are you here?"

I don't say anything, just take him by the elbow and lead him out under the light.

"Who are you?" he asks again, more insistent.

"I'm Daphne."

He keeps clearing his throat, like if he could just get something out of the way, he could speak. Say everything.

"I won't hurt you," I tell him, but it's only a whisper. "Everything's going to be okay."

He looks around, blinking but not seeming to focus. "Jesus. Where are we?"

"The wrong platform," I say. "We need to get back on the train."

He scrubs a hand across his face, shaking his head. "I can't."

"You need to sleep. I'm taking you home."

"Not the train. I can't." He says it in a soft, harsh whisper. "Please."

I stand at the top of the platform stairs, looking out over

dark streets. When I close my eyes, the map is a colored spiderweb in my head, stars showing up where we are, where we came from, where I want to go. His home is close enough, only eight blocks. If he were well we could walk it easily, but he's too unsteady, and even going down the steps is an ordeal. I have to put my arm around his waist so he won't trip.

At the bottom, I let him go and we stand facing each other under the streetlight. As I pull my coat straight, something small and white begins to fall, drifting in front of us. At first, I think it must be tiny scraps of ash.

The flakes keep falling, landing on my cheeks where they sting hotly, then turn to water. And in a rush of delight, I realize that I know what this is. For the first time in my life, I'm seeing snow.

I turn slowly, holding out my hands and letting the snowflakes scatter on my face and get caught in my hair. "Look," I tell Truman, pointing at the sky. "It's snowing."

He just shivers harder and doesn't look up. His head is bowed and he holds himself tightly, arms crossed against his body.

"You're cold." I slip out of my coat, meaning to offer it, but my shoulders are narrow and he's much bigger than me. "Here, you can wear my sweater."

When I pull the Freddy sweater over my head, the air stings my bare arms. The sweater fits him much better than it does me. He doesn't have to roll the sleeves up over his hands.

"Does that help?" I ask.

He nods, but his breath is unsteady. It leaves his mouth and nose in clouds.

We make our way down the dark street, my arm around his waist the way I've seen the Lilim do with some of the bone men, but this is different. It's not about want or desire, and every now and then he pitches forward, tripping over his own feet. I catch him as best I can, but he's heavy and several times he falls hard on the pavement. By the time we reach Sebastian Street, his hands have begun to bleed.

❊   ❊   ❊

On the fourth floor, Truman fumbles in the pocket of his jeans, and when he can't get his key into the lock, I do it for him. I've got him by the arm, but once we're inside, he pulls away and I follow him down the hall. His room is small, with one window and a mostly empty bookcase. There's a narrow, lumpy-looking bed pushed against the wall and Truman collapses on it, sighing and rolling onto his back.

"Can you help me?" He whispers. His voice is slurred. "I need to take off my shirt."

"Why do you need help?"

He starts to laugh, a hitching, inexplicable sound. "I can't—I can't move my arms."

I help him pull the sweaters over his head, first my Freddy sweater, then his gray one. They're warm inside from being close to his body. When I sit down beside him, the mattress creaks under my weight and he rests a hand over his eyes. Below it, the line of his mouth is soft and lovely and terribly sad.

112

I study him, brushing his hair away from his forehead, remembering the feeling of his fingers twined with mine. Trying to find the boy who reached for me in the terminal.

At my touch, he uncovers his eyes and looks up. "Do I know you?"

"No."

"That's funny." He smiles, just a little. "You look . . . familiar. If I don't know you, why are you doing that to my hair?"

I watch my hand, stroking his hair away from his face again and again. "It's nice. It feels soft."

Truman laughs like he's trying not to cough. "Nice. It does feel nice." He takes a long breath. "Please, don't stop."

And so I keep touching him, feeling the softness of his hair, the warmth of his body. I press my fingers against his temple and find the whisper of his pulse.

"Why are you taking care of me?" he asks with his eyes closed.

I don't know how to answer. I'm not the kind of person who's supposed to be taking care of anyone. Even the question feels wrong, so I let my hand fall and stand up. "Stay here. I need to wash your face."

He nods without opening his eyes.

I cross the hall to a cramped bathroom. There's a washcloth beside the sink and I wet it under the faucet. I don't look at the mirror, in case my mother appears with more ideas about what exactly I should be doing to help Truman.

When I go back into the bedroom, he's still lying where I

left him. I wash his face as gently as possible, but his breathing doesn't even change. His palms are raw from falling so much and when I touch his hands, they feel hot. His face looks better clean, and the hollowness inside me beats against my ribcage like a living thing.

I hate the empty feeling, but more than that, I hate the way my mother smiles knowingly, like this is simply to be expected. Like there's no way I can control it. Hunger echoes inside me and I need to prove—to myself and to my mother—that I can resist the pull of his sadness.

Leaning down, I press my mouth to Truman's.

His lips feel cracked against mine, but warm, and I move closer. Hunger fills my throat and I can almost taste the complex flavor of his sorrow. I breathe it from his lips and as I do, I know without a doubt that I could drink it if I let myself, draw it out of him like venom. But it isn't mine to take.

He sighs in his sleep, and I pull away quickly and turn out the light. In the dark, I lie down beside him on top of the blankets, turning on my side and folding my hands under my cheek like praying. I close my eyes, something I have barely ever done.

So close to Truman, I can hear him breathing.

BRANCHES
CHAPTER TWELVE

Outside, the light is getting brighter. In the street, the snow has turned wet and grimy, spraying away from the tires of passing cars. I stand at the window and watch the sun balanced on the horizon. From so far away, it looks edible. It gets higher, becomes a tangerine and then a piece of hard candy lighting up everything. Truman's still on the bed. He's been sleeping for hours and I wonder if I should wake him up. He looks pale in the early light and I don't want to disturb him, but I'm getting hungry.

In the pockets of his jeans are an assortment of things. There's half a package of breath mints, keys on a metal ring, a blue plastic lighter, a crumpled receipt for coffee and cigarettes, a dollar bill, and two safety pins.

I eat the mints, which taste overpowering and do almost nothing to satisfy my hunger. Then I sit on the edge of the bed, rolling the wheel of the lighter with my thumb and watching the flame spring up, then disappear again as soon as I let go. When I touch the metal to the inside of my arm, it hurts the way light reflects off glass. The skin turns red and blisters, then almost as quickly, it smoothes over, seals back up. Is perfect again.

Beside me Truman starts to mutter, whimpering against the mattress. I take his hands in mine, one and then the other, palms turned up. Something's wrong with his left. Even when I press the fingers open, they won't straighten. They stay curled, like he's always holding something.

His wrists are lined with long welts that overlap and connect with each other. It's as though someone has drawn branches on the insides of his arms, carved them carefully into his skin.

I touch the branches, making him sigh and cough, but he doesn't wake up.

I wonder what I would do if he died right here. Then what? Then I would take my bag of things and leave this room. I'd find myself a hotel, and another person who knew my brother. It took six hours to find one boy. I can find someone else if I have to, someone more resilient, less damaged. I'll find someone better, like Moloch said, and all I'll have left behind is a body and twenty-four hours of my time.

Truman looks strangely peaceful lying facedown on the mattress and I don't want to leave him.

"Don't be dead," I whisper with my mouth close to his ear.

"I'm not." His voice is husky and kind of shocking, muffled against the bed.

He takes a breath and begins to cough in the middle, then sits up, raising one hand to his temple, feeling the purple lump where his head hit the floor in Dio's bathroom.

We sit in the tangle of blankets, looking at each other but not saying anything.

"Hey," he says finally, squinting against the sun. "What are you doing here?"

"I brought you home. It was snowing and I stayed. Is that okay?"

He regards me blearily and nods, not like a person nodding in agreement, but like he has to because there's nothing to say. Then he swings his feet off the bed.

"Um, I'm going to take a shower," he says, sounding awkward.

"Okay."

He stands up slowly, like he's getting his bearings, before stumbling across the hall to the bathroom. I hear the door close behind him and then the shower comes on.

I look at his rumpled blanket, the dent in the pillow. When I put my hand in the depression, it feels warm. If I were home, a girl like Petra would have already slipped in to smooth away the creases. I straighten the sheet, pat the blankets flat, but it just looks lumpy and uneven.

From out in the apartment, there's the scrabbling sound of someone working the lock to the front door, and then the sounds of stomping feet, jangling keys. I stand up.

Out in the hall, the man from yesterday is standing in the entryway, boots leaving puddles on the mat. Charlie, Alexa called him. When he turns and sees me, his eyes get wider, but nothing else changes.

"Hi," he says. He's in the process of taking off his coat

and has stopped, arms held awkwardly behind him. He looks like he's waiting for something.

"I brought Truman home," I tell him.

"Found him, huh?"

I nod. "He's in the shower."

"But he's okay?"

"Mostly."

Charlie breathes out. Then he takes his coat off and hangs it on a hook. He jerks his head sideways. "Hey, do you want some coffee, or some breakfast, maybe?"

I nod, trying not to appear overeager. The only thing I've eaten since yesterday is Truman's package of breath mints and I'm ravenous.

The kitchen is small and grimy, linoleum peeling up from the floor in all the corners. Charlie keeps his back to me, running the faucet, opening cupboards and drawers. He pours water into a plastic device on the counter and presses buttons until the air smells fragrant. Then he hands me my coffee in a ceramic cup and sets a milk carton in front of me, but still doesn't say anything.

The coffee is hot and velvety, with a flavor that reminds me of something burned until it got clean. It reminds me of home.

"I'll make you something, if you want," he says, leaning on the back of a chair. "You like eggs?"

"Yes," I say, but I have no idea if it's the truth.

He digs around in the refrigerator and starts lining things

up on the stove. I recognize the egg carton from television and it makes me smile. Eggs are my favorite grocery.

Charlie breaks three of them into a bowl and gives them a cursory stir with a fork. Then he leans against the counter, watching the ceiling and not my face. "So, what happened to him last night?"

"He almost died."

Charlie doesn't even look surprised. He just nods and turns away, twisting a knob on the stove. On the wall above the doorway is a wooden crucifix attended by a metal savior. Jesus, they call him.

I keep my eyes down while Charlie cooks. I want to watch him use the stove, but he's making so much noise that looking at him doesn't seem right. I stare at my coffee until he puts a plate in front of me. On it, there are two slices of toasted bread and a mass of yellow. He sits facing me and I begin to eat.

"Eggs okay?" he asks, after I've taken several bites.

"They're good."

He smiles across the table like something's unwinding inside him. He's unshaven, the bristles glowing reddish along his jaw as the sun keeps rising, shining into the kitchen from a window above the sink.

"I've tried," he says suddenly. "I know it doesn't look like it. But I tried to so hard with him."

There's the sound of the bathroom door opening and suddenly Charlie is picking at his fingernails, pointedly not looking toward the hall.

When Truman appears in the doorway, they don't acknowledge each other. He doesn't come all the way into the kitchen, just leans there with his hands in his pockets. He looks better this morning, clear-eyed and alert, and his color is much better. His hair is damp and clean, falling over his forehead in a way that makes me want to brush it back.

I stand up, smoothing the front of my dress automatically, even though it's ridiculous to think of decorum when I'm looking at a boy who does nothing but shiver and tremble and damage himself in useless ways.

"Do you want some breakfast?" Charlie says finally, still looking at the table. "I'll throw in a couple eggs for you if you want."

"Thanks. I'm not . . ." Truman swallows, his voice trailing away.

When he starts to fall down, he does it slowly. Then he's sitting on the floor, hanging his head between his knees and breathing hard like he's been running.

Charlie pushes back his chair. "You want to tell me the last time you ate something besides cereal?" His eyes are warm and kind and sad.

Truman just sits in the doorway, taking deep breaths and pressing his hands to his face. "Look, I'm fine. Everything is *fine*."

When he tries to stand, he has to reach for the wall to get his balance. I cross the kitchen and tuck my hand into the crook of his elbow. The skin is cold and slick. He doesn't protest and I lead him back down the hall.

In his room, Truman pulls away from me and lowers himself onto the mattress. He rolls over so that his back is to me, and draws his knees up. Through his T-shirt, his shoulder blades are like something by Rodin or Bernini.

"Are you asleep?" I ask, trying not to sound loud, but I can't help it.

The room is hollow with how quiet Truman is. He doesn't answer. If he is breathing, I can't hear it.

"Are you all right?" I take a step toward him, and when he doesn't move, I touch him gently on the arm. His skin feels warm and he flinches.

I stroke his hair the way I did before. It's still damp. He smells different now. Clean, like water.

"Could you please not do that?" he whispers.

"You liked it last night. You asked me not to stop."

"Yeah, well last night I was wrecked. Now, I'm asking you to stop."

I take my hand away. His eyes are closed and his mouth looks tight, like he's biting down on something to keep from crying out. It's hard to know how to touch him. His bones look delicate under his skin.

"What's wrong? Will you talk to me?"

He rolls over, looking up into my face. "I don't even know who you are."

"I'm Daphne."

And he smiles at me for the first time since he's been awake, a sad, tired smile. "That doesn't *mean* anything, okay?"

"I have a brother, though. His name is Obie."

121

"Obie." Truman's eyes are flat, suddenly. Far away. "From the hospital?"

"I don't know. Probably. Can you tell me where he is?" All at once I feel desperate for whatever information he can give me, even some small, offhand recollection, some little story.

Truman sighs and pushes himself up on one elbow. "Look, I haven't seen Obie in more than a year, okay?"

And for a moment, I just sit looking at him, because a year is a long time. I understand that. A year is a very long time, and part of me is still certain that I saw Obie only recently—a week ago or a month. But that was Pandemonium, and in Pandemonium, centuries slip by like no time at all. Here, time matters and any number of terrible things can happen in the space of a single year.

"Please," I say, trying to make Truman see how much this matters. "You have to help me. I think something awful's happened to him."

He shakes his head, looking helpless—almost apologetic. His eyes are a clear, icy blue like running water, and it's in this moment I know for sure that I've found him. Last night, that was someone else, dazed and unresponsive. *This* is the boy who looked up at me in the terminal. The boy who reached for my hand.

Only now, I'm the one reaching for him. I turn his arm to expose the inside of his wrist, tracing the branches with my fingers, but he twists away and won't look at me.

"What do they mean?" I ask. "Do they mean something?"

"They're scars," he says softly, says it to the wall. "They don't mean anything."

"Will you tell me about the hospital?"

But Truman goes rigid and still, staring past me toward the window. "Leave."

"But—"

"Get out of my room." He says it in a flat, measured voice, without looking at me. Then he rolls over, turning so that his back is to me, and doesn't say anything else.

I want to protest, or at least ask him what it is I've done, but my tongue feels stuck. I want to make him take it back, but I don't know how. Neither of us says anything and time stretches out.

After much too long I stand up, shaking the creases from my skirt, and I start for the door.

MARCH 8
2 DAYS 22 HOURS 25 MINUTES

Truman faced the wall, listening to her footsteps as they faded down the hall, away from his room. Then he rolled onto his back, one arm resting across his face. All the numbness and the sick, heavy stupor were gone and now he just felt cored-out. The daylight was bright and chilly, making his eyes hurt. He was so unbelievably tired.

With his eyes closed, he had a brief flash of the girl—Daphne—standing in an empty L station, looking up at him. There was a clearer memory of her fingers sliding through his hair. Her fingers on the insides of his wrists, tracing the lines there, exploring. How she hadn't looked at him with horror or pity, and she hadn't recoiled. She'd simply traced the lines with her fingers. He closed his eyes, swallowing against the ache in his throat.

How did you get your scars?

Her voice was an urgent whisper, repeating in his head, and he thought of Obie because he couldn't help it.

The emergency room, the hospital—everything seemed rubbed-out around the edges. He knew there'd been Jell-O every day, but he couldn't remember exactly how it had tasted.

He knew the sheets had been blue, but he couldn't say if they'd been blue like sky or like detergent.

The first night in the ICU was barely a coherent memory, but now and then, parts of it came back in excruciating detail. That night, he had dreamed of dark hallways and a blue-lipped-cadaver version of his face. Himself smiling at himself. In the dream, he'd closed his eyes, cringing away. And that was when the shadow man had appeared for the first time, only Truman didn't understand the consequences yet—didn't understand that he would come back, dragging Truman out of bed or whispering from the closet. From now on, they would excavate the jumbled garbage dump of Truman's deepest fears almost every night.

"Look," the man whispered gently, taking Truman's chin is his hand, turning him back toward his own decomposing corpse. "Open your eyes and look at yourself. That's you, undisguised. That's your black, revolting heart."

Truman had woken up shaking, seasick with pain medication.

Obie had come into the room then, rumpled and friendly looking in his chalk-green scrubs. When he'd seen Truman sitting up with the blankets pushed back and his hands held awkwardly in front of him, Obie's eyes had turned worried. "Hey, what's up? Is something wrong?"

But Truman was much too shaken to answer, shivering so hard his teeth chattered, and every time he closed his eyes, he saw his own grinning body—rotten, covered with a thin slime of grave-moss. Maggots squirming where his eyes should be.

Obie was patient. He sat on the bed while Truman shuddered and tried not to think about his dream. When twenty minutes went by and Truman couldn't stop shaking, Obie prepped a syringe and fed it into the IV line.

"What are you doing?" Truman whispered. It was the first thing he'd said since he'd woken from the dream, and his voice was dry and hoarse.

Obie stood over him, ready to depress the plunger. "I'm just going to give you something to help you sleep. It'll knock you right out. You won't even feel it."

For a second, Truman could only shake his head, struggling to make his voice work. "Don't," he whispered. "Please don't give me that. Don't make me sleep."

Another attendant would have given him the sedative anyway—easier to drug him up, put him out—but Obie only nodded. He pulled the syringe from the IV without asking any questions.

Then he sat back down on the edge of the bed and began to talk. He did it easily, leaning forward with his elbows propped on his knees, telling Truman strange, fantastical stories about astronomy and botany and God, until the sky lightened and Truman could finally close his eyes.

❅   ❅   ❅

The first time Truman almost died, he'd been Obie's responsibility. Obie had overseen the tubes and monitors, doled out the medication, changed the bandages.

Now, everything was different. Truman was in his own room. His sheets smelled stale and smoky, and it had been the black-haired girl kneeling over him on Dio's floor, holding out her hands. When he closed his eyes, the pressure of her fingers was still there, exploring his skin, finding all the things that he needed to forget.

Truman got up.

His ears rang and he saw little starbursts at the corners of his vision. Twinkling bugs went squirming by every time he turned his head. The room glittered with fatigue.

He pulled on one of his school sweaters and smoothed down his hair. There was a bottle of aspirin in the bathroom cabinet and he swallowed two, drinking straight from the faucet. After a few minutes, his head began to feel better.

In the kitchen, Charlie was standing alone at the counter, eating scrambled eggs. He cleared his throat and took a swallow of the coffee at his elbow. "Sounds like you had yourself some kind of night. Not gonna take it easy for awhile, have some breakfast? Maybe try sleeping?"

Truman shook his head and opened the refrigerator. "I'm not tired."

Charlie shrugged and hunched over his plate. "Whatever you say."

Truman nodded, staring at a plate of leftover pizza, a half-full carton of milk. Then he closed the refrigerator again. He waited for Charlie to explode, throw his coffee cup or his knock his breakfast on the floor, to do something. Even shouting would loosen up the knot in Truman's chest, but Charlie just scraped the last of the eggs onto his fork and shoved it in his mouth.

For a minute, neither of them said anything and then Charlie spoke again. "Hey, did that girl take off then?"

"Daphne? Yeah."

"She was a weird one. What'd she want?"

"This guy I used to know a while back, she's his sister. She just wanted to know if I'd seen him."

He didn't mention the hospital. He didn't mention last winter, but the temperature in the kitchen seemed to change anyway. Truman stood at the end of the table and waited for Charlie to notice, but Charlie only put his plate in the sink and started out of the room without looking at him.

"Unless you need something," he said on his way out, "I'm taking a shower and going to bed."

Truman nodded, making fists so that his nails dug into his palms. He watched Charlie walk away down the hall to the bathroom, wishing that Charlie would punish him or hug him or slap him or do something to show that he'd noticed Truman was gone. Charlie shut the bathroom door and the apartment was suddenly so quiet that it seemed to hum. Then the shower came on and the pipes clanked and Truman breathed out.

He opened the refrigerator again and took out a half-gallon of Gatorade. He drank from the bottle in long gulps, stopping when he started to feel sick. Then he sat down at the table and rested his head on his arms.

Before Truman's mother died, Charlie had been different. He'd laughed all the time, slinging an arm around Truman or tousling his hair. They'd gone places together sometimes, ballgames or movies. Charlie had been more like a father.

But that wasn't the whole truth. Before his mother died, they'd *both* been different. Even afterward, Charlie had done okay, for a little while at least. It was the other thing—the razor and the bathtub and the hospital. Then everything had changed.

Truman remembered the months between his mother and the other thing like one long, unbroken dream. In bed at night, he would curl around himself and the missing was so desolate and raw it was like a physical pain. Sometimes it was three in the morning before he slept. Sometimes the sun was already a glowing slice of orange on the horizon. Alcohol helped. He mixed it with things, fruit punch or strawberry Crush or cherry Kool-Aid. They all tasted like cough medicine.

Charlie kept a stash of decent bourbon in the cupboard over the refrigerator, but he hardly ever drank it. Truman helped himself, topping the bottles off with water until what was left was barely even the right color anymore. There were parties on the weekends, and if Truman was desperate, Dio could usually be counted on to scrounge something up. That was the thing about being bereaved. People were overcome with sympathy. They did things for you without even considering whether or not it was the right thing to do.

At school, the teachers still called on him, but he'd stopped trying to answer the questions about colonialism or factors. Their voices came from far away and all the assignments seemed pointless and much too hard. The knot in his throat that kept him from talking didn't feel like bitterness or defiance. It was just another part of the sensation that everything in the world was moving except him. Even breathing had begun to make him feel very tired.

In January, he'd had the idea for the first time.

By February, it had become a plan.

The bathtub seemed the best way, but there was something awful about being found naked. He'd stripped to his undershirt, left his jeans on. He spread towels on the floor around the tub, in case they made a mess lifting his body. He didn't want to make the whole thing any harder on Charlie than he had to.

Blood loss was both terrifying and gentle. The overhead light began to shimmer and the lines of the room seemed to run together. Truman had lain back in the bright bathtub water and closed his eyes. And that was where Charlie found him, barely twenty minutes later, but already Truman's heart was slowing down, a weak butterfly in his chest, fluttering, faltering, on its way to stopping.

The bathroom door was flimsy and narrow. It closed with a sliding bolt and when it didn't open, Charlie had kicked the panel below the knob until the bolt gave way and the screws peeled out of the drywall.

Truman didn't remember the noise the door made when it banged against the wall. He didn't remember Charlie dragging him out of the bathtub, squeezing Truman's wrists so hard that later, there were bruises. The bathroom was awash and they were both pink with bloody water.

He remembered the ceiling light, and his dream of the

black-haired girl. Everything else only fell into place later, when he lay in a dark hospital room, piecing together what had saved him.

Alexa had been on her way out to buy cereal. She'd heard Charlie yelling, calling for someone to help and had gone right back into her apartment and dialed 9-1-1. Truman had always wondered about that. Wondered what made her go straight for the phone, how she'd known to make the call instead of waking up her mother or running downstairs to get the super, but he'd never asked her about it. It was just one more link in the dubious chain of events that had saved his life.

All the tiny, lucky things.

MORNING
CHAPTER THIRTEEN

When I come out of Truman's apartment building, Moloch is standing on the steps. His back is to me and his hands are in his pockets. He's looking out over the snowy neighborhood like it offends him.

"Are you following me?" I say, adjusting my grip on my bag. "Because you're wasting your time. I'm not giving Truman back."

Moloch combs his fingers through his hair and turns to face me. I'm expecting another one of his sly, aggravating smiles, but his expression is strained. In the daylight, he looks younger and more uncertain than he did last night. "Look, I just figured someone had better warn you. Things have gotten kind of ugly."

I survey the empty street, the parking lot of the Avalon apartment complex. Everything is exactly as it was yesterday, only whiter. "I think the snow looks nice."

That makes him laugh, but only in the harshest, shortest sense, and then he stops. "I'm not talking about the weather. You just—you can't go wandering around like this."

"I'm not wandering," I say. "I'm being thorough. Truman was the last-known person to see my brother."

Moloch takes a deep breath, blowing the air between his jagged teeth. "And how are you getting on with that?"

"Not well. He told me to leave. To get out of his room, actually."

"Then thank the devil for small mercies. Honestly, that kid is a piece of work all on his own. He doesn't need you hanging around."

I look away, glancing up at Truman's bedroom window. It regards me blankly, curtainless and covered in smudges. "I think he'll die if I leave him alone."

I expect Moloch to scoff at that, but he just shrugs. "More to the point then, you don't need *him*." Then he shoves his hands in his pockets and looks down at me. "I think you should get out of Chicago."

"What are you talking about? I can't leave *now*—not until I find Obie."

"Daphne, you have to listen to me." Moloch's voice is low. Urgent. "A collection crew found one of you girls frozen and bloodless a block from the Garfield Street L this morning. It was a bad scene. I'm skipping town tonight, and so should you."

I stand numbly on the steps, shaking my head. "How could something like that happen? Lilith didn't say anything about it last night. She showed me a door I have to find. Is there any way you can help me look for it?"

Moloch's eyes shift toward the street and then back to me. "If you think I'm hanging around here, you're crazy. I've got one more local job tonight, and then I'm getting out of town. If you need sage advice or rapier wit before then, catch me over on the West Side." He gestures in the direction of the train. "Otherwise, I'm good as gone and you should be, too."

"West side of what?"

For a moment, he just stares at me. Then he produces a pad of yellow sticky notes and pen. He scribbles something on the top note, then peels it off and sticks it to my lapel. "There's a decent club in North Lawndale after dark. If you need me, there's the address. Now tell me you're going to get out of here."

I pluck the paper off my coat and shake my head. "I can't, not until I find Obie's apartment and search it."

Moloch sighs. Then he takes the note back and scrawls another address. "Look, that's for a hotel. This way, at least I know that you've got a place to stay." He shoves the note into my hand, looking sober. "Just, please be careful."

And he turns without another word and walks away down Sebastian Street.

※　※　※

The hotel on Moloch's list is to the north, a tall, cadaverous building called the Arlington.

The woman at the front desk gives me a key, which opens the door to a filthy little room on the sixth floor. There's a narrow bed, a tiny bathroom, threadbare curtains squirming with a pattern of roses. The wallpaper is peeling down in strips.

In the bathroom, there's a cramped shower stall and a pair of scratchy towels. I'm forced to admit that in the wake of my first day on Earth, I don't smell very good. I undo the top buttons of my dress with some difficulty and yank it over my head.

When I step into the shower, the water is delightful and shocking, falling over me in a warm cascade. It soaks my hair and when the spray hits my scalp it feels like tiny, glorious points of light. I touch a little bar of soap sitting on the edge of the tub. Its wrapper is lying crumpled on the linoleum, and the soap slides under my fingers, coating them in a slippery film.

I hold the soap and run it over my skin, touching it to my arms, my ribs, my collarbone, my face. It smells strongly like something I don't recognize. When I hold it close to breathe the smell, there is a tingling feeling in my nose and the back of my throat. The soap makes bubbles on my skin, and the shower washes them away, the suds streaming down my legs and ankles until they gather at my feet and disappear. At home, everything was clean and I never had to think about it. Here, clean is something you have to work at.

When I turn the knob, the spray above me shuts off.

There's a low, sucking gurgle as the last of the water runs down the drain. Then I'm just standing there, dripping wet and suddenly very cold.

By the time I change into my dress, I'm shivering a little. I go out into the main room to find my sweater. A battered television sits forlornly on the dresser, bolted in place. The silhouette reflected in its dark surface is not my own.

"What are you doing here?" my mother says, her voice brittle. There's a glare on the screen and I can't make out her features. "You need to come home."

I stand frozen in the middle of the room, hands half-raised to dry my hair with the towel. "But I'm still looking for Obie. Last night you said we had to find Estella and the door."

"That was last night. The city isn't safe anymore."

"I know. Moloch told me. He said I shouldn't go wandering around, and I'm not—I'm being careful, but I can't leave yet."

"Of course you can." Her tone is absolutely frigid. "This isn't some kind of game."

"I can't just forget about Obie," I say to the dark television. "And you can't just change your mind!"

My voice sounds plaintive and much too loud, but I don't care. Yesterday, she showed me the door, she gave me Estella. We were conspirators. We had a mission. Now, she's telling me to walk away, to give up on my brother, and slink back to Pandemonium like nothing happened.

"What was I thinking, sending a child?" she says. "This was a terrible idea."

I don't tell her that I'm not a child. I don't tell her that sometimes, things worth doing involve risk. "If you won't help me, I'll find the door without you. And if I can't figure it out myself, maybe Truman knows what Estella is."

Lilith laughs morosely. "Don't count on it. He has other things to worry about just now."

"What are you talking about? He's fine. I left him asleep in his room."

Her silhouette is unreadable, half turned away. "And I'm sure you would know better than I."

The way she says it makes me go cold. Without stopping to think, I shove my feet into my boots and yank my sweater on over my head.

"Wait," she cries. "Don't you dare go running off!"

I throw my damp towel over the television to drown her out, then reach for my coat.

BIRDS
CHAPTER FOURTEEN

At the train station in Cicero, snow is everywhere, filthy from the city. I start for the Avalon Apartments, almost running, but as I reach the intersection, there's a harsh chorus of screeching above me and I stop and look up. A flock of crows has gathered overhead, rising noisily from an alley between two buildings. They swoop around me in a wide circle, flapping and cawing. One wheels past, uncomfortably close, and in its round eye, I see a reflection of my mother. I jerk away, half-choked by the storm of feathers. The tip of one wing slaps hard against my cheek.

Their flight is raucous and frantic, herding me away from Sebastian Street, and I bat at them, trying break through their noisy circle. "Stop—just stop it."

"Go back," says my mother's voice from somewhere in the dark flurry of feathers. "Go home."

Then, as the crows get louder and the circle grows tighter, I realize they're not chasing me away from Truman's apartment at all, but away from the alley. I pull my coat up over my head and fight my way through them.

Wind sweeps down through the narrow space between

the buildings, kicking up trash and sparkling clouds of snow. I burst into the alley and then, open-mouthed, surrounded by crows, I let the coat fall.

Truman is standing in the dead end, under the fire escape, cornered there by three boys with hard shoulders and worn-out jackets. Two of them are holding wooden bats and as I watch, the third grabs Truman by the front of his sweater and shoves him against the wall.

"What are you doing to him?" I ask, and my voice seems to be coming from outside myself.

The boy closest to me turns and stares. "What the hell?"

"Daphne." Truman's voice sounds tense. "You need to leave. Right now."

The crows take off in a disorderly flock, and then I'm just standing there, alone in the mouth of the alley. "They want to hurt you."

He takes a deep breath. "I know."

The boys are all staring at me, squaring their shoulders to make themselves bigger.

"Well, I can't stop them if I leave. Why are you doing this?" I say to the one who has Truman pinned against the wall.

He glances over his shoulder. "I sold this punk forty bucks worth of booze last week. He said he'd pay me later, and guess what—he didn't. Now, I want my money." He adjusts his grip, pressing a scabbed hand to Truman's throat. His eyes are hard and without depth.

"Twenty-five," Truman says, looking angry and resigned. "It's twenty-five and you know it."

I consider the two of them. The thick, broad-shouldered boy and Truman against the wall with a hand at his throat and no reason to lie. The number itself is immaterial. If he owed forty, I would pay forty, but I have no patience for deception. With exceptional care, I take the roll of money from my pocket and count it out—two ten-dollar bills and one five.

I offer it, and am increasingly uneasy when no one takes it. "Here," I say, waving the bills. "Here's your money. Now give me Truman."

But the boy only watches me, eyeing the rest of it. When he doesn't look away, I snap the rubber band around the roll and put it back in my coat.

"Whoa, whoa, whoa—look at you," he says. "Don't you maybe want to spread some of that around?"

But the question is ludicrous. I don't. I offer the money Truman owes him, shaking my head. "You can't just take what doesn't belong to you. It's not *acceptable*."

"Daphne," Truman says. He looks noticeably worried. "They'll hurt you too. Don't you know that? They're just going to hurt you too."

But the boys only stand there, gaping dumbly, and I'm thinking about the lighter and the way my skin sealed up again.

The one closest to me has turned, positioning himself between me and the mouth of the alley. Not blocking my path exactly, but like he's about to. He says, "You might want to think it over. There's penalties if you don't pay the toll."

For a moment, I can only shake my head. I may be new

to this world, and catastrophically inexperienced, but I'm not stupid. There is no toll. There is no penalty, no justification except that he wants to take something that doesn't belong to him.

When he moves, it is with uncommon ferocity, like I'm a deer he's hunting, something delicate he wants to break for fun. He catches me by the elbow and the shock of his touch makes my whole body feel outraged. My hands fly into motion of their own accord, finding the pockets of my coat. The straight razor is flat on the end, but the other knife, the thief's knife, is made to slide neatly between ribs. I spin away, and that's all I mean to do, but suddenly, he's cringing against the wall and the other boys are falling back around me.

I have the point of the blade against his chest, already nosing through the heavy fabric of his jacket when Truman catches me by the wrist. "*Stop*."

"Why? He's not your friend. I don't think you even like him."

Truman looks at the other boy, whose eyes show white all the way around his irises. "But I don't hate him either."

Because this seems reasonable, I lower the knife and fold it carefully shut. I reach for him, the boy Truman doesn't hate, and pat his cheek. His skin is rough and he shies away from my hand but doesn't speak or make a sound.

"I only did this because you were about to make a terrible mistake," I tell him. "I only stopped you because you weren't about to stop yourself."

I mean it as an explanation, an apology, but he shrinks

against the wall, a spot of blood showing on his jacket now, very bright, but also small. A negligible amount.

"It's okay," I tell him finally, handing him the money, a five and two tens. "Just go home."

They leave at a run. One looks back, but the others only seem intent on putting distance between us.

"Christ," says Truman when we're alone. "You're insane, do you know that?"

"I'm not insane. I'm just making sure you don't die." Aloud, the admission sounds uglier than I would have expected. Without my mother's guidance, I'm alone. I need him to help me, and I can't ignore the feeling that he needs me to help him, too. He looks drained, like the confrontation under the fire escape has taken a lot out of him.

"Would you like some lunch?" I ask. "Let's go have lunch."

"I don't have any money."

I smile and touch the pocket that holds the roll of bills. "But I do. Please," I say, and I mean it in all the ways that a single word can carry a multitude. I mean it so much I sound close to tragic. "I'm just trying to keep you safe."

The look he gives me is hard and hurt and complicated. Then his face relaxes and he holds his hands up, like people do when they want to show they have no weapons. When I start to walk, he follows.

Neither of us speak for several blocks. We're stopped at the corner, waiting for the light, when Truman turns, looking at something over my head. "What you did back there in the alley," he says, staring past me. "That was pretty crazy."

"Crazy to keep them from beating you?"

"You were so fast. Like you knew exactly what you were doing. You stab a lot of guys before?"

"No, just that one. And I didn't *stab* him, really—only punctured him a little."

I want to explain the hours I've spent with Beelzebub, watching him get ready, but I don't think Truman would understand. It's hard to explain that this is normal, sticking knives into people. That where I come from, they do it all the time. It's hard, because it suddenly seems like an awful thing to do.

The light changes, the cluster of traffic moves on. I try not think about how bad I am. All my life, I've understood the nature of where I come from, but I never thought I might be wicked until now.

MARCH 8
2 DAYS 18 HOURS 22 MINUTES

The diner was a festival of tile and chrome, and all the waitresses wore ruffled aprons.

Truman hunched over his plate, mashing his hashbrowns into a paste. Across from him, Daphne was devouring bacon like she hadn't eaten in years. He was profoundly not hungry.

"Who were they?" she said suddenly, dipping the last of her bacon in a puddle of egg yolk and shoving it into her mouth. "Those boys—who were they?"

Truman didn't look at her. He reached for the salt and pepper shakers. They were made of cut glass, with metal screw-tops. The weight of them was comforting. "No one."

Daphne leaned forward, propping her elbows on the table. He could feel her staring at him.

"Look," he said, keeping his head bent. "I've known those guys a long time. I could have handled it."

"No, you couldn't have. You would have stood there not paying them, and then they would have beaten you."

He shrugged, trying to keep his face under control. "So what?"

She put down her fork, looking dignified like some kind of

princess. "So it makes no sense to get beaten up over twenty-five dollars."

Truman stared back at her. His gaze was steady, but his hands felt jittery and he spun the pepper shaker on its base.

She leaned closer, studying his face. "Or was it forty?"

"Maybe. Yeah, it might have been forty. So *what*?"

She took the saltshaker from him and tipped some into her hand. "That was money you owed them. Why would you lie about it? Did you *want* them to beat you?"

"No," he said, but his voice sounded defensive, even to himself.

"Truman, you have to stop inviting peril." She leaned back in her chair and licked the salt off her palm. "The world *is* actually dangerous, after all. Why are you looking at me like that?"

"You're eating salt."

She finished what was in her hand and shook out more. "It's good. I like it."

"Your brother told me once that salt was one of the divine substances of the world." Truman smiled, even though talking about Obie made his throat hurt. "He was always telling me about history and philosophy and stuff when I was . . . well, after."

"After what?"

He picked up his toast, then put it down again. "Nothing. Just after." His voice sounded empty and he stared at his hands.

"Can I see them?" she asked.

"See what?"

"Your scars."

After a second, Truman nodded and turned his hands palm up. Daphne reached across the table and took his wrist. Then she rolled back the sleeve of his sweater and began to trace the scars with her fingertips. When she touched him, Truman felt a rush of exhaustion, relief, and also like if she kept doing it, he might cry. He pulled his arm away.

"What made them?" she asked, and her voice was soft and almost tender. He had the idea that if she kept looking at him like that, he wouldn't have to tell her. She would just see the truth, the whole ugly story, right there in his face.

"I cut myself." The words ached in his throat, but his voice was steady and calm, like there was nothing inside him.

"Why? What made you want to—" She hesitated. Her smile didn't change, but her eyes were knowing and a little sad. "To cut yourself?"

"My mom died. I was a mess. I couldn't sleep, I couldn't eat, and Charlie's okay, but he isn't like a dad or anything. After she died, I was just . . . I didn't have anybody anymore." He was grinning now, a liar with a movie star smile, but the smile wasn't fooling her. His throat hurt so much he was afraid he might choke, and he squeezed the pepper shaker hard enough to make his knuckles go white.

Solemnly, Daphne offered him the salt and he took it, holding a shaker in each hand, looking down.

"But you did it because you wanted to die too."

"Yeah, that's why I did it. Now, can we not talk about it?"

She leaned across the table, watching him over her French toast. He stared back and stopped trying to charm her. The smile didn't matter, the warm, easy voice didn't matter. Her gaze was kind and steady. She was seeing right through him.

When she spoke, her voice was almost a whisper. "I'm sorry. We won't talk about it anymore. Have you finished eating?"

He looked down at his plate. Two eggs over easy, two pieces of bacon, hashbrowns. All he'd eaten was the toast. "Yeah."

Daphne nodded, then put down a twenty-dollar bill and stood up.

Outside, she smoothed the front of her coat and began adjusting the buttons. "There's something I need to ask you."

Truman passed a hand over his eyes. "Look, I already told you, I'm really sorry, but I don't know what happened to your brother."

"It's not that. Can you tell me what Estella is?"

"I'm not sure what you're talking about. Do you mean Estella like a person?"

"No." She stared up at the sky, looking anxious. "It's a place, on a yellow sign, and there was a door where my brother lived."

Truman started to tell her he had no idea, but then something occurred to him. "Hey, it's kind of weird, but in the city some of the really old street signs aren't green, they're yellow. Do you mean he lives on Estella Avenue?"

She looked away and shook her head. "He didn't tell me

things like that. Anyway, I don't think he's even there anymore, but maybe we can find something that he left behind. A clue."

Truman sighed, resisting the urge to press his fingers against his eyelids. "A *clue*? Daphne, it's not like he's some kind of spy—he's a hospital orderly. Why would he just disappear?"

She stood in front of him with her hands clasped against the front of her coat and her chin raised like she'd just been called on to read aloud in class. "Please, I need to explain something now, and you have to listen very carefully."

He took in her grave expression and started to laugh. "It can't be that confusing."

"Just *listen*," she said. Her voice was higher than normal and Truman was surprised to realize she was nervous. "My father—you've probably heard of him—his name is Lucifer. He's very famous."

Truman laughed harder, shaking his head. He took a crumpled pack of Luckies out of the pocket of his jeans, fishing for his lighter as he held a cigarette in the corner of his mouth.

"That's all right," she said at his elbow. When he turned, she was staring anxiously up into his face, gaze steady and unguarded. Her lashes were so dark they were almost sooty-looking. "It's perfectly understandable if you don't believe me."

But in a strange way, he did believe her. Maybe not that she was the daughter of the actual devil, but Obie had been unusual, and now here she was. And she was pretty unusual too.

"Here, I'll show you," she said, holding out her hand. "Give me a cigarette."

Truman raised his eyebrows and handed her one. The pack was almost empty.

He offered to light it for her, but she shook her head, indicating that she wanted to do it herself. Sticking the cigarette in her mouth, she bit down on the filter and cupped her hand around the lighter.

"Have you ever smoked before?" he asked, watching as she proceeded to ignite the tip of the cigarette and then shake the flame out again, looking mildly surprised.

"No." She tucked the now-smoldering cigarette back into the corner of her mouth and inhaled abruptly.

"Well, take it easy then. You're not going to like it and if you keep sucking on it like that you're going to make yourself sick."

Daphne tilted her head and gave him a perplexed look. She wasn't coughing. Her eyes weren't watering. In fact, she looked like a perfectly normal girl, smoking a cigarette like it was something she did every day.

Except, she didn't breathe the smoke back out.

It had to be a trick of the light. Or the breeze was coming from a funny direction, or she was only pretending to exhale just to mess with him. She was not holding the smoke inside her lungs, because that was a physical impossibility.

"Okay," she said. "Now I need to show you something. Are you watching?"

Truman squinted down at her. "Wait, this isn't already the thing?"

She shook her head and rolled up the sleeve of her coat. Then, with the cigarette clamped between her teeth, she flicked the lighter again. As Truman watched, she held the flame to her wrist and kept it there as the skin began to blister.

"Oh, God!" He grabbed her arm, jerking it away from the hand that held the lighter. "What's *wrong* with you?"

Her eyes widened and the cigarette dropped from her mouth. "Nothing. See?"

She held out her wrist and he examined it, ready to wince at the scorched flesh. But she was right—there was nothing. He stood in the middle of the sidewalk, cradling her hand in both of his and staring down at her unmarked wrist.

"How did you do that?"

She smiled finally, her industrial death-metal teeth glinting in the sun. "I'm a demon. It makes me durable."

Truman bent closer, brushing his fingers over the inside of her arm. The skin was smooth and warm, with no interruption in the texture, and his heart was suddenly beating much too fast. It had been a long time since he'd wanted to touch anyone, including Claire. Daphne's hair smelled like soap and something light and summery. Flowers, maybe.

He dropped her hand and stepped back, trying to shake the feeling of having been here before, having held her hand and then let go. "You wanted to go to Estella Avenue, right?"

She rolled down her sleeve and nodded.

"Come on," he said, starting for the train. "I'll take you."

THE SNOW GLOBE
CHAPTER FIFTEEN

Estella Avenue is just a narrow street that runs between two busier ones and we walk along it, looking for the door with the scalloped trim.

I'm thinking the search might take all day, but we've only gone three blocks when we find it, attached to a squat brick building, with a whole fleet of taller buildings around it.

Beside it, there's a numbered panel like the one at the Avalon, but unlike the one at the Avalon, this panel is in perfect working order. Next to the buttons is a list of names, but all of them are last names and I don't know which one to choose.

I'm deliberating when Truman steps in front of me.

"There," he says, pointing to a paper label marked in black pen. "O. Adams, that's him."

I press the number beside the label but am not really surprised when no one answers. When I try the scalloped door, it doesn't budge.

"This is ridiculous," I say, leaning against the front of the building and debating using a hairpin to melt the handle. "Why does everyone here lock everything all the time?"

Truman gives me a sardonic look and then proceeds to hit every call button on the panel, one by one, until finally, a woman's voice crackles out at us through the speaker. She sounds querulous, and very old. "Hello? Hello? Who is this?"

I open my mouth to ask if she can let me in so I can look for Obie, but before I can speak, Truman holds up a hand.

"I have a package for 224B," he says into the speaker, double-checking the apartment number for the button he just pushed. He sounds pleasantly official, and somehow older.

For a moment, nothing happens. Then there's a short blaring sound, and the door to the building unlocks with a loud click. We step inside, assailed by the smells of cleaning products and unidentifiable food.

"Isn't that dishonest?" I say, looking around the lobby. "You tricked her."

"You wanted in, I got you in."

"But won't she be disappointed that there's no package for her?"

At this, Truman's expression softens and for an instant, I think he might even feel regret, but then he just shrugs and starts up the stairs to Obie's floor.

After the incident with the lighter, he seems to have accepted my fiendishness, at least on a cursory level. He stands watch behind me while I melt the inside of the door knob, but he doesn't say anything. Then I push the door open and we step into my brother's apartment.

The place is damp and cold and very dark. It even smells abandoned.

Truman slips past me, feeling along the wall until he finds the switch. Immediately, the room is flooded in dull yellow light.

We're standing in an empty kitchenette. It has a pass-through that looks out over the counter into the living room, which is furnished with a threadbare couch and a matching chair, but no throw rugs or lamps or knickknacks. In the kitchenette, the cabinets are all standing open, empty of dishes.

With the overhead light shining down on him, Truman looks cautious and thoughtful.

"Power's still on," he says. "If Obie checked out, he can't have been gone more than a couple of months. Any longer, they would have shut off the electricity."

The empty living room is strangely unsettling, still full of furniture, but with no clutter or decorations, none of the trappings of daily life. Even Truman and Charlie's apartment, bare as it was, had a layer of miscellany, a feeling of being lived in.

I move through the apartment, looking for evidence of a struggle, or even just some proof that my brother spent the last year living in these rooms. That he's been here at all.

The bedroom is dark and cramped, most of it taken up by a double bed stripped of blankets and sheets, a dresser with the drawers hanging open. The closets are all empty except for a few odds and ends—an occasional button or a stray sock.

Truman stops to investigate the little alcove by the

kitchenette, peering into a plastic bin filled with glass bottles and aluminum cans. He holds up an empty soft drink bottle. "Whoever lived here, it looks like they moved out in a hurry. They didn't even take out the recycling."

We turn over sofa cushions, checking under them for clues but finding only paper clips, push pins, loose change. In the bathroom, the countertop is bare and the shower curtain hangs askew, torn partway off its rings. We go through cupboards and drawers, but our search is perfunctory. By the time I open the cabinet above the sink, Truman is already on his way back out.

I'm expecting another empty shelf, but the mirrored door swings out to reveal my snow globe. It's sitting alone in the center of the cabinet, shining softly in the florescent light. For a moment, I think I see my mother's reflection distorted in its surface, but then she disappears.

I take the globe down and examine it. The dancer still stands under the tree, face serene and arms held aloft. When I shake it, the cloud of flakes snows down like always. Only now, there's something lying in a jagged little hollow at the base of tree, nestled under the roots. All I can see is that it's flat and metallic.

I flip the globe over, trying to shake the thing loose. Snow filters down, collecting in the curve of the globe, but whatever's hidden stays tucked securely under the tree roots.

Holding the globe upside down, I notice something stuck to the base, taped to the circle of felt covering the bottom. I peel it off and examine it, but it's only a narrow slip of paper.

The word *Asher* and the number *206* are written on it in pencil, in a dainty, feminine hand that is not Obie's.

The script is graceful and precise. I move closer to the light, studying it—the delicate curve of the *r*, the straight, unfaltering *A*, the carefully rendered *2*. These few pencil marks are telling and somehow vital, the only evidence of Obie's clandestine love, Elizabeth. The woman that my brother left Hell for.

I fold the ends of the tape over, then tuck the paper into my pocket and offer the globe to Truman. "Do you know what that is? That thing under the tree?"

Truman squints into the hollow tangle of roots. "I can't see it very well. It looks like a necklace, maybe?"

"How do I get it out?"

He hands the globe back to me. "I think you're probably going to have to break it."

I hold the snow globe, feeling the weight of it, the knowledge that this is something Obie gave me. I might never have another belonging that reminds me so deeply of him, might never even see him again, and I don't want to break it, but the dome is sealed and I'll need to if I want to retrieve what's inside. When I smash the globe against the edge of the counter, water and glass spray everywhere and Truman jumps back, looking startled. He stands in the doorway of the tiny bathroom, staring at me. Then he starts to laugh.

"I didn't mean right this second."

"Was there a special way to do it?"

"Well, to start with, I probably would have done it in the sink."

I crouch down and pick through the broken glass and shattered resin. The dancer lies on the tile a few feet away, snapped off at the base. There's glass everywhere and I pull the sleeve of my sweater over my hand and rake through it carefully, alert for whatever amulet or charm was hidden under the tree.

When I fish it from the heap of glass though, I feel a little jolt of disappointment. It's a key. Not even a grand old-fashioned one, just a flat piece of die-cut brass, nickel-plated and unremarkable.

"Do you know what kind of key this is?" I ask, holding it out to Truman.

He shakes his head, but doesn't take it from me. "It looks like it goes to a door, but that doesn't really tell us a whole lot. Is this another one of those things where we walk up and down streets looking for someplace you've never been?"

I shake my head and wipe the key dry with my sleeve. "I think my cousin might be able to tell me what it's for."

"Just by looking at it?" Truman has his eyebrows raised. He sounds skeptical.

But what Moloch can do is a little more complicated. With only a single drop on the point of a knife, he told me all the secrets of Truman's blood, the history of it. "No, not by looking at it. But he's really good at finding out where things come from."

I mean it to say it lightly, but my voice is higher than normal and the words come out too shrill and too fast to sound casual. For some reason, finding the carefully hidden key is suddenly more frightening than finding nothing. Out in the apartment, the emptiness is like a solid thing.

Truman stands looking down at me. He hunches his shoulders and his jaw is suddenly tense. "Daphne, what's going on?"

I raise my hands, waving the key and feeling helpless. "My brother's been taken. He wasn't supposed to be here, and I think someone found out. There's only one person I know of who hates demons enough to hunt them down, but I don't even know how to find him. He's an archangel."

Truman doesn't respond right away. Closing his eyes, he rakes his hands through his hair. Then he bows his head and I just kneel on the floor of the tiny bathroom, looking up.

Finally, he opens his eyes and lets his breath out in a long sigh. "Uh—" He clears his throat and starts again. "Okay, this is bad. I mean, I shouldn't . . . I don't think I can be here anymore."

"What are you talking about? You seemed fine earlier, when I told you who I was. You didn't even mind that I'm a demon."

Truman stands straighter, still clenching his jaw. "Yeah, well that was before we were looking for someone who was kidnapped by an archangel. Angels are *holy*, Daphne. They're good, and they're *right*. Their whole point is to protect the world from the bad stuff."

He stands there looking down at me. It's a long, searching look, and even though his expression is kind, I can't think of anything to say. Then, without any warning, he turns around and walks back through the apartment and out the front door.

For a moment, I just keep kneeling on the floor of Obie's bathroom, surrounded by glass. Then I pocket the key and get to my feet, following him out into the stairwell and down onto the sidewalk. He's already halfway down the block, and I walk quickly enough to keep up without getting too close.

We pass crowded bars and a Chinese restaurant, a nail parlor that's closed for the evening, or maybe for good. Truman doesn't seem to have a particular destination in mind. He's just walking.

When he finally stops, he's breathing hard. He leans back against the wall of a dark electronics repair store and closes his eyes. After a moment, he slides down until he's sitting on the pavement, covering his head with his hands.

I sit next to him, our shoulders close but not touching. The cement is cold through my dress. "You almost died," I say, watching the traffic signals change color in the intersection. "My brother was the one who brought you back. He saved you."

Truman takes his hands away from his face. The look he gives me is anguished. "I know. Do you think I don't *know* that?"

"Then help me," I say. "Please, Truman. I know a lot of really terrible demons, but Obie isn't one of them. You *know* he's good. He needs us, and you can't just walk away."

Truman clenches his jaw and stares out over the rooftops.

"I *can*, though. Checking out is the easiest thing in the world. It's kind of what I do best."

"Well, did you ever think that maybe it's time to get good at something else, then?"

Truman slumps forward, shaking his head. "Unbelievable," he mutters.

But I know that after the lighter trick, he finds me perfectly believable, so I don't say anything.

We sit on the sidewalk without talking. Time passes. A van with a green florist's logo rumbles by and I get to my feet. "I have to meet my cousin at a club. Are you coming with me, or not?"

When he acts like he hasn't heard me, I turn and begin walking toward the train station.

I'm almost to the corner when I hear his footsteps. I don't slow down, but I don't walk faster either. After a minute, he catches up with me, shoulders hunched, hands in his pockets.

"Okay, this isn't because I think I can be a whole lot of help," he says. "But you need someone to keep you from going around stabbing guys."

"Well, at least you've picked something new to get good at."

"Wow." His voice is low and I don't look over, but he sounds like he might be smiling. "*You're* all about the tough love tonight."

Love. The word makes me feel unsteady, like something is moving under my skin. I'm not about any kind of love, but

I don't tell him that. Love is for people with a certain amount of humanity. It's for someone else.

I glance over and am surprised to see how solemn Truman looks and how wistful. In the glow of the streetlights, his profile is straight and handsome, oddly familiar. I have a sudden nagging sensation that I know him, and not from here in Cicero or from the floor of the terminal. I know the look on his face, the angle of his head, the way he's staring off into the distance, seeing farther than the intersection ahead of us or the deli across the street.

I'm not about love, but in this moment, I wish that I were.

THE PROPHET CLUB
CHAPTER SIXTEEN

"Are you sure this is safe?" Truman asks. He has his back against the wall and is smoking, because it seems like he never stops.

We're in a ramshackle neighborhood on the West Side, and this is the second time Truman's asked. The address Moloch has given me is for a place called the Prophet Club, but the only thing there is a grimy storefront, boarded up and abandoned-looking. The number is spray-painted over the plywood in bold, scrawling strokes, running downhill. There's no name, no sign or marker anywhere.

"It's fine," I say. "I just need to figure out the way in."

Truman takes the cigarette out of his mouth and squints at me. "What way in? It's condemned."

But I'm bending close to the wall, examining the plywood for some clue to the password, and don't answer.

Just below the painted numbers, someone has scratched *Gluttony* in letters so small they look like odd, uneven pinpricks. I place my palm flat against it and close my eyes.

"Moderation," I whisper. Nothing. "Abstinence, restraint, abnegation, nephalism." No response and I consider the possibility that Moloch was only teasing me, luring me out to an abandoned street corner because he thinks it's funny to watch me flounder. But Moloch is nowhere to be seen and I can't imagine him perpetrating a joke he couldn't watch, and the counter-word is there, scratched on the plywood. There must be a way in.

Truman pushes himself away from the wall and puts out the cigarette. "What are you doing?"

"Trying to speak the word." I press my hands against the wood, squinting at the tiny crooked letters. "There should be an obverse, something to counteract gluttony."

"Temperance," he mutters, reaching past me to rest his hand on the board.

At his touch, a handle materializes, followed by the outline of a battered door.

"How did you do that?"

Truman shrugs and looks away. "Gluttony's a sin. All the deadlies have matching virtues." My expression must show my confusion, because he raises his eyebrows and mutters, "Catholic school."

When I reach for the handle, it's cold and solid in my grasp. Inside, the club is dim, hazy with smoke. It settles over everything like a veil. A wiry man covered in blue tattoos is managing the door. He stares into my face with pale eyes, then smiles a toothy smile. "Good to see a young lady of your breeding. It's not often that we get the aristocracy in here."

He waves us into a large, crowded room with an oppressively low ceiling. All around, people are grouped in twos and fours, drinking from a startling array of mismatched glasses.

On a little stage over in the corner, a seven-piece orchestra is playing rock music with a cello and two violins. Everyone is packed together, laughing, talking, dancing. They're pale and alike, all ghostly copies of each other. Truman moves closer to me, staring around at all the people. My people.

I slide my way through the crowd, scanning the room for Moloch's crest of red hair. The whole place seems to be nothing but black and white.

When another tattooed footman pushes by us with a tray of drinks, I catch hold of his arm. "Excuse me, I'm looking for my cousin Moloch. Have you seen him?"

The server hefts his tray over the heads of a pair of giggling Lilim and gazes down at me with bored eyes. "I see a lot of people."

"Well, he doesn't look like any of them. He works for the bone shop and his hair is very red."

The server makes an ambiguous noise and points in the direction of a low doorway, nearly hidden by smoke and people. "He's in the back."

We make our way toward the door, past packed alcoves and crowded tables. The floor is rough, sloping gently downward, and it's hard to tell if the room is cut straight from the ground, or if it's just covered in so much dirt that whatever surface lies below has been buried for centuries. The walls and the ceiling are painted a dark, flaking maroon.

Truman stays close, following me into another room and

another. I wonder how far the Prophet Club goes. It sprawls indecorously, winding back on itself. At the end of a maze of hallways, we come out in a low-ceilinged room with a long, heavy bar along one wall.

At a table in the far corner, Moloch has his back to us and is leaning toward a girl with long black hair and an astonishing amount of cleavage. He's got his coat off and his sleeves rolled up. As he talks, he gestures with what looks like a long strand of beads. The girl sitting across from him is Myra.

I make my way toward them, edging through the crowd and pulling Truman behind me. As we come up behind him, Moloch glances over his shoulder. He smiles when he sees us, but it looks subdued.

"Well, hello there, sweetness. I see you've brought your Romeo with you." He tips an imaginary hat at Truman. "Feeling better then? It looks as though death didn't agree with you."

Truman nods, but still doesn't say anything.

We situate ourselves at the table, and Myra gathers up the string of beads, moving her chair to make room for me. Beside her, I finally have a chance to study her face and I can see that something is very wrong. Her mouth is a strange shape I'm not used to, soft and lost-looking.

"Aren't you going to introduce me to your friend?" Her tone sounds oddly timid. It doesn't at all match the hunger in her eyes as her gaze darts to Truman, then back to me.

He's staring at her like he's never seen a girl so shockingly beautiful, and he probably hasn't.

"This is my sister," I tell him, because it's true and because I have to say something.

Myra leans forward, holding out a hand. "Charmed," she says in a tremulous voice as he reaches for her.

For an instant, her fingers seem to flicker past his palm, stroking the inside of his wrist. Then they're back where they belong, clasped in a prim, well-mannered handshake. Her expression goes from vulnerable to something else and back again too quickly to say for sure. I may have mistaken the movement of her hand, reaching to stroke his scarred wrist. But I am almost positive that I did not mistake the look of calculation in her eyes.

"What's wrong?" I ask, holding her gaze as I reach over and carefully disengage her fingers from Truman's.

He gives me a startled look, but Myra only glances down, closing her hand around the string of beads. "Deirdre's gone."

The words are flat, without intonation, and for a second, I don't understand. Then realization sinks in, underlining the difference between gone and *gone*. Obie is gone—gone from Pandemonium, gone from his apartment. And that's grave, but not insurmountable. It simply means that his location is unknown, and I'm here on the chance that wherever he might be, I can bring him back.

Deirdre has gone someplace she won't come back from.

Across from me, Moloch's face contorts for a second, then goes back to normal. The fleeting expression is one of sorrow, or maybe pity, but one thing is sure. I know now who the girl they found near the Garfield Street station was.

Beside me, Myra fidgets with the beads, then puts them down, cupping her elbows one moment, touching her hair the next. Her hands look uncertain without someone to hold onto. Without Deirdre, she's just a girl in a short dress, tugging on her own hair. I remember them together, slinking into my room, rearranging my souvenirs and terrorizing Petra. How bright and fierce they looked. How permanent.

"How did she die?" I ask, and my voice sounds thin, like I don't want to know.

Myra's lip trembles. "Horribly." Nothing but a whisper. "They left *this* nasty thing."

Her eyes are glistening, but she brandishes the beads at me with savage intensity. Her wrist clatters with bangles and cuff bracelets and a thin silver chain covered in tiny charms. When I look closer, I see that each one is a vial labeled with a different deadly sin. LUST is worn away, as though she has spent a long time fingering it. Despite her apparent distress, she keeps glancing over at Truman, touching her lips with the tip of her tongue.

She breathes a heavy sigh and winds the string of beads around her wrist, knotting the ends together. "I apologize for my lack of composure," she tells him with a watery smile. "It's just—it's so sad. Do you think you could get me a drink? If it's not too much trouble?"

Truman nods and gets to his feet. "Do you know what you want?"

Myra smiles up at him. Her eyelashes are long and mysterious. They flutter against her cheeks every time she blinks. "A White Angel," she says in a voice that hints at deep, secret chasms and burning sulfur. "Please."

When Truman looks at me, I indicate Moloch and touch the pocket that holds the key. Truman seems to understand, because he turns and heads in the direction of the bar.

Out in the front of the Prophet Club, the band is playing a song that sounds like birds at night, darker shapes against a dark sky. The music seeps back to us in sultry tones, pulsing and rhythmic.

Myra watches him go, hissing softly when she sees the way the Lilim and the bone men are staring at him. Then she rises from her chair. "I think he needs some company."

When she starts after Truman, her step is light and graceful. Her hips sway like beats on a drum.

"He's got a sort of charm, I'll admit," says Moloch softly, watching Truman slide through the crowd toward the bar, with Myra creeping after him. "Kind of brazenly pathetic."

I nod, but I don't like how the bone men are looking at him or the way Myra follows behind him.

"You two seem to be managing better now that he's not in a coma. Or do you just bring all the dying boys you've stolen from your cousin to demon night clubs? I imagine Beelzebub will be thrilled to hear that you're dabbling in Collections now."

"Is he *here*?" The Prophet Club seems far too dark and grimy for Beelzebub's tastes, but I slide down in my chair, trying to make myself smaller, because if he's here, there's a strong possibility that I am going to be in a great deal of trouble.

Moloch shakes his head, giving me a knowing smile.

"Don't worry, he's mucking around in Bulgaria or somewhere. And no, I didn't tell him that his favorite little protégé is trundling around Earth yelling blue murder about her brother." He leans closer, clasping his hands around his drink. "How goes the brother search? Did you find anything?"

"Nothing good." I fish the key from my coat pocket and slide it toward him. "We went to his apartment, but it was abandoned. This was all that turned up. It was hidden inside my snow globe."

Moloch studies the key, scraping his teeth with a gray thumbnail. "Well, that's enigmatic."

"I was hoping you might be able to help. Do you think you could tell me where it came from?"

He stares back, looking distinctly nonplussed. "You can't be serious."

I only sit taller in my chair, giving him the look my mother uses when she means to be obeyed.

He rolls his eyes and glances around, then reaches for the key. Turning surreptitiously toward the wall, he holds it to his tongue.

"Was Obie the one who hid it in the snow globe?"

Moloch shakes his head. "He's never touched it, and that's saying something. An awful lot of people have handled this."

"Do you know what it goes to?"

He brings the key to his mouth again, holding it there for longer this time. Then he palms it and passes it back to me. "Asher Self-Storage. The unit number is 206, or maybe 209— it's hard to get the specifics sometimes."

"206," I say, remembering the scrap of paper.

Moloch shrugs. "Fair enough." Then he glances over his shoulder to where Truman is standing at the bar with Myra. "By the way, you might want to keep an eye on that. Your sister's in a mood tonight."

I slip the key back into my pocket, trying not to stare too pointedly at Truman and Myra. Her mouth is very close to his ear and I can't help wondering what secrets she's telling him. What dark, seductive promises.

"I feel I've been very good about debasing myself for your edification," Moloch says. "Now, will you think seriously about leaving Chicago?"

His tone is flippant, but underneath is a current of anxiety. I recognize it, but I'm not even close to finding Obie, and now I need to see what's hidden in Asher Self-Storage 206. "Not yet. I still have some things to do."

"Deirdre was flogged," he says abruptly and his expression holds no humor and no irony. "She was beaten to shreds and drained of blood." Every word sounds strained, like it's being wrenched out of him.

I realize that he saw her. When he says that a collection crew found her, he doesn't just mean he heard some grisly secondhand account of her death. He stood over her body and now here we are, sitting across from each other, trying valiantly not to care. I recall Deirdre, laughing, preening, smiling. Then, when the picture gets chaotic and bloody, I stop thinking about her. The memory of her makes something ache behind my eyes.

"It will be all right," I say, because it's what I want to

believe. I know better though. Even if murder were something that happened in Pandemonium, it would take a great deal of strength and stamina to beat one of the Lilim to death. More power than most demons possess.

Moloch looks away. His face is slack. "You've got a funny definition of *all right.*"

"I just mean, this has to be some kind of terrible accident, or the result of a grudge or something. Doesn't it?"

He smiles grimly and shakes his head. "I guess I'm just a little less optimistic than you are. Maybe no one around here wants to admit it, but I'm pretty sure we're looking at the handiwork of Dark Dreadful."

I know her only as the monster on the wall, with her jagged teeth, eyes like comets. Whips and knives and razor claws. The blood-drinker. But it's always seemed too fantastical. Even though I've grown up looking at her portrait, I never actually believed that she was real.

"Whatever happened," Moloch says, "Illinois's looking a bit fatal right about now. It's time to get out."

I shake my head, feeling slightly lost. The only map I have is for Chicago. "Where would I even go?"

"Come to the Passiflore Hotel in Las Vegas. There's a jump-door in the garden there, so you won't have to waste time traveling or mess with transportation. It's a good place for people like us. I've got Myra convinced to join me, and quite frankly, it's a bit suicidal staying around here."

"Is the Passiflore like the Arlington?"

"No." His expression is amused and he leans back in his

chair, smiling mysteriously. "No, it's not like the Arlington."

"If I were to set out for Las Vegas, are there any special words or commands I ought to know? I mean, I had some trouble with the door here. Truman had to open it for me."

Moloch regards me with eyebrows raised. "Did he, now?"

"Yes, he went to Catholic school."

"Be as that may," Moloch says dryly, "I think his ability to open hidden doors has less to do with latent Catholicism, and more to do with being the bastard son of someone with a halo. Blood like that, he can walk through just like anybody else. Now, if you want to get to the Passiflore, all you'll need is this."

He takes a black felt-tipped marker from his pocket and rolls it across the table to me.

For a moment, I say nothing, staring down at the marker. Then I look up at him, trying to determine if he's mocking me. "What do I do with it?"

"You make yourself a door. It just takes an east-facing wall and something to draw with. Render the entryway of your choice, knock politely, and ask for the Passiflore Hotel. If your walking tragedy got you both in here, he should manage the jump all right. The trip probably isn't going to feel good, but it won't kill him."

"He didn't seem to have any problem coming in here. Do you mean the jump-door will be worse?"

Moloch gives me a complacent smile. "I'm not a betting man, but I'd venture the half of him that's human is going to find it quite a bit worse."

MARCH 8
2 DAYS 7 HOURS 13 MINUTES

They sat side by side on the train, swaying against each other as it rocked.

Truman clasped his hands behind the back of his neck and stared straight ahead. "No offense, but your cousin's kind of a dick. Your sister though, she's—" He shook his head, trying to find the words for what Myra was. "Holy shit."

Daphne stared out at the moving skyline. "I know."

Her voice was distant and Truman lapsed into silence. What he didn't say was that Myra had scared him a little. Really, he was just glad to be out of there.

At the bar she'd slipped onto a stool next to him, pretending not to notice that her leg was pressing against his. When she'd offered to buy him a drink, his first impulse was to say no. The night before was still fresh in his mind and he didn't want Daphne to see him drunk again. But his skin felt too tight for comfort and it was just one drink. Myra's smile was wide and inviting, and Truman found it hard to look away. After a second, he nodded.

"Road to Redemption," she told the bartender, holding up a hand. Her nails were painted a sticky, iridescent purple, so dark it looked nearly black in the light from the bar. "And doesn't he look like he needs it?"

"What is it?" he asked Myra when the bartender slid the drink across to him.

The look she gave him was sly. "Don't you worry about the particulars. Let's just say, I could have ordered you a Road to Hell—they're basically the same. The only difference is, Redemption comes with a splash of grenadine."

The drink was a deep mahogany color, topped with a layer of bright, sickly red.

Myra ran one finger along the back of Truman's neck. Her touch was electric and he sipped the drink to keep himself from breathing too fast. It tasted like sweet, salty water and something flammable. He'd never been in a bar before, not even to ask for directions or use a pay phone. The Prophet Club was ancient, and decades of liquor had soaked into the counter and the floors, making everything smell boozy and kind of sickening.

Myra sighed and moved closer. Her own drink was almost black, with a thin column of smoke rising off it. There was a hunger in her face that he recognized. It reminded him of girls at school. The ones who would make out at parties and not expect him to call afterward. It was an unsettling look—sad, but a little too predatory.

She turned to face him and held up her glass. The cloud of smoke had already drifted away. "To Deirdre. I'll remember her for as long as I remember anything."

She said it with a smile, but her eyes were flat as she

downed her drink, then sat toying restlessly with the string of beads knotted around her wrist. A short length hung down separate from the main strand and Truman moved to get a better look. The thing Moloch had given her was a rosary.

"So," she whispered, letting go of the beads and leaning so her chest brushed his shoulder. "How did you meet my sister?"

Her body was warm through his T-shirt and he stayed very still. "We met at a party."

"A party? Daphne? How adorable."

Truman didn't answer. *Adorable* was not a word he generally used to describe anything. But it sort of fit Daphne.

"And what about you?" she said, leaning closer and fondling the rosary. "You look lonely, like you could use a kiss."

He shook his head and inched away. He wanted to argue with her, remind her that her sister had just died and this was hardly the time to be scamming on guys in bars, but even Daphne's reaction to Moloch's news had been minimal. And the truth was, Truman wasn't entirely sure he'd understood the conversation. He knew they'd been talking about someone being killed—murdered, maybe—but all three of them had seemed disturbingly unconcerned.

"Let me tell you a secret." Myra's lips moved slowly, almost brushing his neck. "Girls like me, we are very, very good at making people feel better. We find pain, and we take it away."

"Why are you even talking to me? I mean, what's in it for you?"

"Maybe nothing. Maybe it's all about you." Her lips against his ear were unbearably warm. "I know you want to get rid of something—all the feelings, the memories."

"Like you know anything about it."

Myra smiled slyly. Then she closed her eyes and moved her mouth along his neck, inhaling deeply like she was smelling him. "Linoleum. Liquor, mildew, soap. And water. I smell water and something black and sick underneath." She opened her eyes again. "Guilt?"

Truman stared at the wall of bottles behind the bar and didn't answer. It was unsettling to think that she could see guilt just by looking at him.

"And you smell a little like death. Not a lot, just a little." She held her fingers an inch apart. "Just this much." Then she licked her lips, and her eyes widened in something like delight. "Oh, alcoholism—that's nice."

"I'm not an alcoholic."

She moved closer, running the tip of her tongue along her bottom lip like she was tasting the air beside his cheek. "Well, not yet. Not quite. But it's on its way. Six months—a year, maybe. How Deirdre would have loved you. She always had a taste for addiction."

Myra rested her hand on his knee, pressing her mouth against his ear. "Let me take it," she whispered. "You don't want it. It's just going to hurt you and keep hurting you. Let me take it away and you'll never have to feel it again." Her breath on his neck was electric.

And for one excruciating moment, Truman wanted to say yes. The word was there. He could feel it shaping itself in his mouth.

Then he looked past her. Daphne still sat at the corner table with Moloch, partially in shadow. Her face was turned toward him and she looked very out of place in the dim, seedy club. She looked clean.

Myra's hand on the back of Truman's neck suddenly turned into the way Daphne had touched him the other night. Holding him in Dio's bathroom. On the train platform. In the street. Her hand on his forehead, the insides of his arms. Holding him again, always, no matter how ruined and messy and pathetic. Myra was caressing his shoulder when he stood up abruptly.

He crossed the dance floor to the corner, not looking back.

❀   ❀   ❀

Outside the train, the city flashed by, dark and light and dark. The ghosts of high-rises showed in outline against the sky, but Truman ignored their insubstantial shapes and focused on his own reflection.

"Which one is your stop?" Daphne said, still gazing out the window.

He shrugged, feeling awkward. "It's not for awhile. I mean, I actually have to go back the other way."

Daphne glanced up at him with wide, startled eyes. "You came with me?"

He nodded. "I thought it might be better if you didn't have to go back to your hotel alone. I thought it might be safer."

The decision hadn't been that conscious, though. They'd left the club and walked through the rundown neighborhood to the station and instead of saying goodbye, he'd simply gotten on the train with Daphne, fully aware that he was going the wrong direction.

Maybe he'd done it to make up for how close he'd come to bailing on her earlier. Everything he'd ever learned in church said that angels were the very definition of good. You shouldn't even want to go against them. But Obie was good too, and that was something he knew for a fact.

Beside him, Daphne was quiet, staring down at her hands.

"What happened to Deirdre?" he asked, glancing at Daphne's face. It was hard to tell if the question was a bad one—if it even bothered her.

She took a second before she answered, folding her hands in her lap. "She died. Moloch told me this morning that some of the bone men found a body, but he didn't know whose. I guess they couldn't identify her right away. She was . . . badly mutilated."

"Oh." He wasn't exactly the world's biggest coping expert himself—he understood the temptation to pretend so doggedly, so defiantly, to be above it all because the prospect of being in it hurt too much, but Daphne's calm was bordering on catatonic. "Are you okay?"

She drew a deep breath and said with frightening composure, "I keep telling myself things are going to be fine.

That this was just a freak occurrence, and if Obie were dead, I'd know. Someone would have found a body by now." She looked at him as though daring him to disagree with her. "There'd be a body."

Truman didn't argue. He leaned forward, clasping his hands and trying to think of something to say. Myra's version of grief had been dramatic and mostly fake while, under her frightening calm, Daphne's was stark and disoriented and absolutely real.

He wanted to reach for her and hold on. She looked lost, like she needed someone to tell her everything would be okay. Truman wasn't stupid though. He knew how useless words could be. How even when you wanted more than anything just to hear someone say they understood, it didn't make you feel better. Not really.

"When my mom died—" His voice sounded hoarse and he cleared his throat and started over. "When she died, the only thing that really helped was knowing that all my best times and my memories of her—that I still had those. No one could take them away."

Daphne looked up at him and her face was almost unbearably vulnerable. "Will you tell me what she was like?"

"What's to tell? I mean, she was my mom."

"She was a person, though. People are different. She must have been unique, had her own preferences and mannerisms." Daphne's eyes were fixed on the long window across from them, staring into the glass like she was seeing something besides their own wavering reflections.

Truman nodded, trying to assemble the details that would conjure the image of his mother, accurate and whole, but even before he spoke, he knew it would just come out sounding trivial and flat.

"She was a bank teller. Even sort of liked her job, I think. She could be really funny sometimes. She liked books about China and Japan, and the Civil War. She made good pancakes." His voice cracked and he leaned his head back, covering his face with his hands. "Jesus, it sounds so *stupid*."

"Did she love you?"

He nodded against the window glass. "Yeah, she did." His voice was husky and muffled against his palms. He sounded like someone else.

"How do you know?"

"She told me."

"A lot?"

"Enough."

"You're lucky."

He dropped his hands and looked at Daphne. "Doesn't your mother love you?"

"No," she said, and it was nearly a whisper. "But Obie loves me. That's why I have to find him."

There was a wounded look in her eyes, an ache so deep that Truman felt it in the center of his chest. After a second, he draped his arm across the back of the seat, but wasn't quite brave enough to touch her.

She glanced up at him and didn't say anything. If she'd been a normal girl, he might have put his arm around her, pulled her close or smiled sympathetically or even just told her that the pain of loss would get better eventually. But she wasn't a normal girl, and he could lie to a lot of people, but he couldn't to lie to her. It didn't get better, it just got different.

THE DREAM
CHAPTER SEVENTEEN

The windows in my room at the Arlington are so dirty that I have to make a circle on the glass with my hand in order to see out. I don't know what I'm looking for. Monsters, maybe. The ruthless slaughterer of sisters. Below, the street is full of taxis.

When I turn around, Truman is standing just inside the open door, staring at the peeling wallpaper and the dusty furniture. His expression is exceedingly unimpressed. "You're staying in a *hooker* hotel?"

I slip off my boots and sit down on the bed. "I don't know. What's a hooker hotel?"

"It's—nothing." He gestures to the tattered curtains and the bedspread and the bolted-down TV. "Just . . . it's not that clean."

This revelation is apt, but unsurprising. Nothing else in Chicago is that clean either. The Arlington isn't any dirtier than half the places I've seen since arriving on Earth, but Truman seems reluctant to come farther into the room. He stands by the door, looking disoriented, like he's waiting for someone to tell him what to do, but I don't know the answer any more than he does.

"It's late," I say, and when he still doesn't move, I look down, plucking at the bedspread. "Maybe you should stay here tonight. If you want to."

For a second, Truman just stands there, looking around like he's considering the carpet and the bed, like he's counting all the ways it's not his own room. Then he steps inside and pushes the door shut behind him.

"I have a toothbrush," I tell him, trying to make him feel at home. "You can borrow it, if you like."

He just looks at me. Then he smiles a little, shaking his head. "Toothbrushes aren't the kind of thing people usually share."

"I know. I haven't used mine yet though, so it's new. It could be yours instead."

"Thanks. I actually might take you up on that." He runs a hand through his hair, making it stand up. "Man, I could probably use a comb, too. I guess I'm pretty much a mess, huh?"

At first, I don't know how to answer. His hair is disheveled but clean, and something about his eyes reminds me of ice-melt. An arctic freeze, thawing. I could fall into them.

That seems too complicated though and I'm about to reply that he looks fine, when he catches sight of the television. "Why is there a towel on the TV?"

"My—" I start to say *my mother* and then realize how ridiculous that sounds. "No reason. It was bothering me and I had to cover it. Did you want to watch something?"

He stands there, combing his hands through his hair and eyeing the shrouded television like he might actually be thinking about accepting the invitation. Then he shakes his head and turns away, yanking the top blanket off the bed and taking one of the pillows. "I don't know—not tonight. I'm pretty beat."

He drops the blanket in a heap and then sits on the carpet, prying off his shoes. When he lies down, he doesn't undress, just curls on his side, shifting against the floor like he's looking for something more comfortable.

The lamp by the bed makes a dismal circle of light. After minutes pass and Truman doesn't move, I take off my dress and fold it carefully, tie my socks together so they don't become separated. My underthings are flimsy and old-fashioned, made of silk and lace. They're not like anything my sisters would wear, but standing there in the lamplight still makes me self-conscious. The slip is nearly transparent. These are the particulars that boys are supposed to find riveting, but Truman doesn't look up from the floor. He curls around himself with the blanket pulled over his head. He isn't looking when I flip the light switch and turn down the bed, standing in the dark in my underwear. If I were Myra, my body would be like a magnet, unavoidable. He hasn't used my toothbrush.

I tell myself it doesn't matter. That we are just two people, on a mission to find someone in danger. We're rescuers, plain and simple, and Truman's disinterest makes no difference. Under the covers, I close my eyes and practice breathing. The habit of falling asleep is one that I am already learning.

✳   ✳   ✳

The world is made of chrome and even in the dark there are no stars. Below me, the city sprawls vacant and pitch black.

"You're dreaming," my mother says behind me, and I know that it's the truth because although she might tell wild, fanciful stories, she never tells lies.

We're standing on the roof of the Spire building, in a garden that is not my mother's garden. It's built of metal and something clear and smooth that doesn't exist at home. It looks like glass.

The whole roof is covered with flowers, real ones, and when I look up, carnations fall in cascades from a sky that should be orange or gray but only looms a deep, solid black.

When I turn to face her, Lilith is standing in front of the portrait of Azrael, which blazes a violent red on the wall behind her. The glow is so bright that at first, I can't make out her face. Then she turns, looking out toward the terminal, and I see the familiar line of her profile.

"Something's coming for you," she says, gazing over the dark city. "And you don't even have the sense to be afraid."

"What is it?" I whisper, because her expression is too stony to mean anything good.

She bows her head, letting her hair fall forward like a curtain coming down on a stage, obscuring her face. "Azrael's been busy, and none of you are safe, not now that he's unleashed Dark Dreadful."

The sky burns red as roses suddenly, lit with a glow so much brighter than the furnace. I reach into my coat pockets and they're full of flowers. As I pull my hands out, loose petals cling to my fingers. Violets.

I brush them away and step closer. "She's here in Chicago, isn't she? She's the one that killed Deirdre."

Around me, the air is suddenly heavy, pressing in. Flowers burst into flames at my feet. I'm crossing the garden through drifts of ash. It powders over the tops of my boots and my mother doesn't have to answer for me to know it's the truth.

"Did she take Obie? Is that what happened to him?" But if that was what happened, I wouldn't be looking for him now. He'd already be dead.

Lilith just turns away, staring around at the burning flowers and the glass garden. "I think I understand your talent now," she says, smiling down at the layers of ash. "I never stopped to think that perhaps it could only manifest on Earth. Have you discovered it yet?"

The answer seems obvious and I nod. "I can burn things by touching them. I did it to some doorknobs and a man under a bridge."

She laughs, shaking her head. "That? That's just a parlor trick. Half the family can do it. I'm thinking that your true talent is far more complex."

I want to ask why she's so much nicer here in my dream, but the question is a stupid one, because dreams aren't real. She's reaching for me now, her expression almost eager, and I back away, suddenly terrified of what she's going to say next.

"I don't want to hurt him," I whisper, shaking my head, but even as I say it, I can't shut out the thoughts that creep into my head. Truman—his hands, eyes, arms, mouth. I don't want to be this greedy thing, hungry and mercenary, preying on people who are too damaged and too desperate to resist.

Lilith moves closer, towering over me, and her smile turns scornful. "I'm not talking about a craving for the fix. You have that to deal with—make no mistake—but so do all your sisters. This is something far more exciting, something that could only ever manifest outside of Pandemonium. Now close your eyes."

I'm reluctant to look away, but I do as she says, standing with my arms at my sides, waiting for her to tell me a parable or do some trick to show me the nature of my gift. Instead, I feel her reach for me, cradling my face between her hands. With exquisite care, she bends down and kisses me on each eyelid.

"You don't have to take," she whispers. "Sometimes it's enough just to see. Now, help him go back to sleep."

CRAVING
CHAPTER EIGHTEEN

I wake suddenly. Like a blanket being lifted from my face, it happens all at once. In my hotel room, the streetlights make wavy patterns on the wall.

"Daphne." The word is hesitant, choked.

It takes days or hours or seconds to realize that someone is speaking to me, and when I roll over, I still feel half-asleep.

"Daphne." Truman is leaning over the bed.

"What is it?" I ask, sitting up and patting around for the lamp, but I can't find the switch. "What's wrong?"

"Can I sleep with you?" Even though the room is dark, he turns his face away when he asks it.

When I lift the blanket, he climbs in beside me. His whole body is shaking.

After a little, when he doesn't stop, I reach out and pull him closer. He gasps, but lets me do it. I remember him falling into my lap in the bathroom, how he shook and the tears leaked out of his eyes. Now though, his back is to me. His shoulders are hard, and under my hands, his shirt feels damp.

"What's wrong?" I ask again, speaking very quietly against his neck.

"I was dreaming." His voice sounds dry and hoarse, like he might be thirsty. "I—I was just having really bad dreams."

There's a fog of agitation around him, almost a palpable thing, and I pull back even though I don't want to. The feeling of him lying next to me is almost agonizingly appealing and I'm gripped by the same desire I felt last night, when I leaned over him in his room. When I kissed him.

We lie against each other in the sagging middle of the bed and even though I know it's not the right thing to do, I open my mouth and breathe the air coming off him. Not a smell or a taste, but something deeper. When I hold onto him, I don't let myself touch my lips to his neck. If I do, I'll taste the thing that makes him shudder. I will drink it from his skin like liquid, and that's unconscionable. When I press my forehead to his back, the shape of his pain is alluring, almost visible. It forms him, tells him to protect himself, makes him everything he is. He needs to keep it.

I close my eyes against it, resisting the urge to put my mouth to his skin. I close my eyes so tight that I see tiny lights, like sparks—the embers of his sadness.

When he shivers, he makes a noise in his throat like something is loose and knocking around inside him, a piece of broken machinery, clanking and grinding. I press closer to him in the dark, and after awhile, his breathing is slower again.

MARCH 9
2 DAYS 5 HOURS 10 MINUTES

With Daphne curled against his back, the shaking was better, a little. The bed was warm, and he was so tired. He stared out into the dark room, fighting to stay awake.

As soon as he blinked though, he was right back in one of his nightmares. This time, it was the hospital. He was standing over an adjustable bed with his hands shoved uselessly in his pockets, and his mother was dying.

"Look at you," she said. Her voice was ragged, but filled with a fierce kind of pride. "Oh, look at you, my brave, sweet boy."

He went to her even though a deep, guilty part of him was repulsed by the ruin of her face. She was not who she'd been even a month ago, and the sickness was everywhere, in her blood and her bones. It would keep eating until there was nothing left. He let her reach for him, leaning over her in the cranked-up hospital bed.

"Truman," she whispered. "Please take care of yourself."

And he lied—assured and reassured her that he would. Against judgment and reason, he would. Her arms around his neck were much too tight.

"Please," she said again. "All I want for you is some kind of redemption."

The words were stiff and not quite right—a little off, and then a lot off.

"Wait," he whispered. "What are you talking about? What does that mean?"

But she didn't answer. Her breathing got hoarser and louder, until it wasn't his mother at all anymore. It was the shadow man, gripping him roughly by the neck, but even inches from each other, Truman still couldn't see his face. The only feature not swallowed up by blackness was his eyes.

Above them, the lights blew out in a burst of glass and chilly florescent sparks. In the dark, the man grabbed him by the wrists, wrenching Truman's hands so the palms were turned up.

"Do you think *this* is what your mother wanted for you?" His eye sockets were deep and when he blinked there was the glitter of cold light and then, nothing.

The hospital faded abruptly and when the setting resolved again, they were in a dimly lit church and Truman was half-choked by the familiar smell of dust and stale incense.

The shadow man faced him across the center aisle. On either side were rows and rows of wooden pews, carved with saints and flowers. The place was lit only by candles, but Truman could tell from the way the air around them seemed to echo that it was big, and it was empty.

"You really should listen to me," said the man in a conversational voice. "I'm trying to help you."

Truman stared back at him, needing so badly to see what

he looked like. If he could just see the man's face, everything would be okay, but no matter how hard he tried, there was nothing but darkness. He breathed out in despair and frustration and looked away.

Over on one side of the dais, a heavy table was shoved against the wall and Truman's heart lurched. The church wasn't empty after all.

Someone was lying on the table—a man with pale skin, black-haired and barefoot. He was wearing jeans, a T-shirt, and a frayed blindfold that covered most of his face. At first it was hard to make out features in the flickering candlelight, but Truman recognized the messy hair, the shape of the chin and jaw. It was Obie, but not like Truman remembered him. At the hospital, his hair had been shaggy, but clean. Now, it was tangled and skeezy-looking. His cheeks were hollow and his jaw was dark with stubble. His arms were covered with shallow cuts and his wrists were bound with wire and fastened to a metal ring above his head. His hands were bloody where the wire dug into the skin.

Without thinking, Truman lunged for the dais, but the shadow man's palm caught him in the chest, shoving him backward.

Truman stumbled, then caught his balance, breathless. "What are you doing to him?"

"Only what he deserves, trust me. So you let me worry about him. You and I have our own issues to address."

Truman shook his head, still staring across the church to where Obie lay motionless on the table. "Please, I don't want to be here. This isn't right!"

The man caught him by the wrist and held tight, speaking close to his face. "No, it *isn't* right, but I'm stuck with you and you're stuck with me."

"What do you mean, stuck?"

"Stop flailing around and listen. First, I want you to stay away from that disgusting little fiend."

"What?" Truman struggled to pull his hand away. "Are you talking about Daphne?"

The shadow man smiled and the pale shine of his teeth in the dim light made Truman shudder. "I'm here to save you."

Truman swallowed hard but stopped struggling. "Save me from *what*?"

The man traced a finger down Truman's forearm, and as he did, blood sprang up in a thin trail along his scars. "You have what few people in this world will ever get—a second chance. And now you want to throw it away because some wicked girl looks sideways at you? Well, I'm here to make sure you have a life lived right this time."

Truman shook his head, staring past the shadow man to the figure on the table. Obie lay perfectly still, and every now and then, a few drops of blood pattered down onto the floor, running from the shallow cuts that covered his hands.

The shadow man leaned closer, so close that his nose was almost touching Truman's. "Pay *attention*. We're stuck with each other, and I suggest we both make the best of it."

Without warning, he slapped Truman in the face.

* * *

Truman woke up in the dark and couldn't breathe. Beside him,

Daphne was making confused, anxious noises and he realized that their hands were clasped together, fingers intertwined. His cheek throbbed where the shadow man had hit him. The insides of his wrists felt raw.

"Where was it?" Daphne mumbled next to him. "Was it here, or were we there?"

He sat up, slipping his hand free from hers.

"It's nothing," he said, running his hands over his face and squeezing his eyes shut. "You're talking in your sleep. Everything's fine." His voice sounded dry and husky though, and he was pretty much sure that nothing was fine at all.

Daphne pushed herself up on one elbow and reached for him, pulling him back down onto the mattress. "Don't be scared," she said in a vague, drowsy whisper. "I'm just going to breathe the bad stuff away. But just a little—just because it's nice. I won't hurt you."

"What?" Truman said, trying to get his head clear.

He felt like he would never sleep again, but when she put her hand on his arm, he lay back, letting her roll against him and hold on. Wanting her to.

"You don't have to be scared," she said again and yawned.

She pressed herself against his back, draping an arm over his shoulders. Her breath on his neck was warm. Without thinking, he reached for her hand, gripping it against his chest. Her touch made him feel strangely calm. The cold wash of panic was lifting. He lay close to her and closed his eyes, and this time, sleep was deep and it was dreamless.

ASHER SELF-STORAGE
CHAPTER NINETEEN

In the morning, we take the train south, sitting with the row of windows to our backs.

I'm mindful of my mother's warning that Dark Dreadful is loose somewhere, but it seems unlikely that she'd attack in the daytime. Still, it makes me nervous not to see what's behind me and I turn around, kneeling on the seat to press my nose to the glass. Outside, the city whips by at a fantastic speed.

My memory of the night before is fragmented and I stare out at the passing scenery, thinking about dreams, about prophecies and visions. After Truman got into bed with me, I fell back asleep and, when I did, I dreamed of Obie. The recollection is just a disconnected jumble of pictures, but the harder I concentrate, the more clearly it comes back—the heavy wooden table, the candles and the church. Only the more I think about it, the more I have the nagging sense that it wasn't my own dream. The scene felt fixed in place, like I was watching something on television. Even when I wanted to, I couldn't turn my head. It was nothing like the dream of my mother on the roof.

Beside me, Truman is quieter than usual.

I slide back down into the seat, trying to think how to address the subject of a dream that isn't mine. "Were you having nightmares last night?"

He laughs softly, shaking his head. His hair is uncombed, falling in his eyes and I don't brush it away, even though I'd like to. "You have no idea."

But last night, when I stood across from Lilith in the dream garden, she said that my inborn talent was the kind that could only manifest on Earth, and I think I do have an idea.

"This is going to seem strange," I tell Truman.

"What doesn't?"

"Last night, after you got in bed with me, I think I dreamed your dream."

Truman laughs again, but his expression is skeptical. "Daphne, people don't dream each other's dreams."

"I think I might. At least, I think I might dream yours. I saw you there, in a dark church, standing over my brother."

For a moment, Truman says nothing. Then he turns to face me. "How did you know I dreamed about Obie?"

"I told you, I dreamed it too. I think we need to find that church."

"What?" He sounds dazed. "What do you mean find it? It was a *dream*. Dreams aren't the same as real life."

"Yes, but this wasn't like other dreams. It felt . . . solid. And there was a man there, and a warm, dusty smell, and furniture. I think it's a real place—out in the world somewhere. Now we just have to find it." The prospect of having a mission is relieving. It's attainable, and despite the danger and the difficulty, I can't help smiling. This is the first indication we've had of Obie's whereabouts, and I wouldn't have been able to see it without Truman.

Truman doesn't smile back. "Look, I need you to understand something," he says, and he sounds tense and worn-out. "Every night, I dream crazy, horrific things, and then I wake up and I do my best to convince myself they're not real, because if they're real, that's a whole lot worse than just having some messed-up switch inside my head. I dreamed your brother was on a table, tied up and bleeding. And you're telling me that if it's true, that would be a *good* thing?"

"Yes," I say, even though *good* is not precisely the right word. "It would mean he's out there somewhere. It means we know he isn't dead, and if he isn't dead, then we can get him back."

Truman stares down at me in disbelief. "*How?*"

"I don't know yet, but there has to be a way. Maybe Obie's key can help us."

"Daphne," Truman says. "It's a key. The world isn't full of clues, it's just full of stuff."

I don't answer, just stare out the window, thinking about the church and what the key might lead us to. I know it's something important.

I know I'm right.

❊   ❊   ❊

The storage facility is on a frontage road, with warehouses lining both sides of the street. There's a chain-link fence and a gate. A man is sitting in a small booth beside it, wearing blue coveralls and reading a magazine.

When we walk up to his window, he sets the magazine down, looking deeply disinterested. "Help you kids?"

I hold out the brass key. "We would like to see the storage unit, please."

For a moment, he just looks at me like he's waiting for something. Then he raises his eyebrows and holds out his hand. "Do you have your access card?"

"No," I say, still offering the key but he doesn't take it.

Truman steps in front of me. "Look, our mom just asked us to pick up some stuff. I know it's against the policy, but come on. It's not a big deal."

At first, I'm confused by his self-assured tone. We are so patently unrelated. When the man compares our faces, I can see him debating. Doubting. Then Truman smiles at him— really smiles, wide and honest. Even though I know it's a just a way of getting the man to trust him, the smile makes something flutter in my chest.

"You have to be careful," he says under his breath, once we're past the booth. "You have to stop telling everybody the truth all the time."

We walk through corridors made by rows and rows of small garages. They all have aluminum sliding doors at the front, with joints in them like armor, like the sections of a snake's belly. At number 206, we stop.

"How does it work?" I ask, looking at the door. It's blank and wide and windowless.

Truman takes the key from me and crouches down, gesturing to an unobtrusive lock at the bottom. When he tries the key, it turns with a squeal. He straightens again and the door clatters up, revealing a dark concrete shed behind it. "Like that."

The shed is small, but overflowing with things. There are cardboard boxes everywhere. An acoustic guitar is propped against one wall, strings snapped and curling up its neck. Everything looks lonely and unused. Desolate. As we step inside, the dust puffs up in clouds at our feet.

I pull back the flaps of one of the boxes to reveal a cracked snow globe, a copy of *Grey's Anatomy*. Clothes. Cotton dresses and strappy shoes, combs and barrettes covered in glossy enamel flowers. The shoes and dresses must belong to Obie's girlfriend, then. Elizabeth, the woman he left Pandemonium to be with.

Truman is standing back in the opening, looking skeptical. "This is it? We came all the way out here when we could have just found a garage sale?"

"This is all from the apartment. It's all the stuff that should have been there."

The guitar, the books on medicine and botany, the black-and-gray-striped pullover sweater. These are Obie's things. This is what's left of my brother's new life, wadded up and piled in the corners of a tiny cement room.

I pick up one of the barrettes, turning it over in my hand. It's pretty, but cheap. Compared to the workmanship at home, it's unwearable, all rough edges and uneven, incompetent solder. Some of the stones will fall out. It will look broken and temporary and used. The woman who owned it will throw it away, move on to something else. I set it down again and wonder where she is now.

Then, from the back of the storage unit, I hear a noise, low and almost stealthy. Something in the shadows is rustling, something that is not us. I pick my way forward, dust rising around my boots with each step. Dust and dust, a cardboard box in the shadows, its folding flaps crumpled, hanging open. The rustling is coming out of its dark, gaping mouth.

"Rats," says Truman behind me. "Probably a nest. Be careful," he says and then I know that he doesn't believe in the rats, but in something bigger or worse. He catches at my sleeve as I step closer. The feeling is unexpected, and then my arm pulls out of his grasp.

In front of me, the box rustles softly, trembling in the dim light. I kneel on the floor, peeling back the flaps to look inside.

A baby is sitting at the bottom of it.

Just a baby, blinking up at me with eyes like aluminum. Its face is a fat, pale moon, framed by the deep black of its hair. It reaches for me with tiny hands. Its fingernails are the cool polished silver of chrome.

It's a demon.

"Oh my God," Truman whispers into the box. He's crouched on the floor beside me, staring down like he's waiting for a bomb to go off.

"Not God," the baby whispers in a weird, creaking voice, dusty like the room. "I'm Raymie."

It's shocking to hear her speak. In the city of Pandemonium, I've seen a lot of things, but never this.

I don't remember growing up, or how I came to exist. My memory doesn't stretch that far back. All I know is that demons are born from chaos. They're born from rage or blood or fire, or ruined holy water. They're born from eggs. They come into the world as wisps of smoke or in grotesque forms that splinter off and multiply. There are all kinds of origins, all different ways to be born, but the only story I've ever heard that talked about an actual baby is the story of my brother.

In the cardboard box, this baby is looking up at me patiently. When she raises her arms, I reach to pick her up.

Beside me, Truman is crouching forward like he doesn't know whether or not to run. "Wait." He acts like he'll grab my sleeve, but then doesn't. He doesn't tell me what I'm waiting for.

I lift the baby from the box. She's wrapped in a piece of dingy cotton, thick with dust. She feels cool and heavy.

"Who are you?" she asks me, mouth full of sharp gray teeth. When she shows them, Truman gasps.

"Daphne," I tell her, holding her against me, touching her hair. My hand comes away covered in cobwebs and I understand that this is why my brother had to leave. He made his choice when he learned he'd be a father.

Raymie puts three fingers in her mouth and sucks. Underneath the piece of cotton, she's wrapped in black plastic. There are holes for her arms and thick gray tape at her neck to hold the top shut.

I stand up, holding her to my chest. "I'm taking you out of here," I say. "We need to clean you up and then get you some food."

As we retreat toward the door though, Raymie begins to squirm, the plastic crinkling against me as she moves.

"No," she says in her thin, creaking voice. "No, don't leave my bed behind."

"Get the box, please," I tell Truman.

He starts to speak and I think he'll object, but he reaches down and lifts the box by one flap. He opens out the bottom, folds the box flat and then folds it in half again without looking at me or the baby.

Once we're out in the road though, he turns to me. His eyes are helpless and a little shell-shocked. "What are we going to do now?"

"Do? I don't understand what you mean."

"What are we going to *do*? How are we going to take care of her? She's a baby." He measures the space of Raymie with his hands. "I don't know anything about babies and I don't think you do either. She needs clothes."

"She's already dressed."

"Daphne, she's wearing a garbage bag."

The baby is so dirty that she leaves smears down the inside of my forearms and all over the front of my blouse. She keeps sucking her fingers, which are gray with dust.

✳   ✳   ✳

At the Arlington Hotel, I run water into the bathtub and mix in soap. When I ask Truman to cut Raymie out of her garbage bag, he gives me a doubtful look.

I use the thief's knife to slit the gray tape at her neck. The plastic falls away in layers and I dunk her in the tub. Her face goes under the water for an instant and then pops up again just as fast. She is blinking rapidly as the water streams away from her eyes.

"Jesus, be *careful*," Truman says. "You're going to drown her."

But Raymie is sitting up now, unconcerned. "What's this?" she asks, patting at the water, at the bubbles, the steam.

"This is a bath. It's water and soap. Do you like it?"

She nods, clapping the soap between her hands in white fluffs and watching the bubbles burst. On her face is an expression of deep concentration.

"Maybe Raymie should have some other babies to play with?" I ask Truman. "We could find some people who have babies."

Truman starts to speak, then stops again like he's trying to decide how to phrase something. "Raymie has a mouthful of metal teeth and a better vocabulary than most of my friends. She does not want to play with other babies and even if she did, other babies don't want to play with her."

"This is difficult. I don't really know how to treat babies."

"Neither do I," he says, giving me a long look. "So it's a good thing Raymie is basically not a real baby."

"I'm not a baby?" Raymie asks, catching a cluster of bubbles and trying to eat it.

"No, you are," I tell her. "You're just a different kind. Special."

She looks at me with suds dripping from her chin. Then she nods. "Special," she repeats, like the idea pleases her.

Her hair is bristling crazily around her face and she's pale and grimy, but solid. The dust on her skin makes her look abandoned—discarded, even—but she doesn't look starved.

"Raymie," I say, wiping her face clean with a washcloth. "Do you know how to count? Like one, two, three, four?"

Truman is watching us like we've both gone crazy, but Raymie nods. "I can count like in the song. One for sorrow, two for joy, three for a girl, and four for a boy."

"Do you know how long were you in the shed, then? How many days?"

Raymie shakes her head. "It was dark all the time, like one long night."

"Christmas," says Truman suddenly, and we both look at him. "Were the Christmas lights still up when you went into the shed?"

"No," she says, with grim conviction. "The lights had already gone."

Truman nods. "Okay, what about hearts?"

Raymie glances at me and scowls. "A heart is a muscle," she tells me. "It has four chambers—two atria and two ventricles. It pumps oxygenated and deoxygenated blood." And this, I can't disagree with.

But Truman shakes his head and holds up his hands, joining them together with his thumbs pointing down and his fingers curved to make the shape of a candy box. "Like this," he says.

Raymie watches his hands, still scowling. "That's not a heart, that's a valentine."

"Okay, fine. But were there valentines like this when someone took you to the storage shed?"

She nods and I smile encouragingly. I'm waiting for her to go on, when Truman turns and walks out of the tiny bathroom. He sits down on the bed, raking his hands through his hair and staring fixedly at the wall.

"Jesus," he says in a small, dry voice, like the words are stuck in his chest. "That's not even possible. She was in there for almost a *month*, with no food and no water. How is that possible?"

"Well, she's a demon," I tell him, leaning sideways to talk through the open door. "We're almost impossible to kill through adverse conditions or neglect. I mean, you have to actually want us dead. This is more like someone just ignored her for awhile."

Raymie nods in staunch agreement and piles bubbles on top of her head like a hat.

"Who put you in the shed?" I ask her, cupping my hands, pouring water over her to rinse the soap off.

"My mother." She scrubs at her eyes. "She told me I'd be safe and to wait for my father. But he never came."

Something is humming uneasily in my chest. It beats against my ribs like a bird, and I kneel beside the bathtub, looking down at her.

If I hadn't found the key, she'd still be sitting there in the dark and the cold, waiting for her father. How long? Maybe forever. I imagine Raymie's mother, bringing her to Asher Self-Storage, tucking her away to wait for a man who can't come for her, who's chained to a table in a dark church.

I have a litany of reassuring stories, things to tell myself— that the situation is not completely dire and Truman's dream is definitive proof that my brother's still all right. But deep down I know that Truman may be right. A dream is no substitute for the real thing. Maybe Raymie is not a clue after all, just a complication.

"I want to be dressed again," she tells me.

Her plastic bag is in tatters on the floor and I can't put it back on her. In my head, I make a list of all the things we need, soap and shampoo, clothes for Raymie and for Truman, and the list makes things seem orderly. The world, falling into place.

"I'm going shopping," I tell Truman. "Raymie ought to have clothes, and I'm going to get you a toothbrush and some socks and shirts. What else would you like?"

He smiles at me and shakes his head. His eyes are very blue. "Nothing. Don't buy me anything."

"You need things, though. I'll get you a comb, at least. Is there anything else you can think of?"

"Yeah," he says, nodding toward Raymie. "Yeah. Maybe a toy?"

THE ROSARY
CHAPTER TWENTY

I find a drugstore without much trouble and wander the aisles, choosing things and putting them in a plastic shopping basket. The store is mostly empty and the overhead lights are harsh and florescent. The whole place smells like cleaning products.

I find sleepers for Raymie and a toothbrush for Truman and a white cloth rabbit with black button eyes. The orderliness of the shelves is comforting. It helps me think. By the time I'm done comparing the relative merits of two different sun bonnets, I've decided that we have absolutely no choice but to leave Chicago.

It's dark when I start back to the hotel, and the street is a sea of headlights and traffic lights. It bothers me how nervous I've become. I feel skittish and on edge. Every shadow of every building could hide the monstrous form of Dark Dreadful.

When I open the door to our room at the Arlington, Truman's sitting on the bed with Raymie. They're watching television while he holds her in the crook of his arm and explains about fish, how they live underwater. There's a towel tucked around her like a nest.

I tip the shopping bags out onto the bed. "Here, I got some things for both of you."

Truman sets Raymie on the pillow, bundled in her towel, and begins to pick through my purchases, examining a black book bag with shoulder straps. He holds up a fuzzy baby suit with long sleeves and built-in feet.

"Do you like it?" he asks Raymie.

"Maybe. What's that?" She points to a synthetic duckling appliquéd on the front. "The yellow thing?"

"A duck," he tells her. "Are you telling me you know how many chambers a heart has, but you don't recognize a duck when you see one?"

Raymie shakes her head. "My father knows about hearts. He told me all the kinds of muscles and blood and bones. Why is there a duck?"

"It's a decoration. You know, something fun."

"No." Raymie shakes her head. "I don't know fun."

Truman stands over her, still holding out the yellow sleeper. "So, do you want to put it on?"

She looks over at me. "May I?"

"Yes, that's why I bought it." I pop a plastic comb out of its packaging and toss it into my black bag. "Now we need to get you dressed and pack our things."

Truman is wrestling with the yellow sleeper, trying to remove the price tag, which is fastened on with a little plastic cord. I yank it out of his hands and snip the cord with my teeth. Then I tuck Raymie into the suit, zip it closed, and deposit her on the bed. Looking down at herself, she pats the appliqué duck with both hands, then begins to rifle through the pile of recent purchases.

"What's this?" She holds up a small vinyl package.

"It's a sewing kit," Truman says. "See the little scissors, and all the thread?"

Raymie clutches the package to her chest, rocking back and forth with it.

"It's not a toy," I tell her, offering the rabbit instead. "That's for Truman to fix his clothes. This rabbit is for you."

Raymie considers the rabbit, watching it flop in my hand. When I shake it at her, she drops the sewing kit and takes it. Squeezing it against the front of her sleeper, she bites the top of the rabbit's head. She's still looking at the little vinyl package on the bedspread though.

"Did you have a good time watching television with Truman?" I ask, tidying my purchases—one pile for Truman, one for Raymie.

"I like him," she says. "He's lost, like my mother."

Truman is examining the four-pack of socks and the T-shirts, but that makes him look up. "What does that mean? What's she talking about?"

I collect the new toothbrushes and drop them in my bag. "Nothing. It's not important. Right now, we need to be concentrating on our next move. On leaving town."

"Will you take me with you?" Raymie asks, gnawing on the rabbit.

I stare down at her. "Of course I'll take you. I'm not going to just leave you here."

"Last time, I stayed," she says. "We were pretending to move away, but I stayed with the things. My mother said to wait until someone came for me. It was a trick."

I kneel by the bed so I can look directly into her face. "Do you know what you were hiding from, or if it was bad?"

Raymie scowls, shaking her head. "I don't know what it was."

Truman gives me a sharp look, still holding the package of socks. "She just spent at least four weeks in a storage shed, in sub-zero weather," he says in a low voice. "She didn't *eat* for a month. If her mom thought the best solution was to put her in a cardboard box and leave her there, then yeah, it was bad." He drops the socks on the bed, watching me carefully. "Maybe even the same thing that killed Deirdre."

His expression is challenging, like he's waiting for me to tell him all the secrets of Dark Dreadful. But I find myself reluctant to describe her. It suddenly seems reckless even to speak her name.

"Deirdre was the victim of a terrible attack," I say, keeping my voice flat and matter-of-fact. "We don't know who or what killed her."

"What about that rosary? Myra said they found it on the—" His voice falters then and he looks past me, toward the window. "She said it was with your sister."

I remember Myra's nervous behavior at the Prophet Club, fidgeting with the token Moloch had given her. "You mean the string of beads?"

"Yeah, only it wasn't beads. I mean, they were *beads*, but it was a rosary."

The word is Latinate and only marginally familiar. I know the meaning, but not the significance. "Are you saying the thing that killed Deirdre adorned her body with a holy artifact?"

Truman shrugs, looking apologetic. "Not exactly an artifact, more like an accessory. I mean, they're pretty common. People—Catholics—use them for church all the time."

As soon as he says it, my skin goes cold and I'm transported back to the dream of my brother, bound to the table. Church. The rosary—whatever it signifies, whoever left it—came from a church. For a moment, I only stare up at him. My eyes feel wide and dry and electric.

"Hey," he says catching me by the arm. "Why are you looking like that? What's wrong?"

"We need to go to Las Vegas," I say, forcing myself to stand still when what I want is to wrench away from him and start packing. "Myra's there. She has the rosary and maybe she can tell us what it means. It must be some kind of a clue to finding Obie."

"Wait, what? How are we going to Vegas?"

"I'll draw a jump-door. We just need an east-facing wall."

"Daphne, do you realize that you are totally not oriented in reality?"

I grab the book bag off the bed and shove it at him. "Just pack, please. We have to go."

He puts the socks in the bag without conviction. Behind him, Raymie just sits placidly on the bed, watching us. He reaches for the package of undershirts next, then stops.

"We. I'm assuming *we* means you, me, and her. Christ, I can see so many problems with this. I can't go."

"Why not?"

"I just—it's too weird and school's starting back up and I live here and I barely know you."

I want to tell him that I'm worried about him. That he's come too close to dying too many times and that if I leave him behind, he's going to manage it eventually. But that's not the only reason I need to bring him with me. His dreams are crucial, the only link to my brother, and no one in my family has the slightest knowledge of holy articles or churches. None of us are equipped to handle this.

I suspect I need him almost as much as he needs me.

"Please come with me," I say, and my voice sounds very small. "I need your help."

He takes a deep breath and glances from me to Raymie and back again. "Can I think about it?"

"That depends. How long will that take?"

He touches his mouth, looking someplace else. "Daphne, this is a big deal. I can't just walk away from my life." He says it like he's trying to convince me, but when he looks back at me, his face is stoic and resigned. We both know that he can.

MARCH 9
1 DAY 10 HOURS 10 MINUTES

Daphne was pacing around the room, gathering up the things on the bed and tossing them into her bag.

Truman watched her open a package of plastic barrettes, drop them, pick most of them up off the floor, and shove them into her coat pockets. He felt a surge of sympathy for this new version of Daphne, a twitchy and agitated version. Her eyes were wide and unfocused. It was a stare he recognized—that glassy, panicked look, like the room was shrinking.

"Daphne," he said, keeping his voice low and calm. "Daphne, stand still. It's going to be fine."

She stopped pacing and looked at him. Her eyes were wide and she was breathing fast and shallow. She glanced away and whispered, "Things aren't fine."

"Okay, that's okay. But just for a little, let's pretend they are anyway. Do you know how to do that?"

She shook her head, still giving him that wild, uncomprehending stare.

"Okay, you start like this. Whatever is freaking you out, stop thinking about it."

She gripped the bag with both hands. "What do I think about instead?"

"You think about whatever comes next. Think about what you have to do to keep going."

"Is it really that easy?"

"Yes," he said. But it wasn't.

He'd spent all afternoon while Daphne was out trying not to think about her and mostly failing. It was impossible not to think about her, and thinking about her led to other things. Thinking about her meant thinking about home and Charlie and Dio's bathroom floor and before that, the bathtub and the hospital and her brother.

Finally, he'd bitten the inside of his cheek, and that helped a little. Then he sat down on the floor across from the baby, who was still wet-haired and dripping, wrapped in a ratty bath towel. Truman propped his elbows on his knees and they sat looking at each other.

She was nothing like the babies whose mothers lived in the Avalon. Those ones were sticky and neglected-looking. They screeched or cried and their noses were always red and dripping. Raymie was grave. That was the only word for it— grave, and a little severe, and now, without the layer of dirt from the storage, very clean.

They sat across from each other on the dusty carpet like they were waiting for something. Truman desperately wanted a cigarette, but if one thing had been drilled into him, it was that you were never supposed to smoke around babies.

Probably even crazy-looking nightmare babies with metal teeth.

"So," he said, after a long pause. "Obie was your dad, huh?"

Raymie nodded solemnly. "Did you know him?"

"Yeah, I knew him."

"Were you one of the wounded?"

"I don't know what that means."

"Wounded. Hurt, injured. A process in which the skin is cut or broken."

"No, I know what it *means*, but I don't know what you're talking about."

Raymie stared up, blinking at him. "He helped people sometimes, in the hospital. They were wounded. Did he help you?"

Truman looked back at her. "Yes," he said.

✷   ✷   ✷

At the hospital, they'd sewn Truman back up, pumped him full of someone else's blood. They gave him pain medication that made his wrists numb and his dreams terrible. Surgery had saved him, but before the operating room, there'd been Charlie, dragging him out of the water, slowing the blood. Alexa, with the phone to her ear, speaking rapidly. Truman himself only had vague recollections of hands, voices, sirens, an oxygen mask. Nothing.

He'd been afraid of a lot of things—afraid that he would go to Hell and that he would ruin Charlie's life. He'd been afraid that his mother, watching from some undetermined location, would be disappointed and ashamed of him. He'd been afraid it would be messy and disgusting and weak and cowardly, but never at any point had he been afraid that he would survive. That first night, he lay in the adjustable hospital bed and watched the beat of his heart blip up and down across a black screen.

Obie had come into the room very late, in his chalk-green scrubs, bringing water in a plastic cup. It was Obie who made the whole thing seem much more real than Truman's stitches or his blood in the tub or the sick way the room seemed to spin around him.

"So," he said that first night, when Truman was still dizzy from blood loss and painkillers. "Worst day of your life, huh?"

And Truman had laughed at that, because something was building in his chest and laughing was, of course, easier than crying. Then he began to cough.

Obie offered him the water, shaking his head when Truman tried to raise a hand to take the cup himself. "Don't," he said. "You'll disturb your sutures."

He held the cup while Truman drank from a straw with an accordion joint. He rested his hand on Truman's shoulder and the weight of it felt warm through the fabric of the hospital gown. That was the part he remembered best. How, when Obie touched him, it hadn't hurt.

"I see you went for the bleed-out." The look on his face had been knowing and wise and very sad. He'd smiled and then turned away, busy with the monitors and the IV drip.

Hearing *bleed-out* said aloud felt like being hit hard in the stomach. Truman had begun to cough again and Obie came across to him and pushed the button that raised the bed.

Truman closed his eyes and when he opened them again, Obie was still there, standing over the bed, looking down at him. Obie's hair was shaggy, longer than the way most of the other men on staff wore theirs. He clasped his hands behind his back as though he were waiting for something.

Truman winced. "How are my arms?"

"You've got a bunch of superficials and a couple not-screwing-arounds. You would have died if your stepdad had stopped to pick up a newspaper or something."

Truman cut his eyes away, taking in the linoleum floor, the pastel garden wallpaper. "Where's Charlie?"

"I don't know. Home, maybe." Obie was still looking down at him—intense gray gaze and sad, indeterminate mouth. "What do you remember?"

Truman stared up groggily and shook his head. "Like . . . before the tub? I remember waking up. There was ice on the windows because the furnace is broken. Charlie was still at work. I didn't go to school." Other memories surfaced slowly, and he winced. "I remember getting drunk—really drunk."

He looked away, waiting for Obie to point out that drinking before five was bad news and drinking before noon was just sad but drinking before eight in the morning was completely unstable.

Obie didn't mention it though. He only sat down on the foot of the bed, looking expectant. "But that's all? Nothing unusual or strange? What about after?"

Truman glanced away. He didn't point out that pretty much everything about the day you decided to kill yourself could be considered unusual. "Nothing. I don't know."

That wasn't quite true. He remembered the flooded bathroom and the oxygen mask. He remembered a dream of a girl. She had wide, dark eyes and black hair. He imagined reaching for her hand, grasping it in his, and smiled dazedly at the ceiling.

Obie leaned close, snapping his fingers in Truman's face. "No, no, no, you're getting dopy. Focus. I know it's hard, but stay with me. I need you tell me what you remember."

"*Nothing.* Please, I can't think. I need to sleep."

Obie raised his eyebrows. "You really don't remember anything—anything at all?"

Truman shook his head, trying to forget the chaotic dreams of blood loss. The girl was still there, pale and perfect, surrounded by a huge smear of metallic gray. "Nothing."

"Okay, that's all I needed to know. You did good. You can go to sleep now."

And with a kind of miserable relief, Truman did.

Later on was when the night got bad. The shadow of the dresser seemed to stretch out, oozing over the floor, filling up the room, and then he heard a voice. A real one, and not the kind that echoed up out of drug states or dreams.

Come with me. I have something to show you.

And as drugged-up and exhausted and afraid as he was, he'd gone. Despite the monitor wires and the IV, he felt himself stand up and cross to the corner of the room, only mildly surprised that when he looked back, he was still lying in the hospital bed. Then he'd stepped through the black door and into a derelict church, where the shadow man and his own smiling cadaver were waiting for him.

In the days that followed, his room was full of nurses and orderlies. They wandered in and out constantly, but Obie was the only one who looked at Truman like he was actually seeing him—all of him—and not just what he'd done. Obie told jokes and stories and laughed easily, smiling his wide, rueful smile. Holding Truman's hands still while he shook, careful not to tear the sutures. Truman slumped sideways over the bedrail with his head resting against Obie's shoulder. It had been more than a year since he'd let anyone touch him like that, not like a stranger, but like family.

✳   ✳   ✳

Truman closed his eyes, mentally recited the first two lines of the Hail Mary, and stopped remembering. Daphne was sitting on the edge of the bed with her hands folded in her lap, staring at the wall. Her back was straight and tense.

"Is it working?" he asked.

She took a deep breath and nodded. Then she got up and crossed quickly to the other side of the room. "Here, move the dresser."

"Daphne, it's bolted down."

"It's okay," she said, dropping to her knees. "I'll do it."

She reached underneath, fumbling around. After a few seconds, something began to smoke blackly. Then she stood up and pushed the dresser away from the wall, revealing mangled scraps of blackened metal where the bolts had been, just like she'd done to the door of Obie's apartment.

With the dresser out of the way, she took out a felt-tipped marker and drew a high rectangle on the wallpaper where the dresser had been. Then she stepped back and stared at it.

"What are you doing?"

She pointed to the rectangle. "Making a door."

"That's a rectangle."

"Well, most doors are."

Truman watched incredulously as she added a handle and then a pair of hinges. "What are those for?"

"It's important to include details. Do you have everything you need?"

Truman looked around the little room, and realized it was empty. Everything was packed. The drawing of the door seemed very final, suddenly.

He thought about Charlie coming home from work, finding Truman gone for the second morning in a row. He'd get worried after a few days, maybe call the police. But maybe it was better this way. Charlie was a good guy. He could have had a day job if they hadn't needed the money so bad. Maybe even a girlfriend. He could have had a life if he wasn't stuck raising someone else's kid. The thought made Truman feel guilty, and at the same time, he was filled with a wave of love for Charlie. He missed him already.

Walking away from his school and his friends and his whole messy, stupid life—that was easier.

He picked up the backpack and slid his shoulders into the

straps. Then he scooped Raymie off the bed and moved to stand behind Daphne.

She knocked once on her fake door. "Passiflore," she said clearly, and then reached for the handle, which turned into a brass doorknob as her hand closed over it.

THE PASSIFLORE
CHAPTER TWENTY-ONE

Stepping through the door is like stepping into the dead of night. Everything is black and cold and empty. Then the stillness is broken by a rushing sound and a gust of wind. Somewhere ahead of us, a door swings wide, revealing a rectangle of dim, yellow light.

It opens out onto a stone path, and as soon as we're through, I'm struck by the smell—a clean, fresh aroma, like dirt and water and growing things.

We're standing at one end of a huge garden. All around us, raised beds spill over with orchids and lilies, and the path is flanked with carefully shaped rose trees. The sky above us is dark, but the place is lit with bamboo torches and paper lanterns, and by their light, I see that the garden is walled in by a courtyard. On all sides, the building towers above us, studded with windows. The door we've just stepped out of is painted a lush, peeling green. When I let it swing shut behind us, it vanishes into the wall. Somewhere nearby, a stream is rushing along, chuckling over rocks.

The garden is full of shadowy figures grouped in twos and

threes, but if anyone's noticed our sudden appearance, no one seems surprised.

Over by a huge stone fountain, a pair of the Lilim are clinging coyly to a man who is clearly not a demon. He's young and handsome, with artfully disheveled hair and features like a movie star. One of the girls winks at me and smiles a conspiratorial smile. The look she gives Truman is more predatory.

He stands beside me unsteadily, staring around the garden and resting his hand against the wall. He's still holding Raymie, who has her arms around her rabbit and is making little growling noises. He looks disoriented.

A plaque in the stone path at our feet announces that we are presently in the Kissing Garden at the Passiflore Hotel in Las Vegas, Nevada.

Truman is making me nervous. He's very pale and keeps glancing around like he sees something I don't.

"Are you all right?" I ask. "Was the jump-door very hard on you? Moloch said that might happen. Do you feel sick?"

He shrugs and shakes his head. "No, I'm fine."

When Raymie starts to squirm in his arms, I take her from him. Somewhere nearby, there's a restless clanging that never stops.

"Come on," I say. "We should see about getting ourselves a room."

The path leads out through an archway at the other end of the garden and into the hotel, which is impressive, even by the standards of Pandemonium. The ceiling is vaulted like a train station, covered in paintings of Greek gods. Everyone's helmet has wings. There are slot machines everywhere, clanging and flashing. People crowd shoulder to shoulder around felt tabletops, counting their chips. We make our way across the casino floor, surrounded by lights and bells and cocktail servers in short dresses.

"Flower," Raymie says wistfully, watching a tray of brightly garnished drinks glide by, balanced on the upturned palm of a waitress.

Everything smells like smoke.

A painted sign points us toward the reception desk, its words framed in intricate scrollwork and round, art deco roses. But when we try to follow it, the way is crowded and confusing. I try a likely route, only to discover we've turned the wrong way. Instead of finding ourselves in the lobby, we're standing in a deserted hallway.

It's red—the whole thing, ceiling and carpet and walls, which are covered in a mismatched collection of mirrors. They look jumbled and slightly chaotic against the wallpaper, some in heavy gilt frames, others completely unadorned. Out of curiosity, I continue on and turn the corner, only to find that it doesn't lead anywhere. The hallway ends in a solid wall, paneled floor to ceiling with mirrors, and I have a feeling that if we don't leave immediately, my mother will show up and demand that I come home.

When I start back the way we came though, Truman hesitates, looking over his shoulder at one of the gilt-framed mirrors.

"Are you coming?" I say, pausing in the mouth of the hallway to wait.

He blinks and glances back at me. The mirrors are empty except for his own reflection. One too-thin boy with hollow eyes and lank, shaggy hair.

"Did you see something?"

"No," he says, then hesitates. "I mean, it was nothing. Just my mind playing tricks."

With Raymie balanced on my hip, I retrace our steps and locate the reception desk.

We cross the lobby, me and Raymie in front with Truman trailing behind. Raymie is reaching for him over my shoulder, but she has the good sense to stay quiet.

The clerk at the front desk is young, with gold earrings and a small goatee.

"We'd like a room please," I tell him, holding Raymie so that her face is pressed close to my shoulder to hide her teeth.

The clerk nods and enters something into the computer. He's wearing a brocade vest and a gold nametag that says CLARENCE and gold rings in both his ears. He reminds me of a genie or something else magical, but after a close inspection, I decide that he's human after all. His teeth are straight and white, and his eyes are a mild hazel.

He studies me politely. "I haven't seen you around before. You just come in through the Kissing Garden?"

I nod. He says *Kissing Garden* like he is completely unconcerned by what goes on there. The idea of a garden where girls like my sisters prey on gamblers and tourists is unsettling and the fact that this doesn't seem to bother Clarence in the slightest is almost as disconcerting.

I'm filling out the information card when Truman starts to cough. It's a harsh, hacking sound, and Clarence leans on the counter, looking concerned. "Hey, you all right, man?"

Truman clears his throat, smiling brightly. "Yeah, I'm good." His face is red, though, and his eyes have started to water.

Raymie is watching him. When she opens her mouth to speak, I glance around. There's a couple waiting in line behind us and I press my finger to my lips. Raymie stares back at me but doesn't say anything. When she tries to wriggle out of my arms, I adjust my grip. I don't let go, even when she bites me through my coat.

"Are you really all right?" I ask Truman when we're away from the counter.

He shrugs, looking awkward, turning his face away. "It's just—nothing," he says softly. "A cold, the flu or something. It's normal. I mean, I haven't exactly been taking care of myself. That kind of thing'll make you sick, is all."

I nod, even though I'm privately convinced it was the jump-door that made him so unsteady and so pale. Raymie is wriggling in my arms, looking back at the corridor to the Kissing Garden, where the air is cool and smells like flowers and cold water.

✵   ✵   ✵

The room is like a gangster movie and doesn't feel like home. I never thought I'd miss my room in the Arlington, but I do.

The bedspread is a lurid gold, sprinkled with purple blossoms. There are mirrors on the walls and on the ceiling, framed in ornately carved wood and gold leaf. They look like windows where three people just like us are looking in. The mirrors are complimented by a dressing table, a hulking wardrobe, and a small velvet couch. I set Raymie down on the couch, tucking her into the corner so she doesn't tip over onto the floor.

Once the bags are situated, I realize that I'm dangerously hungry, nearly breathless with the gnawing in my chest. Truman's standing beside the bed, watching the bedspread as though it has hypnotized him with its flowers. He shivers, cupping his elbows in his palms.

"Should we get something to eat?" I ask him. "I'm very hungry and it might be good for you to have something too."

We order dinner from room service and eat sitting on the floor. Raymie is stubborn and wants to feed herself. I offer her little bites of sandwich and try to keep my fingers out of the way of her teeth.

"It's nice," she says, snapping at me, trying to catch crumbs and scraps of lettuce as I pull my hand away.

Truman eats half of his, then shakes his head, pushing the plate across the carpet toward me.

"Are you done?" I ask. "You didn't eat very much."

"I guess I'm just not that hungry. You can have it." And he smiles at me, a sad, tired smile, like shrugging with his mouth. It occurs to me that sometimes he smiles when he means the exact opposite.

We don't say anything else and I finish my sandwich and then the rest of his.

He's quiet, leaning his back against the bed frame. His shoulders are hunched like he's expecting someone to hit him and he keeps picking things up and putting them down again, twirling a cigarette between his fingers or playing with his lighter.

"What's wrong?" I ask, picking up my plate and taking a seat next to him on the carpet.

"Nothing. It's just weird, actually being gone. I spent all this time thinking about leaving, but I never really thought I'd leave, you know?"

I nod, picking a stray tomato from my plate and putting it in my mouth. "I know exactly what you mean."

Truman leans back against the bed, glancing sideways at me. "How are you so calm all the time?"

The question is difficult and I don't know what he wants me to say. I'm not like this because of effort or design. I wish that the world affected me like it affects him—struck me to the core. But it doesn't.

"I don't know," I tell him. "I just am."

Truman nods and starts to cough again. He stands up, looking pale and worn-out. "I'm going to bed," he says, pulling back the covers.

I'm glad he's not sleeping on the floor. In the bed means next to me, even if he's still in all his clothes. In the bed means together, with only inches between us and no obstacles, no barriers. I could touch him, even if I shouldn't. Even if it isn't the right thing to want. And there's the matter of his dreams, the chance that if we sleep beside each other, I can dream them with him.

When Truman lies down and puts the pillow over his head, Raymie gives me a curious look, chewing her rabbit distractedly.

"He wants to sleep," I say, then wonder how to explain the idea. "We should all sleep."

I drop Raymie into her box and give her a pillowcase.

She only sits there, holding the pillowcase away from herself with a dubious expression.

As the numbers on the clock move, and the television programs roll by, Truman's breathing turns slow and ragged and his skin gets much too hot. I help him take his sweater off. He tries to tell me no, to leave it, but his voice is ragged. He shivers. When he sleeps, he grinds his teeth.

Out our window, I can see a black hotel, pyramid-shaped, shining as lights race up and down the inclines of its gleaming exterior. At the very top a spotlight shines into the sky, bright at first, then fading as it goes higher, winking out, getting lost. The whole boulevard is bright with lights and I pull the curtains closed.

"Truman is sick," Raymie announces to no one in particular.

And I recognize that she's right.

I sit beside him on the bed and when I touch his chest, I can feel his heart slamming under my hand. I hold a cold washcloth against his face and bring him water. He won't drink it. I want to buy medicine, but I don't even understand what kind he'd need. I keep thinking this is the most ridiculous thing. I'm sitting in Las Vegas with my disaster of a boy, watching while he burns up on the purple bedspread. I'm trying to act kind and sensible, like a human girl, but I don't know how to take care of anyone.

From the box, Raymie cranes her head to see up onto the bed. Finally, I pick her up and set her on the blanket beside him. I let her swab him ineptly with the washcloth.

"What makes people sick?" she asks, touching Truman's bare arm.

"Germs."

"Did the germs hurt him in his skin?"

"I don't understand what you mean."

"This." When she points, it is vague and clumsy, her fingers twitching as they try to follow his scars. "This hurt."

"No. That wasn't germs."

"Then what?"

I look at Raymie, sitting beside him. Her face is a round moon, fat and white and blank, but sweet. I don't want to frighten that out of her with the truth about Truman and the razor, how he was done being himself.

"It was something else," I say. "He doesn't like to talk about it."

I put Raymie back in her box. She doesn't resist, but the look she gives me is dubious, like maybe she doesn't believe what I've told her.

"It's time to sleep," I say, "so close your eyes."

But when I've taken off my dress and changed into my sweater, she's still just sitting there, staring over the edge of the box like a slightly ominous doll. Her gaze is steady, and it's unnerving to try and sleep with her watching. When she shows no sign of moving, I pick her up, box and all, and shut her in the wardrobe. Then I crawl into bed next to Truman. When I close my eyes, the street roars on and on like water.

THE STRANGER
CHAPTER TWENTY-TWO

I wake up, and for a second, I can't think what's woken me. The room looks strange in the dark, too full of furniture. It would feel claustrophobic if it didn't feel so cavernous.

I lie on my side, staring numbly at a collection of high-backed wooden benches. They stand in orderly rows, facing the television, and I know this isn't right but can't quite remember what's wrong about it. Our bags are lying on the carpet between them and the bed feels much too big.

When I roll over, Truman is on his side with his face turned toward me, a lighter spot in the dark, and very far away.

Then the panic hits my blood and I am wholly, frantically alert.

There's a man in the room, a man standing beside the bed. He's bending over Truman, whispering in his ear with an expression that is almost tender.

When I push myself up on my elbows, the man turns to look at me. The change in his features is chilling. Everything tender and good is gone, replaced by a deep, abiding hatred.

For a moment, he just stands over the bed, staring down at me with bright, crow-black eyes. His eye sockets are deep. His countenance is even and largely unremarkable, but even in the dark, I recognize every line of it. This is the faceless man from Truman's dream, but no longer faceless. Standing here in our room, he is utterly recognizable—as real as if he just stepped out of one of my mother's murals, full of righteous fury.

"Azrael," I whisper, so small it's barely a sound.

He nods and his smile is mild and appallingly lovely.

Suddenly, I understand that he's more powerful than anything my mother could ever aspire to, even at her most intrusive. His power is apparent in the way that he's brought the church with him, filling our room with tasseled hangings and carved pews and the choking smell of incense.

"I saw you," I tell him in a flat, breathless voice. "I saw what you were doing in the church. My brother—" The word stirs something in me—a kind of panic—and I sit bolt upright, staring around the room, but the table with Obie on it is nowhere to be seen. "Where's my brother?"

When Azrael laughs, his eyes glitter for an instant, then fade into shadow. "How very clever of you. But don't get too excited. You'll never find him, just like Truman will never escape me."

I press my back against the headboard, clutching the covers to my chest. "Why are you here? How did you get in?"

Azrael gestures to Truman. "He's burning up. Sleep can make the fabric between places pretty thin at the best of times, but delirium can destroy it completely."

"But why? Why are you following him?"

Azrael is leaning very close and his voice is low and

soothing. "Don't you worry about that. Just know that I'm doing everything in my power to help Truman. And if you interfere or get in my way, I'll kill you. It's nothing personal."

Suddenly, I feel disoriented, uncertain as to whether I am dreaming. The fact of Azrael standing over me, having a *conversation* with me, is utterly unreal and I need to see him in the light, see the face of the man who has stolen my brother. I lean across Truman and reach for the lamp.

Azrael makes a sharp hissing sound and before I can find the switch, he strides around the end of the bed and grabs me by my ankle.

He jerks me out of bed with a force that makes all the joints in my leg ache. Even as I hit the carpet, he yanks me up again, slamming me into the nearest church pew. It tips and the rest go over like dominos, but Azrael doesn't let go.

He drags me across the room, pinning me against the wall by the wardrobe. Behind him, the bed looks small and far away, like the room has lost its proper dimensions, stretching and lengthening as the church expands around us.

As I watch, Truman flings one arm out and makes a fretful noise, but doesn't wake up. I want to cry out, but Azrael's gaze is paralyzing, boring into me. This is how snakes hypnotize birds. Suddenly, everything seems very quiet.

Azrael leans close, so close I think he might press his cheek to mine. His voice in my ear is kind. "Hold still, my dear. This will only take a second. Then we'll see what's under that bloodless skin."

It is then that I register the knife in his hand. He's holding it deftly, almost casually. When he moves, it is straight for my throat. I barely have time to fling my hands up.

The blade is long, slashing across my palm. Pain explodes up my arm and the sound I make is high and shrill—the sound of metal on metal. I can't tell if it's a shriek or a laugh.

For one dizzying moment, the room rushes in on me in a glittering sea of sparks. Stars are colliding, solar systems imploding. I am consumed by a sensation I didn't know existed.

Then the pain crests and washes out, leaving me breathless but clear-headed, standing against the wall. I raise my hand and Azrael backs away. In a kind of dull wonder, I see that I'm bleeding. It spreads quickly, filling my cupped palm, and I realize that in a second, it will spill over, drip down onto the floor, unleashing whatever horror sleeps there. Fire, I think with a giddy hysteria. Acid, plague, pestilence. Whatever form it takes, it will mean destruction.

Too late, I make a fist, squeezing my hand closed in a desperate attempt to hold on. The blood oozes out between my fingers anyway.

One drop. Azrael has backed away from me and is standing in the center of the room, arms motionless at his sides.

I slap my hand to my chest, smearing blood across my collarbone, pressing the cut flat against my own skin, but it's too late. We stand facing each other across the toppled benches, waiting to see it. My mother's gift to me.

One drop, and time stretches out.

It lands on the carpet, its impact soundless. The seed,

planted deep in the scrambled pattern of the carpet. Where it fell, the floor begins to smoke and a girl materializes in front of me, pale and crouching. She's almost naked, veiled in smoky wisps that move and swirl around her as she straightens. Although her features look like mine, her eyes are steel-gray like my mother's and her teeth are dull silver, bared like fangs. Then she lunges, knocking over the end table. The lamp crashes to the floor. She scrambles over scattered luggage and carved benches, leaping and clawing her way toward Azrael.

When she rakes at his face, he doesn't even flinch. He just stares back at her, expression stony, blood running down his cheek.

"Get ready to regret that," he says, striding toward her, kicking the shattered lamp out of his way.

The girl snarls, showing her teeth like a dog, but he doesn't hesitate. The knife makes a graceful arc, up and in, flashing brightly one second, sunk deep in her chest the next. He lifts her, skewers her to the hilt, holding her nearly off her feet, then peels her neatly off the blade. She lands on the carpet with a boneless thud, then smokes briefly before collapsing into nothing. Dust and ashes.

"Try it again," he says to me, over the pile of ashes. He's smiling now and it's a bad, festering smile. It makes me think of bodies. Blood is running down his face. It looks black in the dark room. "Think you're clever? Think you're so *fierce*? Try it again, because I can do this all night."

With my hand held to my chest, I step between him and the bed, where Truman lies sleeping. Standing in the sliver of light thrown by the gap in the curtains, I feel disoriented and very small, but I also feel brave. And it is a good feeling.

"Cut me then. I'm not going to let you hurt him."

Azrael laughs, and it's the coldest sound I've ever heard. "Noble little thing. Your brother would be proud. But then, he always was a hopeless sentimentalist. Pain is necessary, my dear. It's *good* for you."

With another icy laugh, he steps sideways into the shadow cast by the wardrobe and is gone as surely as if he'd passed through a door.

I want to go after him, but I only get as far as the ruined lamp before my knees start to tremble. I stumble to the bed and I sink down beside Truman, who's sitting up now, staring around in panic. I reach across him and turn on the lamp to find the room is in shambles, filled with toppled furniture. In the light, the benches fade like afterimages, then vanish completely.

Truman is sitting with his back pressed against the headboard. His whole body is shaking and I put my arms around him, holding my injured hand away from us. The bleeding has already stopped. The wound is raw, but closing.

"Daphne," he says in a harsh whisper. "Wake me up. Please, wake me up." He's holding onto me now, his fingers deep in the fabric of my sweater. He's staring at someplace in front of him, trying very hard to breathe.

"How?" I ask. "Aren't you already awake?"

His eyes are wide and dazed, drifting past me to the little pile of ash on the carpet. "Talk to me."

But the room is spinning and I don't know what to say. My hands feel weightless and numb.

His breath is warm against my skin and I hang on tighter because the scene is fading in and out and I've started to shake. My whole body is trembling, like I'm coming apart at the joints and after a while, I can't tell who is holding who. Truman's arms feel tense and wiry, but safe.

The carpet is chalky and pale where the girl fell. Dusty with a layer of ash.

MARCH 10
1 DAY 0 HOURS 6 MINUTES

Truman sat on the edge of the hotel bed. According to the clock on the bedside table, it was just after seven in the morning, which meant nine o'clock at home. It was the latest he'd slept in a long time.

He sat with his hands pressed against his forehead, staring around in disbelief. The carpets and the furniture were all upholstered a deep burgundy, and there was nothing wrong with the actual decorating scheme, as long as you liked velvet. But even with the curtains closed, he could make out the general state of the room. It looked like it had been recently destroyed by one of those guitar bands from the seventies.

Lamps and room service guides and packets of instant coffee were all over the floor. Over by the TV was a mess of broken glass that might have started the night as a hotel ashtray. The throw pillows had all been knocked off the couch and one of the burgundy armchairs was lying on its back.

Beside him, Daphne was still asleep. He was about to wake her up and ask what had happened, but the sight of her face stopped him. Against the white backdrop of the pillowcase, she looked fragile. Her hair was spread out around her, framing her face. When he leaned over her, she burrowed into the covers and smiled slightly, but didn't wake up. Her eyelashes were dark against her cheeks and suddenly, Truman wanted to kiss her.

The desire was immense and wordless. It filled his chest, making it hard to breathe. She was the one peaceful thing in the whole demolished room and he sat beside her, breathless with how much he wanted to press his mouth against hers.

Then the closet door swung open and Raymie peered out at him from her cardboard box. She was sitting up, holding onto the folding flap. When she leaned her weight against the side of the box, it tipped forward and she flopped out onto the floor. She wriggled around a toppled lamp and began to paddle her way toward him, perilously near to the pile of broken glass.

Truman slid off the bed, careful not to wake Daphne. He picked his way through the chaos and sat down on the carpet, lifting Raymie into his lap. She was very warm and her back felt soft and fuzzy when he rested his palm against it.

"I was tired of being shut in," she whispered. "Why is the room so messy?"

Truman looked around at the overturned furniture, and didn't know how to answer. His memory of the night before was fuzzy at best. After Daphne had drawn the door, things had gotten very weird.

The trip through had not been pleasant, and by the time they'd gotten up to the room, he was pretty sure he'd been running a fever. He'd fallen into a bad, restless sleep. Then the shadow man had shown up. Only he wasn't a shadow anymore—now, he had a face. Truman had woken up to a dark room and a lot of noise, and in the chaos that followed, the only thing he'd been sure of was that the intruder had stuck a knife in Daphne's chest.

Only he hadn't, because she was curled up on the bed, looking exhausted, but all in one piece. So the vision of her death must have been a dream, but it was hard to find that reassuring when the destruction of the hotel room was still absolutely real.

"Come on," he said scooping Raymie into the crook of his arm and getting to his feet. "Let's go talk where we won't wake up Daphne."

In the bathroom, he set Raymie on the counter and closed the door. The room was as huge and old-fashioned as the rest of the hotel, with tiny octagonal tiles and a claw-footed tub. The counter, which ran the length of the wall, was one big slab of solid marble.

In the mirror, his reflection stared back at him, hollow-eyed and rumpled-looking. He was wearing jeans and his undershirt, but sometime in the night, he must have taken off his sweater. The sight of his bare arms had the effect it always did, making him feel a little sick. Instinctively, he turned toward the wall, crossing them over his chest.

Raymie sat on the counter with her back against the glass. She didn't look like she cared about his arms one way or another. "Why do you sleep in the bed with Daphne?" she asked, and began to suck on her hand.

Truman pushed himself up onto the counter and leaned back next to her. "It's complicated."

"Do you like it?" Raymie's voice was muffled by her fist. "I have always slept alone."

"Yeah, I like it."

"What makes it nice?"

"A lot of things. To touch someone, to feel them next to you." He laughed, but it was a short, injured sound. "I can actually sleep."

"Someone came last night," Raymie said. "I heard him out in the room, making noise. Is he the one who knocked over the furniture?"

Truman nodded. "I think so. Yeah, I'm pretty sure."

He knew it was bad news when your nightmares started spilling out into real life. The shadow man had always been more solid than any normal dream, but now he'd officially managed to make himself real enough to break things.

Truman knew he should be shocked, terrified even. Under other circumstances, fear would have been easy to come by. But two days ago, he'd met a girl who claimed to be a demon and then turned out to actually be one. Now he was in Las Vegas, with no money and no way to get back, sitting on the counter in the bathroom of what was obviously an insanely expensive hotel, talking to a baby with metal teeth. Surprises were becoming a thing of the past.

Truman looked over at Raymie, who was still chewing on her hand. "That guy—he visits me, I guess, but this was kind of a new thing. He's never broken stuff before."

"Why does he come to see you?"

"He says he wants to fix me," Truman said, and even saying it out loud made him feel ashamed. "And I don't know if I can be fixed."

"I can't help you," she told him.

"I know. I don't know if anyone can. I don't even know if I deserve it."

"You are always tender." Raymie was looking up at him with her strange eyes, a little terrifying in the light that shone above the bathroom mirror. "You are always tender to me."

"I like you, Raymie. Don't you know that?"

"Tender," she said again. "Tender is kind and gentle. It's also sore, like the skin around an injury."

Truman touched his wrists again, but the nerve damage made it hard to feel anything.

BLOOD LOSS
CHAPTER TWENTY-THREE

I wake up feeling light-headed and hungrier than I've ever been, like if I don't eat something now, right this second, I will implode. The whole room is in disarray, furniture overturned and luggage scattered everywhere. A lamp is lying on the floor, shade torn like someone put a foot through it.

After staring at the ceiling for a moment, I drag myself out of bed and pick through the room, opening drawers and cupboards, looking for something to eat. It's light out and Truman is already awake, sitting on the couch with a heap of decorative pillows at his feet.

He watches as I eat two packets of instant coffee from a wicker basket beside the television. Raymie is on the floor by the wardrobe, playing with her rabbit.

"Good morning," she says, reaching for me. I scoop her up and set her on the bed. Then I cross to the window and pull back the blinds.

Our room has a sliding door that opens out onto a tiny veranda. Through the glass, I can see the boulevard, full of cars and crowds of pedestrians, and a row of extraordinary buildings lined up like toys. Castles with a jewel-colored roof on every tower. An emerald city, dark, reflective, massive. There is a cluster of miniature skyscrapers, looming behind a scale replica of the Statue of Liberty. And the black pyramid, onyx-colored in the sunlight.

When I turn around, Truman is sitting on the edge of the couch, watching me. With the sliding door at my back, the sun shines into the room and I can see him very clearly, like he's the only thing in the room worth shining on. He gets up and comes to stand with me.

"Hey," he says, then doesn't say anything else.

He's looking down at me, standing very close. From the bed, Raymie is watching us, and her eyes make me feel warm and self-conscious.

The blood on my collarbone has dried to a crusty, brownish smear. The cut on my hand is long gone. I'm just about to ask if Truman wants to get something to eat, when he touches me, reaching for my collarbone. I can feel the way his fingers tremble, jittering over the smear of dried blood. "You're shaking," I tell him. "Why are you shaking?"

He doesn't answer, just stares down at me with an anxious, complicated expression. "Where'd all this blood come from?" His hand on my skin is warm, moving gently up my neck to cup my cheek.

"From me," I tell him. "From my hand."

He doesn't ask what happened to it, just moves closer. "I had the worst dream," he says, still touching my cheek. "I dreamed you died."

"No, I just got cut a little. I'm all right."

"What's he doing to you?" Raymie asks, shaking the corner of the duvet at me.

Truman jerks back like he's just coming awake. Suddenly his face is colored by a deep flush, and he takes his hand away. He turns abruptly and shuts himself in the bathroom. After a minute, I hear the shower come on. I can still feel the warmth of his fingers on my skin, and I'm hungrier than ever before.

Raymie clutches the duvet, looking up at me. "Why did that man wreck the room last night?"

I stare down at her in surprise. "Did you see him, too?"

"I heard him, but I was hiding. Will you play a game with me?"

I take the rabbit and wave it so its ears flop, but she just stares.

"This isn't a very good game," she tells me. "What is a better one?"

I pick up Truman's plastic lighter, flicking it to life.

Raymie claps her hands, then looks surprised at herself. She's smiling, and I wave the flame above her, drawing swirls and spirals in the air. She reaches with doll hands, trying to catch the smoke. Her teeth are spectacularly gray.

When Truman comes out of the bathroom, he's in his jeans, but shirtless. His hair is wet, sticking to his forehead. I look at his bare skin, wonder how it would be to put my hand on his collarbone. The muscles and bones of his chest stand out like Italian sculpture.

"Are you sure that's okay?" he asks, rubbing his head

roughly with a towel. "I mean, aren't you supposed to keep kids away from fire or something?"

We both look at Raymie. White-faced and black-haired, she is sitting on the bed in her yellow duck suit, staring at us.

I move the flame in a sweeping figure eight. "She likes it."

As if agreeing, she claps again and tries to take the lighter from me.

Truman finishes toweling off his hair and sits down on the foot of the bed. The way he smells is intoxicating, and even after the packets of instant coffee, I'm nearly desperate for something more satisfying. I need to get out of the room.

"I'm going to go downstairs," I say. "I'll find my cousin and ask him if he's seen Myra."

Truman nods, pulling on his shirt. "Yeah, hang on. Just let me get my shoes."

"I want to stay here," Raymie says to the nightstand. "I don't like the bells."

"Can you please stay with her?" I ask Truman, even though he's already putting on his socks and Raymie is perfectly used to staying alone.

He looks at me, but doesn't ask why I don't want him to come with me. He doesn't ask why, when I start for the door, I'm nearly running.

*   *   *

I find Moloch on the main level, in a little bar called the Paradise Lounge.

He's sitting on a barstool, watching a man in a sharkskin suit sing Sinatra while accompanied by a three-piece jazz ensemble. Moloch is occupying himself with a handful of paper napkins, lighting them on fire by breathing on them, and then extinguishing them between his fingertips, and although I have difficulty believing that setting fires is permitted in casinos, no one seems to notice. I decide that it's one more way the Passiflore welcomes our kind, like the jump-door and the Kissing Garden.

As I come up to the bar, Moloch drops the burning napkin and hooks his thumbs under his suspenders.

"Good to see you made it," he says, resting his hand on the flaming napkin. The paper smokes between his fingers, then goes out. "Still got your fatally self-destructive friend in tow? How did the jump-door agree with him?"

I shrug and climb onto a stool beside him. "Not well, but he made it."

It makes me feel strange to think of Truman. Not his disorientation after we passed through the door into the garden, but the way he held me last night, rocking me while I shivered and tried to catch my breath. The memory makes me feel light-headed and my hands are starting to shake again.

Moloch leans on the bar, playing around in a pile of ash left behind by the napkin. Then he turns on his stool and studies my face. "Cousin," he says, and it doesn't sound ironic, the way it would if he were calling me *pet* or *sweetness*. "You don't look very well. Are you feeling all right?"

I stare down at the palm of my hand, trembling but unmarked. For just a second, I want to tell him about Azrael, but I can hardly breathe when I think of those dark, glittering eyes boring into mine, and I can't bring myself to say the words out loud. How could I explain the girl or the knife blade?

There's a long mirror behind the bar, showing our reflections, Moloch red-haired and me monochromatic. It frightens me to realize that even though I am not calm anymore, it doesn't matter. My reflection is thoughtful and serene. I might be trembling to pieces underneath, but on the outside, I still look the same.

"I bled on the floor last night and it turned into a girl." The words sound cool and detached. They match the person in the mirror and not the way I feel inside.

For a moment, Moloch just stares at me with his mouth slightly open. Then he raps his knuckles on the bar and calls to the bartender. "Get me some salt, some bread, and a piece of steak, rare as you can make it."

"We don't serve food here," the bartender tells him, looking apologetic.

"Then give me garnishes—whatever you've got. Just get her something to eat."

The bartender produces the salt, along with Spanish olives, cocktail onions, gherkins, lemon wedges, and two glasses of tomato juice.

Moloch waits until I've drunk them both, then inspects me closely. "That's your protection—yourself in replica?"

I nod, salting the olives and eating them in handfuls. "It was kind of scary. And exhausting."

"Well, the food should help. Eat up and you'll get your strength back. Meanwhile, don't keep us in suspense—what's the story on that key you found. Anything of interest in your famous storage shed?"

"Clothes," I say, starting on the onions. "Mostly clothes. And also, a baby."

Moloch doesn't do any of the silly theatrical things that represent surprise. No hand to his chest, no eyes widening in shock. Instead, he just watches me, his gaze sharp and distrustful. "A *what*?"

"A baby. Obie had a baby. Did you know that?"

But I can tell from Moloch's face that he had no idea Raymie existed. "And it was just languishing in a storage shed? Is it all right?"

"She's fine." I don't know how to explain the feeling in my chest, that someone would leave a child in the dark. Leave her to sit patiently and gather dust while out in the world, things are charging along at a crazy pace, hurtling toward disaster. "She's very indestructible. Not much seems to bother her."

Moloch nods. "Kind of a side effect of our bloodline. Do you know who the mother is?"

I do know, but only vaguely. My knowledge of Raymie's mother is mostly just miscellany—some flowered dresses, some barrettes, and a slip of paper displaying light, dainty handwriting.

"Elizabeth," I tell him. "She's named Elizabeth."

"And I don't suppose you left the beast in the shed?" Moloch says.

"*No!* I couldn't do that. And she's not a beast—she's a little girl. I brought her with us."

249

"So an illicit baby is up in your hotel room right now. Daphne, this is a *very bad thing.*"

"But Obie hasn't done anything *wrong.* Why shouldn't he have a home and a family? He left Pandemonium because he loved her!"

Onstage, the band breaks into a rendition of "Stardust" and Moloch leans closer, folding his arms on the bar. "Maybe he did love her, but that doesn't matter. We're not supposed to breed with the locals." His tone is ironic, toying with me, but underneath, I think I hear shame, or maybe bitterness. He reaches over and shoves the little dish that held the olives. "You made quick work of those. Are you feeling better yet?"

"Yes, much. I was wondering if you could help me with something. I need to talk to Myra." I bite a slice of lemon and wince at the taste. "Is she here?"

Moloch glances around the nearly empty bar and shakes his head. "We came in through the jump-door together, but then she took off almost as soon as we arrived. I think I saw her skulking around the gardens yesterday, looking for some unfortunate reprobate to latch onto, but after that, I lost track of her. Since when are you two bosom buddies?"

I eat the last of the cocktail onions and get started on the gherkins. I'm not ready to tell him about the church. I don't quite know how to describe the importance of a place that only appears in dreams. Especially when the dreams aren't even mine.

In my own mind though, I have no doubt that the struggle with Azrael happened. The hotel room was destroyed, and I woke up with blood all over my neck, which leaves me with hope that the church is a real place—and that we can find it.

"The rosary you gave her is a strange thing to leave on a body. It might be important. I thought if we had it, you could help me figure out where it came from."

Moloch shrugs. "It's not a bad thought, but good luck tracking her down. If she couldn't find a willing victim in the hotel, there's a high probability that she's out prowling around the city."

I close my eyes for a moment and then open them again, trying to ignore the feeling that things are spinning out of control, well beyond the scope of my ability. "How big is the city?"

Moloch just shakes his head and laughs.

THISTLES
CHAPTER TWENTY-FOUR

When I go back up to the hotel room, Truman and Raymie are sitting on the floor, taking turns scraping at the carpet with a black plastic button from the sewing kit. Raymie is laughing, clapping her hands every time the button touches the floor. Truman looks up when I come in. He shrugs, like he has no idea what the game is about.

The room is marginally neater. While I was gone, he righted the overturned chair and swept up the broken glass. The pillows are arranged haphazardly on the sofa and the crushed lampshade sits forlornly in a corner.

"I think we should go out and look for Myra," I say. "We need to go around and check all the hotels."

Truman hands the button back to Raymie and stands up. His expression is skeptical. "Do you have any idea how many hotels there are in Las Vegas?"

"Yes, well it might go faster if we split up."

He presses his fingers against his eyelids and at first, I think he's about to start laughing, or else tell me I'm being unreasonable, but in the end, he just throws his hands up and smiles helplessly. "Sure, we'll check all the hotels in Las Vegas. Let's do it, let's go look for Myra."

We decide that I'll be the one to take Raymie, because it will look less strange than if Truman were carrying a baby around Las Vegas by himself. Once we get outside though, I'm forced to admit that it looks pretty strange anyway.

The day is overcast and cool. Truman stands looking down at me. "Are you actually serious about this?"

"Yes," I say. The city looks much bigger now that we're outside, but I have no other ideas.

We agree to meet back at the room in three hours. Then Raymie and I start off in one direction, and he goes the other.

The boulevard is broad and packed with cars. I only have to look at the sheer size of the nearest hotel before I realize that this is a ludicrous idea. It's true that I had no real trouble finding Truman, but that was because I had instructions. I had a general idea of where he would be and help figuring out where to find him when he wasn't there. The line of hotels stretches down the street for miles, and these are just the ones on the strip.

There's only one person I know of who might have some idea how to find my sister.

I steel myself to face her and sit down on the curb, holding Raymie in my lap. Out in the street, traffic stops and starts and stops again.

"Mom," I say under my breath, shielding my face from passing tourists as I talk. "Are you here?"

She makes me wait. But not for too long.

"Look who's back," she says from the fender of an expensive car, sounding languid.

"I just need a little bit of help," I tell her, doing my best to look contrite. "I'm trying to find Myra."

Lilith's eyes are cold and spiteful. Then she seems to relent. "You're close. Get up."

I glance in her direction, but there are people everywhere, crowding the sidewalk, so I don't answer her aloud. Instead, I give her a quick, decisive nod and get to my feet, adjusting Raymie in the crook of my arm and following Lilith's reflection as it vanishes and reappears, flashing in intervals along the strip.

"Turn left at the corner," she tells me from a plateglass window and I do it, walking faster as the wind picks up.

At her direction, I turn onto an empty street and then another. She's leading me away from the boulevard. After a few blocks, the scenery changes dramatically. Gone are the huge, extravagant hotels. The taxis and limousines have been replaced by scrubby palm trees and boarded-up buildings. All the houses are small and square, with wire clotheslines hanging in the side yards.

When we reach the end of the block, Lilith appears again, this time in the hubcap of a rusty sedan, leading me farther and farther, until finally she says, "Stop where you are."

Obediently, I freeze, teetering on the edge of the curb, and look down.

The bracelet is lying in the gutter, caught in the rusted

trap of the storm grate. It's covered in charms, tiny vials filled with the seven sins. The clasp is still firmly shut, but the chain has snapped. The broken end dangles, trailing down into the grate. I extract it from the mess of candy wrappers and cigarette packages and newspaper.

"How did this get here?" I ask my mother, who is staring up at me from the smooth surface of WRATH. "Where's Myra?"

My mother just shakes her head, gesturing behind me with her eyes. This street is darker and quieter than the one I just turned off of. At the far end of the block is a huge empty lot, fenced-in but full of nothing but weeds and gravel. Over by the back fence, something is lying in the knee-high weeds.

The gate is held closed with a heavy chain. Raymie watches, pressing her hands against her cheeks and staring in wonder as I melt the lock. I pick my way toward the back of the lot, slower now, reluctant to approach the crumpled shape. The sound of my boots on the gravel is very loud and I realize that I'm holding my breath.

"Don't," Raymie whispers. "Don't squeeze me so hard." Then she makes a tiny gasping noise and doesn't say anything at all.

Myra is lying under a scraggly palm tree, between a pile of warped boards and an empty fifty-gallon drum. Her eyes are open, her face strangely peaceful. Someone has arranged her, covered her in a grimy blanket that might have been purple once. Her hair is tangled, her head wreathed in a crown of weeds and thistles.

Carefully, I set Raymie on the ground. "Cover your eyes," I tell her, and my voice sounds almost calm.

I leave her sitting in the weeds with her hands pressed to her eyelids and approach Myra slowly. I pull back the blanket, and at first, I think that her throat has been cut, but the truth is so much worse. She's been torn open from chin to pelvic bone, left ragged and bloodless. Her body is ruined, and all her flirtatiousness and her heedless grace are gone. Her arms and legs are twisted awkwardly. One of her shoes is missing.

I kneel over her, trying to find a sense of loss or grief, but there's only Myra, broken and still in the shadow of the palm tree. There's blood on the ground, spattered around the body, sinking into the dirt, but not much. Not enough. Where it fell, it's started to eat through the gravel.

Something screeches in the tree above me, a hoarse, shrill sound, and I have to make myself believe that it's a bird and not an omen. I reach for Myra's arm, turning it to examine her wrist, but the rosary is gone, along with the rest of her bracelets.

Her face is horrific and delicate, and I hug myself. I want to stop looking, but something won't let me turn away. Her eyes are as flat as clouds.

Suddenly, I wish Truman and I hadn't split up. I wish I hadn't brought Raymie out here to this vacant field.

"This is why you have to run," Lilith says beside me, warped by the curve of the fifty-gallon drum. "Savage things are on the prowl."

Someone's been using the drum to light fires and it still

smells like scorched metal and burning trash. It was red once, but now the paint is flaking off, leaving bare patches where my mother's face shows through. The bow in the steel makes her mouth look wide and hungry.

"How could this happen?" I whisper to the metal drum and the empty lot. "She came here because she wanted to be safe."

"It doesn't matter where you go," my mother says. "Dark Dreadful isn't bound to one place any more than you are. She can always find you. She can hunt you anywhere."

When I close my eyes, I can almost hear the scrape and shuffle of stealthy feet somewhere in the dark. I am alone with the reflection of my mother, imagining the sound, but Myra didn't imagine things. Whatever she heard before the end was real.

I lean closer to my mother's reflection, searching for some evidence of grief, some sign that she feels sadness or loss. Her eyes shine fiercely and I see myself there—two tiny dolls reflected back at me. I stare until the dolls stop looking like me and become blank-faced versions of a girl. Myra, Deirdre. All of us. She blinks, and when she opens her eyes again, the dolls are gone.

I wonder if she's sad. All my life, my sisters have wandered out into the world, wicked and laughing in their extravagant dresses, and sometimes they don't come back. My mother has never seemed to care one way or another. At least, not in the way that Truman grieves for his mother, or parents care in the movies. Her face is unreadable, but something in her eyes is stark and far away. I wonder if she's worried about me. If she thinks I'll be next.

I hug myself tighter and sit down in the dirt. Myra lies empty in front of me, missing, gone, and I am alone. I reach out and cover her back up, even her face.

It's hard to say how long I sit there in the weeds before I'm shaken from my trance by the sound of footsteps crunching over the gravel toward me. I know who it is, even before he says my name.

"You were supposed to go in the other direction," I say without turning around. My face feels like a mask.

Truman crashes through the weeds and stands over me. "Sorry, I—I looked back and saw you turn off the strip. And it was weird, so . . . I followed you." Then he catches sight of the rumpled shape beside me. "What *is* that?"

I don't answer, just reach out and draw back the blanket, exposing Myra in all her gruesome splendor. Crowned and gutted.

"Oh, Jesus," he says, cupping his hands over his mouth and nose so that his voice comes out muffled. "Oh, God."

He sits down beside me in the dirt, keeping a hand over his mouth, and neither of us says anything. In the tall weeds beyond us, Raymie is still sitting patiently, covering her eyes.

I have an idea that if I speak, my voice will break and then so will the rest of me, clattering into pieces. The only thing holding me together is my silence.

"What happened to her?" he says after awhile.

"Azrael," I tell him, hugging my knees. The dry grass scratches my legs and I'm cold from sitting on the ground, but I sound composed.

"What's Azrael?"

"You already know him," I say. "He appears to you in dreams, like in the stories. Angels are always appearing to people, bringing them messages."

Truman makes a dry, wordless sound, like a laugh, but not. "Maybe two thousand years ago, but there haven't been a whole lot of divine visitations just lately. And trust me, the things I dream about aren't like any holy visions I've ever heard of."

"That's because he's not like the angels in the stories. He's unbending and absolutely dedicated to his calling."

"What's he the angel of?"

"Death," I say, gazing into Myra's face. She stares back, glazed and out of focus, looking past me into the middle distance. "He wants to kill us all."

Truman stands up. He lifts Raymie from the weeds and cradles her against his shoulder. Then, without saying anything, he reaches for me, taking me by the arm and guiding me to my feet. He turns me away from Myra's body and leads me back toward the gate.

"Where are we going?" I say, sounding vague and breathless.

His hand on my arm is gentle but unfaltering, and he just keeps walking. "It doesn't matter. Away from here."

✳   ✳   ✳

Back in the hotel, we sit in silence. Raymie is lying on the floor with her rabbit, chewing restlessly on its ears. Outside, it's starting to get dark.

"That was bad," Truman says from the couch, but his voice is so strange and so flat that it takes me a moment to make sense of what he's said.

I cup my elbows and nod. Raymie just chews harder on the rabbit.

When the phone by the bed rings, we all jump and Raymie bites down so ferociously that the rabbit tears and little bits of stuffing come spilling out.

I pick up the receiver and am relieved and slightly disoriented when Moloch speaks on the other end.

"Pet," he says. "Listen. Do you think you can come down to the lobby? I need to have a word with you."

Even thinking about going back down to the casino makes me feel very tired. "Can we have the word over the phone?"

"Well, the thing is, it's not really something I can discuss over the phone. You kind of have to see it. And bring your tragic friend, why don't you?"

When I hang up the phone, I'm still half-dazed, shaking my head. "We have to go downstairs and meet Moloch in the lobby."

Truman looks up from his seat on the couch. "Are you sure? What about Raymie?"

Raymie shakes her head and gnaws harder on the rabbit. "Bells," she says, sounding willful and sullen.

I pick her up and carry her over to the closet. "I think she'd rather stay here."

The fact is, I would rather stay too, but Moloch is waiting for me and with any luck, he'll know what to do. My only solid hope of finding my brother is gone. All we have left are Truman's dreams, and who knows where those will lead us.

MARCH 10
0 DAYS 10 HOURS 25 MINUTES

Moloch was waiting for them down in a little furnished alcove just off the lobby. He looked characteristically punk-rock, his sleeves pushed up, his slacks cuffed to show three inches of black combat boot. Beside him was another man, tall and blond. He wore a dark suit and an incongruously silver tie.

At the sight of him, Daphne stopped abruptly. The look on her face was close to unreadable, but Truman thought he recognized apprehension, or maybe guilt.

The man in the suit turned toward them. His expression was pleasant, but tightly controlled. "Daphne," he said. "How *unexpected* to find you here. And I see you've brought a friend."

When he looked at Truman, it was like a small electrical shock. His gaze seemed to settle inside Truman's bones. It made his teeth hum.

Beside him, Daphne was practically wringing her hands. "Truman," she said, looking at the floor. "This is Beelzebub."

Truman nodded, but couldn't think of anything to say. His throat felt closed up. Beelzebub was too polished, somehow. Too clean. Everything about him looked neat and sophisticated, nearly immaculate, except for a small tattoo on his jawline, just below his ear. It was a single housefly.

Beelzebub motioned to her and said, "May I have a word with you in private, please?" He spoke easily, but his eyes were chilly. His gaze kept returning to Truman.

Daphne nodded, lowering her chin like she was waiting to be punished.

As the two of them left the alcove, she glanced over her shoulder and gave Truman a little wave. Her face was anxious and Truman was about to start after her when Moloch caught him by the arm and shook his head.

"Don't worry about them. He's just going to scold her a bit, and I can't say that she doesn't deserve it. Come on, I'll buy you a drink."

He pulled Truman back into the alcove, guiding him toward the wall, toward a pair of high-backed chairs and a forest of potted plants.

Truman looked back over his shoulder. He could still see Daphne fading into the crowd. She was looking up at Beelzebub, gesturing with her hands. Then the gap in the crowd closed and she was gone.

Moloch leaned against the wall. "Sacrament," he said, but not to Truman.

As soon as he touched the striped wallpaper, a door appeared, but it was nothing like the grimy entrance to the Prophet Club, or even the door he and Daphne had come through when they'd arrived at the hotel. This door was easily fifteen feet high, heavy and carved with elaborate scenes of miracles and saints. It towered over them, but no one passing by the alcove seemed to notice. A red and gold sign above the door read THE CHURCH.

Moloch opened it, gasping against its weight, and waved Truman through ahead of him. Inside, they found themselves in a dark hall at the end of a long line of people.

When they got up to the front, the bouncer gave Truman a once-over and held up a hand to stop him, shaking his head. He was bigger than the bouncer at the Prophet Club, and a lot tougher-looking. His mouth glittered with metal and his eyes were a dangerous shade of red.

"This isn't torment night," he said to Moloch. "If you want screaming, take it someplace else."

"Don't be an ass." Even though he looked younger and smaller than the man guarding the door, Moloch's voice carried an air of authority. "He's just a guest."

The bouncer didn't say anything else. With a sullen look, he waved them in.

Inside, the club was huge and open like a warehouse, but the walls were covered in stained glass and the whole place was lit with giant purple chandeliers. Spaced along the edge of the dance floor were what looked like confessional booths. The curtains had been taken down, but the booths were still recognizable, decorated with carved flowers and gilded cherubs.

Truman followed Moloch through the crowd to the back wall, which was taken up by a long bar. It was packed with a throng of girls who all looked like they could be Daphne's sisters. The men were less identical, but just as obviously inhuman. Just as obviously demons.

At the bar, they had to elbow their way up to the bartender, a short man with glossy black skin and stubby horns poking up through his hair. "What can I get you boys?" he said in a bored voice.

Moloch glanced at Truman. "Bourbon on the rocks and a Bloody Martyr."

Truman expected the bartender to study him like the bouncer had, but he only shrugged and reached for the glasses. "You want the Martyr sticky and sweet or hot as hell?"

Moloch smiled his strange, tight smile. "Oh, hot as hell, *please.*"

The bartender nodded. He poured their drinks quickly, setting down the glasses and turning to the next group. Truman's drink was impossibly cold, burning the palm of his hand. Moloch's was thick and bloody-looking, topped with what looked like a communion wafer. He sipped it experimentally and then drank off half in one swallow.

As they turned from the bar, one of the black-haired girls moved closer, reaching for Truman's arm. "Hello there, stranger. We're just about to go out dancing. Why don't you join us?"

Her face was perfectly proportioned, with smoky eyes and slick red lips. Her dress was like rainbow snakeskin or a butterfly's wing, shimmering every time she breathed.

Moloch shoved her away, looking contemptuous. "Come

on," he said to Truman. "Grab your drink and we'll get a seat before they *really* start to close in."

They crossed the floor to one of the deconstructed confessionals and each took a booth. They were less than a foot apart, but with the wicker screen between them, Truman couldn't see Moloch's face.

With the glass in his hand, it was easier for Truman to pretend he was someplace else, just sitting in a quiet room somewhere. Sitting in his bedroom on Sebastian Street maybe, drinking Wild Turkey out of a coffee cup in an attempt to hide his self-destructive habits from Charlie. Back before he discovered that he really didn't have to. His life would be some bleak, empty place with no bright lights and no pale girls and no men with flies tattooed below their jaws. Unremarkable. Obscure.

For weeks after his mother's death, he'd woken up hopeful. His first thought when the alarm went off was always that he'd simply dreamed the grim parade of days following her funeral, that she was still alive, not sick, not dying, but laughing out in the kitchen with Charlie. Then he'd sit up and the reality of her death would settle into the room again. Each morning, he woke up and the first thing he felt was the headache, the nausea that came and went in sweaty waves. The hangover was miserable, but not deceptive. It only meant one thing: his mother was dead.

As he sipped his drink, a gaping hole seemed to open somewhere under his ribs and he had to stop thinking about it.

Looking out from the curtainless booth, he was suddenly

cold. The whole place was full of dried flowers and wooden crucifixes, heavy altars decorated with red velvet runners and steadily melting candles. Some of the demon girls were using the altars as cocktail tables. It made him think of his dreams and the nightmare church, but the layout was all wrong. Whatever dark cathedral he'd been dreaming about, it wasn't this one.

"What is this place?" he asked, staring out at the crowd.

Moloch spoke through the wicker screen between them. "Like the sign says, it's the Church. The finest club outside of Prague. Or maybe it *is* in Prague. With the jump-doors, it gets a little hard to keep track."

"So, where we are isn't real?"

"Oh, it's real, it's just not measurable. If you checked the blueprints, the extra space wouldn't show up, but that doesn't mean we're not here. The world is full of unused corners."

Truman watched the crowd swaying out on the dance floor. "Will Daphne even be able to find us here, then? When's she coming back?"

"Well, I can't say for sure. I suppose that's up to your father."

"*Charlie?*"

Moloch began to laugh. It was a low, unpleasant sound that made Truman look down at his hands. "No, not Charlie. Come on, do you actually expect me to believe that you didn't recognize your own father out there? For the love of all things ugly, you look just *like* him."

Truman sat in the confessional booth, staring down into

his drink. The ice was melting steadily. In a way, he'd known it the second Beelzebub looked at him. The buzzing in his teeth had been proof even before the long, tapering fingers, the pale eyes. "Does Daphne know?"

Moloch leaned closer, speaking to him through the screen. "No. I had a notion that she would have figured it out by now, but she's always been wretchedly stubborn about Beelzebub's more unpleasant qualities, and that includes his predilection for mortal women. As they say, there are none so blind as those who won't see. Anyway, it didn't seem like any of my business."

"How'd you know, then?"

"It was in your blood," Moloch said shortly. "Just simmering in your veins along with everything else. The folks at home do not give enough lip service to the taste of mixed blood, by the way. Exceptional."

Truman finished his drink, making a face. "You tasted my blood?"

"Only a drop—not like you were going to miss it. Anyway, you were too busy working on your sordid little death wish to mind."

Truman stared out at the crowd of laughing demons, feeling helpless. "That night," he said in a whisper. "That night at the party—I didn't do it on purpose."

Beside him, Moloch made a derisive noise. "Suit yourself. You're the one who toxified your blood with alcohol and indulged in a brief coma. You would have died if she hadn't come sweeping in at the last minute. So don't tell me you didn't have some idea of what you were doing."

Truman stared up the vaulted ceiling, which was bathed in purple light. He stared at the chandeliers. He stared at the empty glass in his hands. It was different, hearing it from another person.

He glanced at Moloch through the screen, trying to make out his silhouette. "Fine, I mean I got fucked up, but it was an accident. I'm not really *like* this."

On Moloch's side of the confessional there was silence. Then he sighed and leaned closer to the little window. "Yeah, you are. Maybe you weren't always, and maybe one day you'll be clean and whole and shiny again. But right now, you're not doing yourself any favors by pretending your downward slide is some freak occurrence. This is you, right here, right now."

Truman didn't say anything. He was thinking of Charlie. Of skinny little Alexa Harding, and of Dio Wan, who had been his best friend once, an eternity ago. Of anyone who'd ever watched him drink and pass out and buy razors and pound himself into little tiny pieces. They'd said the lines, made the right noises, but even when he was destructing right in front of them, no one had ever moved to stop him. In the end, they had always just let him do it.

"Daphne thought you were worth keeping," Moloch said. "Against all reason, against my strenuous objections. She needed a partner in crime, and she went with you. So you'd better get it together, that's all I can say."

Truman made fists, digging his fingernails into his palms. They sat side by side with the wicker lattice between them, while out on the dance floor, the bar was almost hidden behind a crowd of girls with black hair and excruciatingly short dresses. None of them were Myra, and Daphne hadn't smiled since before their ill-fated expedition that afternoon. Before Myra and the purple blanket, the broken bracelet. The search had ended in nothing, in a broken body, and Obie was still out there, tied to a table in a dark, secret place that looked like a church.

Moloch's voice was kinder, suddenly. "She likes you, you know. She might not say so, but I can tell. And you like her."

Truman shook his head, leaning back against the ancient upholstery, wishing his glass weren't empty, wishing he didn't wish for things that could kill him.

"No," he said, trying to convince himself that what he was saying was a fact. That he wasn't completely crazy about Daphne. His voice was so low it was barely audible above the music. "She doesn't. I don't."

On the other side of the screen, Moloch made a breathless noise, almost a laugh. "God, you're such a liar."

Truman closed his eyes and didn't answer.

"You're very lonely," Moloch said and for once, his tone wasn't sarcastic or mocking.

Truman nodded. The booth was too small, suddenly. His throat hurt. "Yeah."

When he looked over, he was surprised to see that Moloch's palm was pressed against the screen, fingers spread. The gesture was strangely tender.

"I'm not a holy man," Moloch said from behind his hand. "I'm not pious, and I'm not good. But if I were, your penance would be to start reaching for the things you want and giving up the things that will destroy you."

Truman didn't answer right away. He was no stranger to self-destruction, but running around with demons seemed pretty bad, even for him.

When he did speak, his voice sounded dry and hoarse. "What if they're the same things?"

THE THEATER
CHAPTER TWENTY-FIVE

There was a time when I would have been relieved to see Beelzebub standing in the lobby with Moloch, waiting to tell me what's happening and how to fix it. But now, his face is stony, and I can only square my shoulders and wait for the consequences.

As soon as we're through the lobby doors and out on the street, he stops and takes me by the shoulders. "What in the name of two unbridled hells do you think you're doing? I've been worried sick about you! No one even knew where you were."

We're standing in the middle of the sidewalk, surrounded by tourists. Every now and then, I think I see a flash of white skin, black hair. Sisters who could die in the shadows as easily as Myra or Deirdre. I don't tell him that my mother knew and that she'd gladly have told him, just to see him look disappointed in me. All he had to do was ask her.

"I came to find Obie."

That makes him shake his head in exasperation. "I'm taking you home. *Now.*"

"No," I say, and it's strange to know that he can't make me

go. The realization is liberating and a little sad. He's always been the one to make the rules and give the advice. The voice of authority.

Beelzebub raises his eyebrows. Then he takes me by the elbow and I think he's going to shake me, but instead he turns me away from the strip, toward the darker, narrower streets, waving me along in front of him.

"Where are we going? I told you, I'm not going home."

"No? Then you and I are going to have a little talk."

We follow the same general route I walked earlier when my mother guided me to Myra, and for a little, I think that he's somehow taking me back to the empty lot. Instead, he stops in front of a boarded-up building. It's tall and windowless with a rickety, unlit marquee. The sidewalk in front is deserted and the glass doors are dark.

When he approaches the entrance, I expect him to do some trick that vanishes the glass or melts the chain that holds the door, but he just takes out a set of keys and tries them one after the other until he finds one that works.

"Come on," he says, ushering me into the dark, abandoned lobby.

There are crumpled playbills everywhere and empty popcorn boxes scattered here and there. Beelzebub ignores the mess and leads me down into the theater.

The stage is shabbily grand, with a festive array of colored footlights. Most of them are broken and the orchestra pit is littered with glass, but the remaining bulbs flare to life when Beelzebub touches a switch, providing enough light for me to

273

look around. The curtains are a deep, volatile red, heavy with dust. The whole place smells distinctly unused.

"Where are we?" I say, gazing at the painted ceiling, the worn velvet seats. The upholstery must have started out red, but now the cushions have all faded to a dusty pink.

Beelzebub doesn't answer immediately. He's standing with his back to me, looking around the empty theater. "This used to be our place, Las Vegas. This whole city was a gangland once, and they welcomed us with open arms."

"But not anymore?" I recall Moloch's performance in the lounge, lighting the napkins on fire. "No one even looks twice at us here. And they have that garden—the Kissing Garden—at the Passiflore."

"Oh, the Passiflore still accommodates us, and there are a few other haunts, but the fact is, Vegas is nothing like it was in the old days."

He helps me up onto the stage, leading me toward the center, where a huge, heavy block of wood sits alone, almost as high as my waist. The top of it is rough, crisscrossed with grooves, and stained a dark, unsettling brown.

"What is it?" I ask, running my fingers over the gouged surface.

"It was the finale to a very popular magic act. A pair of demons with a rare and quite appalling gift would cut themselves in half. Then, to the wonder of the audience, they would join the severed halves together again, not always being particular about whose parts were whose." His expression suggests that the notion is distasteful.

"What happened to the show? Did they retire?"

Beelzebub shakes his head, looking out at all the empty seats. "They died. They got accustomed to living on Earth, and when it was clear that they had no intention of leaving, Azrael had them slaughtered, and he had every single one of the wretched demons who ran the theater destroyed. I'm showing you this because you need to understand that Dark Dreadful is real. She's incredibly dangerous, and if she catches you, she will *kill* you."

"I know," I say, and my voice is so low and hard that I almost don't recognize myself. "I'm not stupid."

Beelzebub nods heavily, lowering himself to sit on the edge of the stage. After a second, I sit down next to him.

"I can make you a door," he says. "I can send you home right now, safe and sound. We've got ways of finding Obie, if you'll just let me take care of it."

But I know with grim certainty that he can't. If he hasn't found Obie by now, he's not going to. He doesn't have Truman's dreams. He doesn't know about the church.

When he says he'll take care of it, he's telling me the thing I wanted to hear more than anything, but it's too late now. I've seen Obie on the table. I stood over Myra's body, looked into her dead eyes, and these are things he can't fix. I reach into my pocket and drop her bracelet on the stage between us.

Beelzebub looks mild and quizzical in the footlights, squinting down at all the little vials. "What is this?"

"It was Myra's. I know you want me to go before things get bad, but they're bad already. Dark Dreadful's been here, so don't tell me that everything is under control or that Obie's going to be fine. I saw her body. Nothing is fine."

Beelzebub runs his fingers over SLOTH, AVARICE, ENVY. He doesn't say anything for a long time. The sins lie spread out on the stage between us.

"Was it horrible?" he says finally.

"No," I tell him, staring down at the bracelet, remembering. The threadbare blanket, the crown of thorns. I knelt over her in the dirt, but it doesn't devastate me. It doesn't feel like anything.

I expect him to tell me I must be wrong, that I'm just reacting badly to the discovery of Myra's body. In shock, maybe. I realize with a kind of unhappy surprise that it's what I want to hear, but he doesn't say it. His face is sober and I can see that in some way, I've disappointed him by my failure to feel grief.

He nods heavily. "Then you really are your mother's child."

"Yes," I say, because there's no denying it. I've always been my mother's child.

The theater is still and empty. The spectacle is gone now. A pair of minor demons will never stand in the pale glow of the spotlight, never cut each other in half and join together again.

Beelzebub glances over at me. "I appreciate your determination, you know. But it's not going to do your brother an ounce of good if you end up dead."

I nod. He's right, but not in the comforting, authoritative

way that proves everything is under control. He's right in a way that makes me feel tiny and helpless, like something terrible is coming.

"I guess I have to let you make your own decisions," he says finally, and his voice is soft and almost sorrowful. "But remember, if Dark Dreadful comes for you, there's no way to protect yourself and there will be no one here to help you."

"I'll be all right," I say, because sometimes saying something aloud is enough to make it feel true.

Beelzebub nods and in the dim glow of the footlights, his expression is stark. He sits looking down at me with grave, troubled eyes, and I know he's not convinced.

THE PAIN TREE
CHAPTER TWENTY-SIX

By the time I get back to the room, Truman is already there. On television, the screen is flashing ads for fabric softener and convenience foods. Raymie is in her box with a blanket over her head, like she does when she's thinking about something or wants to pretend she's a rabbit.

I sit down on the velvet couch with my knees pulled up. Truman is on the bed, leaning against the headboard and staring at the mirrored ceiling. His arms are bare and I realize that since last night, he hasn't been so vigilant about wearing long sleeves. I watch the contour of his lower lip and don't realize that I'm doing it until he glances at me. The look he gives me is puzzled and I feel like I've been caught doing something shameful.

"Are you okay?" he says, standing up.

I want to tell him that I'm fine, but his gaze is tender and something catches in my throat, so I look away, hugging my knees.

"What's wrong?" he says, coming over to the couch. He drops down next to me and then moves closer. "Did you get in trouble or something?"

I shake my head, struggling to put voice to the thing that Beelzebub told me about myself.

"What's wrong, then?"

"I wasn't sad when Myra died." The admission is thin and high-pitched, this tiny, shameful thing.

For a moment, Truman just looks at me, looks into my face like he's seeing the coldness and the guilt there. When he speaks though, his tone is kind. "Sad can look a lot of different ways. You don't have to cry or make a big scene just to prove you're sad. I know it when I see it."

"How?" I say. "How can someone be sad without knowing?"

He doesn't answer. Our heads are close together and he leans in. His eyes are the palest, clearest blue, irises patterned with tiny cracks, like glass covered in hairline fractures. He smells like smoke and something warm and spicy.

"Daphne—" Then he stops. His voice is hoarse, suddenly. Cracked.

He opens his mouth, just a little, and maybe I'm not prophetic, but I know what's going to happen. His eyes are uncommonly transparent. They make it so easy to see the ache in him. It waits in the hollow of his chest, in the dark space between his lips. I can almost taste it.

He leans closer and I twist away and slide off the couch, keeping my head turned so I won't see how he looks at me.

In the bathroom, the light fixtures are shaped like brass tulips, jutting out in a row above the long mirror. I drape a bath towel over them so it hangs down in front of the glass and I won't have to see Lilith.

Then I turn on the taps and stand at the sink with the water rushing down the drain. The sound helps me block out my tingling hands. The towel blocks out my reflection, how it seemed to stare back at me with naive reproach.

Water pours into the sink and I'm leaning over it with my eyes closed when Truman knocks softly on the half-closed door. Then, when I don't answer, he pushes it open.

"Daphne." His voice is low and hesitant. "Please, I need to talk to you."

I turn off the faucet and the room is suddenly very quiet. "Don't."

If he reaches for me, I know that I won't be able to resist it. He'll kiss me and I will let him. I'll kiss him back. I won't be any better than my sisters with their hungry smiles. I will know for sure who I am, and it's someone I don't want to be.

He crosses the room and turns me gently by the shoulders. When he touches me, I feel my blood get strange, too hot and like it's moving faster. He runs his finger along my cheek and I breathe out because if I don't, I think my bones will break.

His hand is warm against my skin, cupping my shoulder, and inside, my blood is racing—racing until I'm sure that I won't be able to stand it any longer. I need him to stop just so I can breathe without suffocating.

When I jerk away, he looks hurt but unsurprised. In a moment, he'll leave—walk out, and then the room will feel big enough again and I can go back to being calm and separate. Safe.

Instead, he puts his arms around me and pulls me close. "Hey," he says against my ear. "Hey, what's wrong?"

"If I kiss you, I might ruin your life." My voice is so small. "I might take all the parts that are worth something. Anything that makes you human. My sisters do it all the time."

When he shakes his head, his cheek brushes mine. "I don't care."

He slides his hand to the back of my neck, tangling his fingers in my hair. His heart is beating hard against my body, thudding in my chest. It almost feels like mine.

His mouth against my ear is warm and I can feel him breathing. "You have no idea how much I don't care."

"I'll see you," I whisper. "Not just your sadness or your scars, but really see you. Everything about you."

Truman lets me go. Stepping back, he gazes down into my face. Then he nods. "Okay." He stands in front of me with his arms at his sides, held a little away from himself. Offering.

When I lift his shirt, I do it slowly. His skin is soft-looking and I touch him because he's beautiful and because, because I want so badly just to touch him.

His arms are wiry, but well-defined. Muscular. He stands in front of the porcelain tub, bare-chested, jeans low on his hipbones. His smile is cautious, and all his normal impatience and his irony are gone. "How do I look?"

"Beautiful."

He glances away shyly, shaking his head. "Do I get to see you?"

"Yes," I say, even though the thought makes an alarm shrill frantically inside my head. No one has ever seen me. But he wants to. No one has ever asked my sisters for this. They saw whether they wanted to or not.

When he pulls my dress over my head, he does it slowly. My skin prickles when the air brushes against me and I have to cross my arms over my chest. Everything is much too exposed.

"Here, come here," I say. I pull back the shower curtain and take Truman's hand. When I close the curtain around us, he raises his eyebrows but doesn't say anything. Behind the curtain, everything feels safer, like the world is very small.

We stand facing each other in the bathtub and he watches me intently. Moves his lips, but no sound comes out. He raises his hands and mine rise to meet them, fingers tangling. Here is the best—the *realest* thing of my life and I don't know how to let him touch me. It scares me, how much I want things.

"What are you scared of?" he says, and his voice is low and gentle.

"Myself." My throat feels tight and guilty when I say it out loud. "Where I come from, this—what we're doing—this isn't good. There's all this noise in my head, all these voices telling me what I should be, and I just want them to stop."

Truman nods and his expression is solemn, like he knows exactly what I'm talking about. Without looking away from me, he reaches behind him and turns on the shower.

Immediately, the bathroom is filled with the roar of water.

It pours down on us, cold and then warm. My hair is soaked and we stand facing each other, bathed in steam.

He smiles. "Let's hear them try and talk at you now."

When he lowers his head to kiss me, I let myself collapse into him. His mouth is careful and he moves slowly, so slowly it sends shudders down my spine. Something electric sings in my veins and I love and hate it. I want to laugh at how terrible I am. I have never wanted anything more than this.

He takes me around the waist and leans me back, our skin sticking and squealing against the sides of the tub. He kisses me hard on the mouth and keeps doing it.

Our bodies are awkward in the cradle of the tub, pointy and slippery, twining each other, peeling ourselves out of our clothes. Even in the steam, Truman is shivering, the tiny hairs on his arms standing up. I close my eyes against the spray.

His lips are warm, trailing down my throat, brushing my collarbone like he's breathing me. His mouth is everywhere, caressing my throat and my face and he is wanting me and finding me and finding me again, every time his lips brush my skin.

His forehead touches mine, and that's when I see it—the shape of his sadness.

It looms with frightening clarity, exploding to life behind my eyelids. A leafless tree, bleached by sun, split open at the base. I kiss him hard and the tree comes closer, rushing at me. My dream self reaches into the heart of it, feeling in the dark for what she knows will be there.

I search until my fingers close on something solid and I

drag it out into the open, this sharp crystal thing, all edges and angles and shards. When I hold it in my hands, white light glows from it like a flash bomb, blinding. Then the light is pouring over me, seeping into my skin. It sinks into me like sunshine and I feel free.

Truman shudders against me, fingers digging into my shoulders. He makes a noise in his throat, a thick, choked noise, and I let him go.

At once, the pain tree flickers and is gone. My hands are empty. My ears are full of a faraway screaming, like static, and I've just done the thing I never wanted to do.

I'm lying on my back in the bathtub with a boy who's trying to untangle his legs from mine. The shower is on and we're both soaked.

"What was that?" he whispers. His voice is hoarse, cracking.

"It was a mistake. I'm sorry—I'm so sorry."

"Daphne." He sounds disoriented and a little shaky, but his smile is one I've never seen him wear before, wide and easy, full of gladness. He props himself on his arms, looking down at me. His eyes are clear and steady and calm. "It's not a mistake. Whatever it was, it was . . . amazing."

And I know for sure that there's a heart inside my chest. I can feel it trying to leap free, to fly out into the room like a giant bird, set loose and flapping.

I saw the extent of his pain, saw all the way to the bottom, and he's still here—smiling even. I still feel like myself, but with a better understanding of what that means. All my life, a kiss has been the territory of demons, simultaneously fascinating and frightening. Evil, unnatural, sordid.

All my life, I've been wrong.

The truth is, something about my mouth against his was terribly, gloriously human.

MARCH 11
0 DAYS 6 HOURS 7 MINUTES

Truman lay on the bed, watching the room reflected on the ceiling.

The top of Daphne's head was tucked under his chin and her damp hair felt nice against his throat. Across the room, the television flickered peacefully, and in the mirror, the two of them looked very tired.

Kissing her had been incredible. Nothing like kissing Claire, or any of the hopeless, needy girls who wanted to make out with him at parties. It had been like sunshine, all warmth and freedom. Suddenly, the world looked much brighter.

"Did I hurt you?" she whispered, moving closer.

Truman had to force back a laugh. "I don't know if you've been paying attention, but whenever I get hurt, I mostly do it to myself."

With one hand, she began to stroke his arms. "What makes you hate your body so much?"

"Nothing. I mean, I don't."

She didn't say anything, just ran her finger along the inside of his wrist. On the television, a pair of tigers were taking turns jumping between painted platforms, while a bunch of girls in sequined leotards waved bright yellow streamers behind them.

Daphne pressed closer to him, sounding half-asleep. "I'm sorry that I'm so scary."

"You're not scary. You're beautiful."

"Why do you always say such good things about me?"

"Maybe I like you," he said, squeezing her against his chest and pressing his mouth to the top of her head. "Maybe when I'm with you, I don't think I'm so bad either."

"What?" Her voice was soft and drowsy. "You're mumbling."

"Nothing, it's not important." Her hair smelled like salt and water. "You're lucky," he said, touching her shoulder, her arm.

"What do you mean?"

"You're so happy, just all the time."

"No." He could feel her lips moving against his skin as she spoke. "I was never happy before I came here."

"What were you then?"

"Lonely. Bored, maybe. It was a strange feeling. I think if I could see it, it would look like a tiny polished castle, full of poison flowers and silver spears."

Truman only stared up at the mirror and shook his head. His pain didn't blossom or shine.

He took a deep breath and swallowed before he spoke. "Maybe it has a shape, I don't know, but mine isn't clean."

"Why not?"

"It's just not like that. It's like a car accident. Anybody normal would look away. It would make them sick."

Daphne wriggled out of his arms and pushed herself up off his chest. "No," she said leaning over him, touching his face. "Yours isn't an accident."

Truman closed his eyes, concentrating on the feeling of her hand on his cheek. "That's not what I meant."

"But you should know what it's like. It looks like a tree, all twisted and leafless and lightning-struck, but it's not dead. It could still get better."

Truman didn't answer, just lay on his back looking up at her. Her eyes were soft and she was smiling, holding his face between her hands.

She kissed him gently, then settled back down, snuggling under his chin. "I just don't want you thinking it will never get better."

He clenched his jaw, holding onto her with shaking hands, pressing his mouth against her hair.

When he watched them in the mirror, their reflection was strange and distant, like he was watching from outside himself. Daphne lay with her head on his chest. Her eyes were heavy, drifting closed. His arms were around her, his hands freckled and bony against her unmarked skin. He looked younger than he had since he was sixteen. Since before his mother died. His eyes were wet and shining, but the ache in his throat was good.

He lay with tears running down his face and neck, soaking into the pillow. Watching himself cry was strange, like watching someone distant but familiar. Someone he hadn't seen in a very long time.

Daphne lay on his chest, oblivious to the hitch in his breathing, the tears on his face. He raised one hand, touching the side of her neck, the curve of her shoulder. She was sleeping. With the remote, he switched off the TV and reached for the lamp.

In the dark, he stared up into the shadows. Almost every night for the last year, he'd woken up shaking, and even the narrow bed had seemed a mile wide. Now, sleep seemed not only possible, but right.

Against his chest, Daphne was very warm. He closed his eyes and didn't think about drugs or Azrael or his bad, desperate year. Not loneliness, not sorrow. Nothing, nothing—nothing and everything.

And he slept. And that was fine.

✳　✳　✳

The candles had all been lit, filling the church with a dim, flickering light. Truman stood barefoot on the dais, cupping his elbows in the cold, dry air. The silence was so deep that it echoed.

Azrael appeared out of the dark and leaned his elbow on Truman's shoulder. "This is nice, isn't it—finally being able to see each other? It's been frustrating, trying to work with you when you couldn't see my face."

Truman stared straight ahead. "I don't want to see your face. I want to go back to bed."

"Then you really shouldn't have let your little friend

289

take you through that door. You might have preferred your ignorance, but delirium is a powerful eye-opener. You saw me and now you can't unsee."

Truman twisted away. He was cold and disoriented, but the usual rush of hopelessness was gone. Over in the corner, Obie still lay on the table, hands bound above his head. His arms were bleeding and the sight made Truman feel shaky and sick, but under that, he was newly, ferociously angry.

Azrael sighed, draping his arm over Truman's shoulders and leaning in so that their heads rested against each other. "Aren't you glad to see your old friend? I seem to have a vague memory of this time you got friendly with a razor and spent four days in the hospital, palling around with a lesser demon. Does that sound familiar?"

Truman shook his head, trying to pull away. Azrael's breath was warm on his cheek and he could smell incense and old, dusty books. His throat felt closed up.

In the candlelight, he could see that the table wasn't a table at all, just a painted board laid across a pair of sawhorses. Obie twisted and then began to struggle, pulling against the wire that fastened his hands to the top of the board.

Without thinking, Truman moved to help, but Azrael caught him by the elbow, yanking him back. "No, no. Let's just watch. I'm curious to see where this goes."

Obie pulled hard against the wire and after a struggle, he managed to yank one hand free. Twisting awkwardly, he used his index finger to trace something on the surface of the table.

"Freedom," he whispered, and his voice sounded dry. Nothing happened. "Home."

Azrael smiled and let Truman go. He crossed the dais to Obie and leaned over him. "Haven't you figured it out yet? You're not going anywhere."

He yanked one of Obie's arms down, holding it out from his body, pressing it flat against the board. The railroad spike appeared from nothing, flashing to life in Azrael's hand. He pressed the point into the middle of Obie's palm.

"Hand me that hammer," he told Truman, gesturing behind him to the pulpit.

Truman looked where Azrael pointed, and there was a Craftsman hammer lying on the pulpit.

"Oh, *God*," he whispered, backing away, shaking his head.

"Fine, I'll get it." Azrael shrugged and was suddenly holding the hammer. He pointed it at Truman, raising his eyebrows. "You sure you don't want to help me? This would go faster with another set of hands."

Truman stood by the pulpit, feeling rooted to the floor. He was breathing fast and panicky, and even the Hail Mary didn't help.

"Suit yourself. I'll just be a minute." Azrael steadied Obie's palm, then brought the hammer down. The spike didn't punch through on the first try and he had to swing twice more before it went, splintering into the board behind Obie's hand.

Obie gasped, curling his fingers, arching his back against

the table, but he didn't scream. Somehow, the silence made it worse. Under the blindfold, his face was pale and gaunt. His jaw stood out like he was clenching his teeth.

Satisfied, Azrael stepped back and suddenly, instead of the hammer, he was holding a pair of long-nose pliers. He sliced through the loop of wire that still held Obie's other hand. Then the second spike was in position, driving home, slamming into the board.

Obie lay on the table, arms spread. His mouth was shut, lips white.

Azrael smiled, looking cheerful and friendly in the candle-light. "Now, time for some fun." He glanced up at Truman, holding a finger to his lips, then leaned his elbows on the table, speaking close to Obie's ear. "Your sister's on Earth. Did you know that?"

Obie didn't answer right away. When he did, his voice sounded dusty. "I have a lot of sisters."

"I'm talking about the little one, with the two adorable metal teeth and no sense of self-preservation. You might remember her?"

"You're lying. Daphne doesn't leave the city."

Instantly, Azrael's expression darkened and a scalpel appeared in his hand. He held it above Obie's arm, leaning on his elbows so that the table shifted and squealed on its make-shift supports. "I never tell lies."

Obie tugged hard against the iron nails and Truman winced as the wood squealed but the nails didn't pull free.

"She's here," Azrael said. "But Dreadful doesn't have to

kill her. Dreadful doesn't have to kill anyone. I could decide we've done enough demon-chasing for a while, send her home. All you have to do is tell me where your little puppy is."

When Obie answered, his voice was broken, cracked and desperate. "I told you, I *can't*."

"Then Dreadful's going to have a really good month." Azrael's hand drifted along Obie's arm, not quite letting the blade touch the skin. "I've got another one for your record-keeping. While you were busy lying here, your various friends and relatives are out there dying."

"My family." Obie's voice sounded parched. "You're talking about my family."

Without warning, Azrael cut another hashmark across Obie's forearm. "Say hello to Myra."

As the scalpel drew blood, something thudded on the dais, making the floor shudder.

Truman moved forward cautiously, crouching to examine the pale form that had appeared at his feet, eerie in the flickering candlelight.

He was looking at Myra, but not the sly, smiling girl he'd sat next to at the bar. This was the body that Daphne had found in the open field. This was a car crash, a girl in pieces. Her eyes were open, staring at the dark ceiling. Her ribs had been peeled open and the wound was ragged and bloodless. There was still a little bit here and there, soaking her dress and dripping down her chin, but not much. Where it had splattered on the steps, it burned away the carpet and then began to eat through the floor. He clamped a hand over his mouth but couldn't smother the low, horrified noise that rose in his throat.

Azrael crossed the dais and stood over him. "Do you see that? That could easily be Daphne."

"No," Truman whispered. "Please, no."

In the corner Obie lay staked to the board. His arms oozed with rows of shallow cuts. "Azrael, please." He sounded hopeless and exhausted. "I don't know where she is. I can't give you what you want. She's with her mother, and you won't find her."

"That's a good guess, but no, she's not with her mother."

Obie went rigid. In candlelight, his face was waxy under the blindfold. His voice was hollow. "What did you do?"

"I took care of her mother." Azrael's expression was warm. Sympathetic. "It was picturesque and ultimately, quick. I came to Elizabeth in the city garden at Garfield Park, and proposed a scheme. I like to think that she even considered it. It would have been a valiant sacrifice, her demon child in exchange for salvation."

The words were weirdly familiar. *Sacrifice* and *garden*, and they tripped something in Truman's memory. He'd been going to catechism for most of his life.

"The Sorrowful Mysteries," he whispered, kneeling over Myra's body. Her forehead was still wreathed in thistles. "The agony in the garden, the crown of thorns—those are Mysteries of the Rosary."

Azrael nodded agreeably. "I thought it had a certain grandeur to it. There's a poetic quality to recreating a religious tableau. It was no good, though. She made the wrong choice in the end."

As Azrael spoke, the body of Myra dissolved, transformed. Now Truman was kneeling over a woman with thick brown hair and half her face missing.

Truman swallowed, shaking his head. "How? How did you kill her?"

Azrael stood next to Obie, and the light from the candles made him look very cruel suddenly. "I never touched her, just told my dark friend where to find her."

"She was good," Obie whispered. His voice was shaking. "She was my *wife*. I *loved* her."

Azrael leaned closer, his voice almost tender in the dark. "Of course you did. You love all the little broken things. Now where *is* it?"

"I don't know. Please—please believe me."

The pain in Obie's voice made Truman's chest hurt. It was too raw, too familiar, and he closed his eyes.

Azrael turned and walked back across the dais to where Truman knelt above Obie's wife. He pointed at the crumpled body, the obliterated face. "That's what happens to people who choose demons instead of salvation. Sometimes, the only way to save someone is to just let them go."

Truman stared up at him, shaking his head. "You can't save me," he whispered. "Nothing can. Church never did, and neither did Obie, or school or my family or being drunk or being dead. And Daphne can't save me either—you can't save other people. But I'm *better* when I'm with her."

"No, when you're with her, you're still just as wretched as you ever were, and she's still a dirty little succubus." Azrael spoke softly, watching Truman with something close to sadness. "But that's why I keep Dark Dreadful around. I can still save you, but I'm warning you right now, this is going to be very hard. It's going to hurt."

Truman felt cold and suddenly wide awake. "What are you going to do to Daphne?"

"Nothing. I won't even touch her. But she's going to die, and it's going to be horrible."

❋ ❋ ❋

And Truman was awake again, heart slamming. In the bed Daphne lay very close, clutching his arm. Her fingers dug into his wrist and he sat up.

In the dark he could see shapes and shadows, the faint outlines of the room. Daphne huddled next to him, making a high whimpering noise. He reached for her, and she reached back, collapsing into his arms. She was shivering so hard that at first he thought that she might be crying, but she made no noise and where her cheek pressed against his, her face was dry.

"He won't kill me," she said and her voice sounded small and ferocious. "Not like that."

"It's okay," he whispered, but he didn't believe it. "Don't talk like that. Everything's going to be okay."

He said it firmly, holding her against his chest. The fact that he was lying didn't matter.

LOVE
CHAPTER TWENTY-SEVEN

It's five o'clock in the morning and we're all awake. Truman was first to get up and now he sits perched on the corner of the bed, not smoking, but looking like he wants to.

Raymie is on the carpet by my feet, playing with the sewing kit and making big black stitches all over her rabbit.

Truman scoops her up. Then he sets her in his lap and covers her ears with his hands. "Okay, I think it's time to talk."

At first, I think that he wants to talk about what happened in the bathtub, but he takes a deep breath and says, "Azrael's the one who killed your sisters, right? Well, he's doing it according to the Mysteries of the Rosary and he's almost done with the Sorrowful ones. He nailed Obie's hands to the table, but he hasn't raised him yet."

"What do you mean 'raise' him? Why would he raise him?"

"Because the last Sorrowful Mystery is crucifixion. He did the agony in the garden and the crown of thorns. He missed the flagellation, but—"

"No, he didn't," I say with a heavy feeling in my chest. "Deirdre was beaten so badly that she was unrecognizable."

Truman swallows. "Then he's going in order. There's still the carrying of the cross, but after that, he'll move on to the crucifixion." As he speaks, Raymie stares around the room, sucking on her fingers, peering at me from between Truman's hands.

"Why are you doing that?" I ask. "Why are you covering her ears?"

"Because this is bad, okay? Do you want her to hear that her dad is nailed to a table? That he's trapped in some busted-up church and we can't even do anything to help because Azrael's a psychopath?" He nods down at Raymie. "And that he's going to keep doing it until Obie tells him where she is."

"I don't think Obie can tell him, even if he wanted to. I think we're the only people who know."

Truman nods, staring off at something I can't see. "I think we're wrong about the church. We keep trying to figure out where to go, like Obie's in a real place, but what if he's not? That club I went to last night with Moloch was someplace else. I mean, it wasn't anywhere, really."

I nod. "It was in the liminal space. The in-between."

Truman presses his hands harder over Raymie's ears and his voice drops to a whisper. "All I know is, I saw a lot of dead people there. Her mother—one of those people was her *mother*, and it was bad, and it was *messy*."

I nod, feeling a surge of sorrow for a woman I never met. For Obie, who lost her.

Truman watches me, looking wary. "I think it's time for you to tell me about Dreadful."

It's disorienting to think that I've known about Dark Dreadful for all my life, but I've never had to describe her. I close my eyes, trying to find the words. "She's a—a kind of holy messenger. She eats demons and drinks all their blood so nothing bad can get out."

Truman lets his breath out in a shaky sigh. "And your sisters, they . . . ran into her, then?"

I nod, looking at the carpet, but *ran into* is the wrong way to say it and we both know that. Azrael is the one who tells her where to go. What to do.

After a moment, Truman leans closer. His expression is tense and I think he's going to tell me that he's sorry, but instead he says, "There's this other thing. Moloch told me something last night. He told me your friend in the suit is my father. Did you know?"

I shake my head, but even as I do, the revelation seems right and logical. Obie was the one who took Truman out of Pandemonium, but it was Beelzebub's decision to send him back. Beelzebub who didn't want hand him over to the Eaters. No, I didn't know, but I should have.

"What's he like?" Truman says, bouncing Raymie in the crook of his arm.

For a second, I don't know what to say. I try to think of details that won't sound terrible. He's asking for the sort of things he told me about his mother. All the little quirks and preferences that define a person.

"He likes Italian opera," I say. "And nine millimeter handguns. Before my dad put him in charge of Collections, he was a war god in Canaan, but now he mostly sends other people to do the killing. He acts dignified and like he's above things, but he's the one who started calling Collections the 'rag and bone shop.' At home, he has a cloud of flies that follows him everywhere. He likes poetry by Yeats and William Blake, but his favorite quote is from Kenneth Bainbridge, speaking to Oppenheimer after the Trinity test, with the mushroom cloud still in the sky. 'Now we are all sons of bitches.'"

Truman doesn't answer right away. He sits on the bed, staring down at Raymie. "What's your dad's favorite quote?"

I don't know how to answer. I could make something up, but it wouldn't be the truth. There are the cliches, the obvious ones—*Better to reign in Hell than serve in Heaven* or *Here at least, we shall be free.* But none of them seems like my father. "I don't know."

"So, you can tell me all that stuff about Beelzebub, but not your own dad?"

His tone is arch, like he's being sarcastic, but it's true. I know more about Beelzebub's opinions on modern art than I know about my father's entire life. All I know about Lucifer is a story of who he once was, a mercenary angel, practically a mythology. I have no idea who he is now.

"Beelzebub's my teacher," I say. "He's the only one besides Obie who ever asks my opinion or even *listens* to me. He's the only father I've ever really had."

Truman grabs his cigarettes from the nightstand and

300

fidgets with them like he can't decide whether or not to take one out of the pack. Then he stops and squares his shoulders like he's finally decided something. "I hate him."

"Don't," I say, feeling breathless. "You can't hate him— you don't even know him."

He sets the cigarettes back down. "Whose fault is that?"

The room is silent and dry like the desert. Cold, like we never lay in the bathtub, hidden behind the curtain. Like I never saw the tree.

Truman sighs and sets Raymie on the bed. Then he crosses to the sliding door and steps out onto the balcony.

For a moment, I just sit on the couch looking after him.

"He's angry," says Raymie, hugging the stitched rabbit. "Or maybe sad."

I nod. Her eyes are wide, but her expression is perfectly blank. I wrap my arms around my knees. When she drops the rabbit and keeps looking at me, I get up and I follow Truman out.

We stand side by side on the tiny cement balcony. I know that something is wrong between us and I don't know what it is. The memory of last night is still fresh. I think of Myra, Deirdre, all the girls who slip into the beds of strangers, take whatever they want. Last night, I was that girl. I did it too, but not because I wanted pain—it was because I just wanted *him*. The current between us feels like something real.

Truman's quiet. He stands with his elbows on the railing, smoking. From below us, there's the hum of Las Vegas Boulevard, the faint chatter of pedestrians, a siren screaming a long way off.

I touch my hair nervously, without meaning to. The cut ends prickle against my fingers and I make myself drop my hand. "Is there such a thing as love?"

The question is thin, almost disembodied. It comes out in a cracked, tiny voice that doesn't sound like mine, but I need to ask it. I need to know what this is.

He turns to look at me, and it's all I can do to keep from flinching. I can finally see into his eyes and I want to look someplace else.

"Love," he says. His voice is hoarse and as soon as he says it, he can't look anywhere but away from me. And when his hands won't stay still, he puts them palm down on the railing of the balcony. "I almost died, because I didn't care anymore."

He stops, shaking his head, and he still isn't looking at me. I watch him anyway, because I need to know the answer.

"I almost died because I *wanted* to. It was so easy, Daphne. It was all I *ever* wanted. And it didn't hurt, it didn't feel like anything. And that—" His voice breaks, but his eyes are dry and far away. "That was amazing."

The air is cool, but nothing like Chicago. We're standing on a tiny balcony, high above the street, surrounded by neon lights and desert, and a boy who has spent his whole life dying is trying to explain to me about desire.

"When I woke up, you were just sitting there watching me. I'd never hurt so much in my life. I'd never wanted to die more than I did right then, but I could feel your hands on my face. I was crying because I wasn't dead, and you were just touching my face, like everything was normal and okay. I've woken up every morning for a year and a half feeling like I have broken glass inside me." He shrugs abruptly, shaking his head. "When I'm with you, it goes away."

I blink and when I do, I see the pain tree. I see how I kissed him and tasted sorrow. I took it, and all I know is that when I did, his smile became so much brighter. "Why are you telling me this?"

"Because it's the truth." His face never changes, but his hands are trembling, trembling on the railing. "You asked about love. I don't know about love, Daphne. I just know I don't want anything but you. I don't want to be anywhere but with you."

Down in the dark street, the traffic is gridlocked, sitting bumper to bumper—a river of red taillights. My heart, the thing that until recently I wasn't sure existed, is beating faster than it ever has before. I turn to him and before I can say any of the ways I feel when I'm with him, he reaches for me.

When he lifts my chin, it's like all the movies, and it's not like the movies at all, because it's actually happening. His mouth on mine is warm and soft. His back is warm under my hands and I don't dig for misery or pry farther into him than I should. I only catch a glimmer of it and that's enough. It's incidental, just one small part of him, and all the other parts matter more.

He puts his mouth next to my ear and whispers, "I just want that, the way I feel when you kiss me. Just having it makes all the bad things better."

All my life, my sisters have bewildered and terrified me,

and still, I'd be like them in a second just to have Truman. I would give up my angelic heritage, my translucent fingernails, my white teeth, and not think twice.

Suddenly, I understand what Petra has always been trying to tell me. The whole time she was mumbling her litany of stories, she was always only telling me one thing. Love is when you care more about something else than you do about yourself.

DARK DREADFUL
CHAPTER TWENTY-EIGHT

At dawn, we leave the room and go downstairs to find Moloch. I don't really expect him to be able to help us, but I don't know what else to do. I'm wearing Truman's sweater because he lets me and because I like that it smells like him.

I know it won't do much good against monsters or archangels, but I bring the razor anyway.

We're on the main level, winding through the crowd, when something flashes into view, yellow-eyed and half-transparent in the surface of a plateglass window. All I can say for sure is that it's not my mother. I approach the glass for a closer look, but there's nothing and I walk faster.

Truman gives me a puzzled look, but doesn't ask what I'm looking for and I don't say anything.

Then I see it again. Not all of it, just a flicker in the floor-to-ceiling windows, a swipe of gray sliding between all the people, and my heart starts to beat much too fast.

The casino is built in a series of indecipherable split levels. If you want to go up, you usually have to go down first. We're in the long corridor that leads toward the mezzanine and I squeeze along the wall, shoving my way past people, holding Raymie tighter than usual and keeping her face turned against my shoulder.

We're almost to the escalators when Lilith appears in the glass face of a slot machine, staring out from where my reflection should be. Her eyes are wide and full of an icy terror.

"Run," she whispers in a voice that makes the fear prickle down my neck. "*Run!*"

And this time, I don't wait. I bolt down the escalator, forcing my way past the throng of people, squeezing along the rail.

I can hear Truman pounding after me.

On the casino floor, I bounce off the elbow of a cocktail waitress and keep going, unbalanced with Raymie in my arms, always on the verge of falling forward. The smell of cigarettes doesn't cover the raw stink of meat. And then I hear the breathing. It echoes around us, hoarse, elated—the sound of every tiger stalking every prey animal in the world. Her footsteps are thunderous and seem to come from everywhere.

"Run, run!" Lilith is screaming it, echoing at me from the tokens spilling out of slot machines, howling from the trays of empty cocktail glasses.

I've run in Pandemonium, but never like this. Never for my life, with the breath jolting in and out of my lungs. Raymie is heavy and unwieldy, making it harder to maneuver, but I jostle her up in my arms and keep going, pounding between banks of slot machines, racing for the stairwell. I see it, the weird five-way intersection, the sign that points to the stairwell. If we can reach the stairs, maybe we can elude her, make it to the hotel room and lock the door, push the little velvet couch against it—or break for the garden, take the jump-door back to Chicago or home, someplace safe.

Truman is close behind, shoving past slot machines and blackjack tables, trying to keep up. People turn to stare at us, but no one stands or calls out. No one tries to stop us.

I make a quick right turn, find myself in a narrow hallway. The carpet is red, the walls are covered in mirrors, and the L-shaped hall leads nowhere. For one instant, I see him—Azrael, with glittering eyes and a fierce, expectant smile. Then he turns the corner and disappears. The hallway gapes empty in front of me. Red, like death is red.

Then Dark Dreadful bursts in to visibility between the casino and the dead end and we're trapped in the hall with the monster and the mirrors.

She looms colossal and gray, with jagged teeth and dirty-yellow eyes, nothing like the pristine giantess of the murals. All around us, the mirrors show her in limitless reflection, repeating to infinity, huge and gaunt and hungry.

The mirrors are everywhere, reflecting us from a hundred places. I can see every Dreadful except the real one. Raymie's breath is light and fast against my ear, and she's making tiny animal noises, scared mice noises, clutching at my hair. Truman steps closer to me, but even as he does, I know he can't protect me from this.

Dreadful's mouth is wet with hunger and she licks her lips. Her eyes are ravenous, like she can hardly stand the waiting.

She's blocking our escape, filling the hall with her massive bulk. Her dress is ragged and covered in bones, no way to tell which ones are Myra's, which are Deirdre's. The sight is chilling and if I don't move now, my bones will hang next to theirs.

I clutch Raymie to my chest, shielding her head with my hand and backing away, backing helplessly into the dead end. Dreadful raises her hand and for one excruciating moment, I think she's going to kill me here and now. Then she catches me by the hair, yanking so hard I rise off the floor, twirl in space as she lifts and slams me against the wall. There's a brittle crunch as the mirror cracks behind me. Raymie leaves my arms like a yellow balloon, sailing away in slow motion, her arms and legs waving, but not as frantically as I'd have thought, not as desperately.

Truman dives for her, catching her by the back of her sleeper before she can hit the floor. He holds her to his chest, staring around wildly at the riot of reflections, all of them gaunt and huge and needle-toothed. I understand that he can't see the real Dark Dreadful at all. I can only see her now that her hand is at my throat.

She has me pinned against the wall, my wrists above me, no way to reach the razor. The texture of the glass is rough, spiderwebbed against my arms. My chest, my throat, are exposed, ready for her curved knife, her teeth, and I have nothing but the cracked glass behind me. I want to smash it, knock the pieces loose, but Dreadful has hold of my wrists and when I kick, the heels of my boots drum helplessly on the wall above the carpet.

She grins down at me and I smell brimstone. She's laughing, and still I can barely hear her through the sound of my own blood. The metal-toothed girls are coursing in my veins and they want to come out. They want to destroy everything, and Dreadful is gnashing her teeth, laughing and snarling. Before now, I never thought that I was not immortal.

Then, there's a faint noise coming from someplace nearby, a rustle in the mirror behind me. My mother's voice is small and panicked, speaking to me, directly into my ear. "Daphne, *do* something. You have to do something to save yourself."

A strange, unfathomable calm falls over me. This is the moment of desperation. The moment when I live or die. I look up at Dark Dreadful and sink my teeth into my bottom lip as hard as I can.

There's the sweet, steely flavor of my blood pouring into my mouth and I spit, spraying it across her face. For an instant, she only stares down at me, blood running into her eyes.

But the white girls are here now. They're in the hallway, unfolding around us, springing up at our feet. Blood drips sluggishly from my chin and Dreadful's forehead as the girls bloom like lilies on the carpet. One of them goes clawing her way up Dreadful's back, leaving ragged slashes. The others close in behind her, hissing and baring their teeth.

Dreadful loosens her grip on my hair and I fall.

The girls are blossoming on the ground, clamoring around Dreadful, scratching at her and baring their teeth. She snares one by the throat and begins to drink its blood in long swallows. The girl goes limp in her grasp, growing paler and paler until I see her bones, shadows beneath her skin. In my head, the only thought is *run, run, run,* like a little song I made up and can't stop singing. It thuds in my skull and it doesn't leave room for anything else. For one disorienting moment, I look up and Azrael is standing over me. He smiles and I feel cold. He turns, reflected a thousand times in the mirrored hall, and is gone.

Dreadful doesn't pay him any attention. She only gnaws on the body of the girl and then lets her fall. Arms and legs jut at odd angles, a pile of mismatched bones. The girl crumples to nothing and Dreadful moves onto the next one.

All around me, the girls are pacing restlessly, making a barricade between me and Dreadful. Their legs are thin and willowy like stalks, and Truman is fighting his way through them, reaching for me. I scramble on hands and knees through layers of ash, flinging myself at him, reaching out for him and for Raymie, the warm, actual shape of her.

"Come on," he says in a hoarse whisper. "The mirror—quick, head for the mirror."

I kneel in the dust, clutching Raymie to my chest. I'm trying to get my bearings, trying to stand, but my whole body is shaking. "Mirror?"

He gestures to the largest, the one with the jagged star where my head hit the glass. "Azrael just walked through, but not like a shadow. He went through a door—a real one." Truman glances over his shoulder to where Dreadful is slashing wildly at the snarling girls. "She's not going to let you back out, we have to go this way."

310

He grabs me by the elbow and yanks me up, steering me toward the end of the hall, toward the broken mirror and the place where Azrael vanished.

I'm trembling uncontrollably, and the dizziness makes it hard to focus. The reflection in the broken mirror looks like my mother. I stumble toward it, reaching for her. It's easier with something between us. Our hands meet against glass, palm to palm, and it's a second before I realize that I'm just seeing myself. Behind the web of cracks, I look white-faced and stunned, reflected in pieces.

I lean into the mirror, and press my forehead to the glass. "Let me in," I whisper.

When I speak it, the glass cracks jaggedly down the middle, then seems to ripple and dissolve, revealing a pair of huge double doors with a pair of brass rings for handles. I grab one of the rings with both hands and the door inches open when I pull, scraping along the floor. We slip through the narrow opening, and step into the dark.

MARCH 11
0 DAYS 0 HOURS 45 MINUTES

Truman leaned back against the door. Next to him, he could feel Daphne shaking. He reached out and pulled her closer, and for just a moment, she let him. Then she took a deep breath and started forward, clutching Raymie against her chest. After a second, he followed her.

Their footsteps echoed on stone. He could tell from the sound that the building was high-ceilinged, but the darkness seemed to press down on them.

With shaking hands, he dug through his pockets and found the lighter. When he struck it, and held it up, the butane flame seemed pathetically tiny, glowing out weakly into the dark. After a few seconds, his eyes began to adjust.

They were in the derelict church, standing at the top of the center aisle. On either side of them, the pews sat empty. The seats were upholstered with dusty velvet cushions, worn bald in places.

Logic told him that nothing could be worse than the huge snarling monster out in the hall, but the silence was deep and ominous. Somewhere on the other side of the church, near the altar, he could hear something dripping.

He turned cautiously, looking to either side, but the shadows were everywhere and part of him didn't want to see. It was the scared part, the small, cowardly part, but it clamored in his head, telling him that he would see Azrael soon. That thought tugged at him like a riptide, drowning him, threatening to block out everything else.

"Is he here?" Daphne whispered in a tiny, wavering voice. "Do you see Obie?"

Beside him, she was still shivering, and in the light from the flame, she looked strangely insubstantial. She was always pale, but now her skin had taken on a transparent quality. Her eyes were wide, but unfocused. She looked unsteady, like she might collapse at any second.

Truman didn't like the way she was stumbling over her own feet, but he didn't say anything. With his free arm, he reached out and took Raymie from her.

Her unsteadiness reminded him of the other night, when Azrael had shown up in the hotel room and Daphne had gotten out of bed to face him. Truman's memory was hazy, but there were a few things he knew for sure. There'd been a girl who looked like Daphne, and a smear of blood on her collarbone. She'd woken up the next morning weak and disoriented.

Now, losing less than a tablespoon of blood had left her shakier than ever, but she shrugged off his offer of help and continued farther into the church.

As they started down the long center aisle, candles flared to life in two rows on either side of them. In the sudden burst of light, the shadows receded and Truman could finally see into the dark space above the altar. For a second, it was hard to understand what he was looking at. Then the full significance of the situation sank in and he just stood in the middle of the aisle, staring up.

FLAME
CHAPTER TWENTY-NINE

My hands feel light and detached, like I've left a part of me out in the red hall, where it will powder into the carpet and I'll never get it back.

The church is dark and it takes a moment for my eyes to adjust enough for me see what's hanging over the pulpit.

Obie is upside down with his hands splayed out, nailed to a wooden panel. The panel is painted with glossy, muted colors depicting the Tower of Babel. It stands on its head in the apse, suspended from the ceiling by heavy ropes, swaying slightly even though there's no wind. The blood runs down in slow, meandering trickles.

I stand in the aisle, staring at the ruined spectacle of my brother.

His outstretched arms are wound shoulder to wrist with lengths of barbed wire. It spirals around his legs, leaving dark spots where the barbs have punctured his jeans. It looks like vines.

Near his head and slightly to the left are words, scrawled crookedly in blood, over and over, covering the part of the scene where the ill-conceived tower pierced the sky. They spell out *family* and *home*. His blood has not burned holes in the wood or eaten through the metal or turned into ravenous, snarling men. It just drips down the panel to the floor.

Above me, the windows are made of colored glass, but the pictures aren't exultant. Some of the panes are broken and all of the saints look somber and tired. They've all been boarded up.

Azrael has taken so many things from my brother—his wife, his daughter. He's maimed Obie, cut him, brutalized him.

I want to set things on fire.

Without thinking, I start for Obie, already planning some way cut him down. As I approach though, Azrael steps out of the shadows by the pulpit. His face is tranquil. He's holding a little boot knife.

"Here we all are," he says. "I have to admit, I was expecting Truman, not you. I thought for sure that Dreadful would have you."

Above a squalid, candle-covered altar, Obie begins to struggle, pulling against the nails and the wire, blind to everything that's happening. "Hello?" he whispers.

His voice echoes around me and every step I take sounds like a mortar going off.

"It's going to be all right," I say, and my voice comes from a long way off. "I'm here now."

"I need you to stop where you are," Azrael tells me gently. He holds the boot knife to Obie's cheek.

Behind them, the carved scene is a reminder of human

frailty, of arrogance. They tried to climb to God. Now everyone is falling.

Azrael stands beside my brother, looking down at me. The candles flicker around us and his expression is scornful, like I'm a ghost-girl or nothing at all. "I used to respect Obie," he says. "Do you know that—that I used to respect a demon? I trusted him, because I thought he was better than his bloodline. Better than all the rest of you."

"He is," I say, knowing beyond any shadow of a doubt that it's the truth. Obie is more virtuous than all of us and more human.

Azrael laughs. It's the first time I've ever heard him laugh. He sounds heartbroken. "He broke the cardinal rule, the only rule I truly care about. I'm doing him a favor, you know, getting rid of that little horror. Do you really think she's meant for this world? That she'll even survive? Why don't you just hand her over and be done with it? It would be a mercy."

Obie's hair is hanging down toward the ground. Around the nails in his hands, the blood does nothing special. It just drips onto the floor. I have a sinking feeling that at any second, I will need to sit down.

Truman comes up beside me, carrying Raymie. "That's not going to happen."

Azrael smiles his kind, terrible smile. "Do you really think you can protect her? Either of them?"

"No," Truman says. "I think you could take her from me. And I think you could hurt Daphne if you wanted. But I'd make you work for it. I think you'd have to kill me."

His expression is so matter-of-fact. Not frightened or angry, not defiant. For the first time, I can see Beelzebub in his expression and in his profile. It seems ludicrous that I never saw it before, but it was always hidden behind hopelessness and grief. Now, in the decrepit church, in the candlelight, he's glorious. He is completely angelic.

Azrael seems to see it too. His face softens when he looks at Truman. "I can always count on you to fall headlong for all the wrong things," he says. "You're just preternaturally attracted to sin, aren't you?"

Truman nods. Then, without any warning, he turns and kisses me.

It's a hard, honest kiss—the way he kissed me on the balcony—and I can feel it flooding my arms and legs, sweeping away the dizziness and the confusion. When he stops and steps back, he looks dazed, but I feel sturdy and whole again.

From the dais, Azrael is watching us with interest. I expected him to be angry, but instead, he seems strangely pleased.

"I was beginning to despair," he says to Truman. "But you really have come a long way from the selfish, self-pitying wreck that you were. Unfortunately, you always seem to pick the one thing you're not supposed to have." He's smiling, but it's cold and joyless. He stands by Obie's head, toying with the knife. "Now, are we all ready to see what happens to the human part of him when I stick this in his carotid?"

Truman squeezes Raymie tighter, turning her against his shoulder so she can't see Obie nailed to the board. She doesn't see when Azrael rests his hand on Obie's forehead, pushing it back like Dreadful did to me in the hall of mirrors, and holds the knife to the soft place under Obie's chin.

I stand motionless on the steps of the dais, staring up at Obie. Suddenly, I know with terrible certainty that I'm going to see him die.

Azrael never takes his eyes off my face. When he presses harder with the knife, blood pools at Obie's chin, runs over his jaw and down the side of his face. It hits the floor and does nothing. Then a drop lands in the hot wax pooling around the candles on the altar. For an instant, it catches and smokes, feathers into blue flame and then burns out.

When I step toward the pulpit, Azrael presses the knife harder into Obie's skin. "You need to stop right there."

But I don't. I just keep going, one foot after the other. "Please," I say, and my voice shakes. "Let me say goodbye."

Azrael looks down at me and his eyes are hard, but not merciless. He lets me approach, holding the knife close to my face, but I know that he won't cut me, because my blood is monstrous. I'm indestructible.

Obie is not. What Obie is, is flammable.

I pass Azrael with the slowness of a dream, crossing to where Obie hangs suspended in his web of wire, hair hanging toward the floor.

"I'm sorry," I say, and I mean it. Sorry for taking so long, for not getting here sooner, but mostly sorry for what I'm about to do. "You should probably close your eyes."

And I rake the candles off the makeshift altar with my

arm. The gesture sends them crashing against the panel in a clatter of flame and wax. His blood is all over the Tower of Babel and it catches like kerosene, flames leaping up the edges of the panel. The wood blackens and smolders, blistering with white-blue flame. The smell is toxic and chemical.

Behind me, Truman makes a strangled sound, and then stays quiet. No one moves. We all stand frozen, watching the blaze.

Obie glows upside down at the center of it, the heart of a blast furnace, and I stand on the dais and watch him burn.

Azrael is motionless beside me as the paint burns and bubbles and the structure weakens. It gives way with a splintering crash and a shower of sparks.

Obie sprawls on the floor, his jeans singed and smoking, his shirt burned away to ashes and tatters.

RESCUE
CHAPTER THIRTY

For a second, we all just stand staring at Obie's smoking form.

Then, without any warning, Azrael reaches out and grabs me by the hair.

"You," he says, yanking my head down so I can't pull free. "I don't care if you bleed an army. I will cut them down one by one for as long as it takes, just to get rid of you."

From a crazy angle, I can see Truman shifting Raymie in his arms like he doesn't know what to do with her.

"Try it," he says, sounding breathless, but absolutely sincere. "I'm not going to just stand around while you hurt her."

Azrael drags me toward Truman, adjusting his grip on the boot knife. "Let me be quite clear. You, shut up. First of all, I'm not going to hurt her, I'm going to kill her. Secondly, you will stand there quietly and watch, because you don't have a choice, and then you'll watch while I do the same thing to her dishonorable brother and the monstrous baby. Last, because

I'm a man of my word, I'll send you to your everlasting reward."

I'm clawing at Azrael with both hands, scrabbling at his wrist. He doesn't even seem to notice. He's about to put the knife to my throat when behind us, the doors to the church fly open, banging back against the wall.

Azrael wrenches me around and we all turn to see Beelzebub standing in the doorway. The church doesn't open onto the red hallway of the Passiflore anymore. Outside, the street is empty under a cloudless sky, bright with the rising sun.

Azrael drags me down the steps of the dais, pressing the boot knife flat against my cheek. My head is bent at an impossible angle. The blade is cold below my right eye.

"Get out," Azrael says in a low, ferocious snarl. "Get out now. This isn't your business."

Beelzebub doesn't move. When he smiles, it's not the smile of a well-mannered collections agent, but of a warrior. "I think it just became my business. Let her go."

"On what authority? You might boss them around at home, but on Earth, the demons are mine."

"If there's one demon in this world who's completely off limits to you, it's Daphne, and there is no circumstance under which I'd let you hurt her. That's Lucifer's daughter you've got there. Let's just let that sink in for a bit. Do you really feel like starting a war this morning?"

Azrael only stands there, fingers tangled in my hair.

"I didn't think so. Now, I think it would be better for everyone if you just went home."

Azrael tightens his grip and when he smiles, it's utterly hateful. "Dishonorable as ever, Beelzebub. I should have known not to count on one of the fallen. Your son is redeemed, by the way. I hope you're happy."

Beelzebub just folds his arms across his chest. "If you don't let her go right now, you're going to find out exactly how dishonorable I can be. Go home. I'll take it from here."

Azrael makes a harsh, wordless sound. He leans down so his face is close to mine, twisting his hand in my hair. The flat of the knife digs into my cheek, but doesn't break the skin.

"My whole life, I've made it a point never to trust demons," he says in a tight, venomous whisper. "I credit them for all the wickedness in the world, but I never seem to learn. The treachery of demons is *nothing* compared to the betrayal of an angel."

He lets me go and it's so abrupt that my knees buckle and I land on the dusty carpet.

From the floor, I watch Azrael's feet as he shoulders past Beelzebub, down the center aisle and out the door.

Beelzebub stands with his arms folded, surveying the crumbling church.

"Get up," he tells Obie, who's lying on the dais with his bleeding hands over his face, smoke rising from his clothes in tendrils.

Obie rolls onto his hands and knees and pushes himself to his feet. When he stands, his arms are torn from the barbs, bleeding in little trickles. He tries to untangle himself, but the wire catches at his skin. He's bleeding from so many places.

Truman is the one who goes to him and draws out the nails. He does it carefully. Then, with uncommon tenderness, he begins to untangle the wire.

I climb the dais slowly, pressing my hands to my head. My whole scalp feels raw.

Beside me, Obie is shaking a little, looking stunned. Truman offers him Raymie and he takes her, staring down into her face like he can hardly believe that she's real.

"Are you okay?" I ask. My voice is unsteady.

He shakes his head, but he's smiling in a crumpled, heartbroken way, holding Raymie to him. She wraps her arms around his neck and doesn't say anything.

Beside us, Truman looks magnificent in the sunlight streaming through the open door. The morning lights his hair a pale, pristine gold. In the bright splash of light, I sit down on the end of the nearest pew, covering my mouth with my hand to keep the sounds from getting out. I don't even know if they're laughing sounds or crying. There is a glorious life out there and everything is waiting for me. For us.

"Come on," Truman says, reaching for me, offering his hand. "Don't do that. We did good." He pulls me so I'm standing next to him. "Everything's fine."

He leans sideways and kisses me on the cheek, a quick, playful gesture. I smile without thinking about it. I want coffee, and also pie. Maybe even ice cream. I want laughter and kissing and everything there is, and it doesn't even matter if I get it. This is the world, for good or ill. This is us not being terrible people.

Beelzebub is standing at the double doors, looking so heroic, ready to lead us outside, like this moment is all he's been waiting for. Truman and I start toward the door, but then I glance over my shoulder.

Obie is standing in the little baptistry, beside the font of holy water. He's holding Raymie against his shoulder, but his eyes are unfocused. The look on his face is desolate. With a nod in his direction, I pull my hand from Truman's and go to him.

There are little carved saints around the archway. They're so old that their noses have worn off. We stand in the dark, facing each other. The air smells like flowers.

"I'm sorry," I say, coming up beside him. "I know what he was doing to you in here. That he was killing—that he was killing people. I'm sorry it took so long to stop it."

Obie nods and looks away. "It's not your fault. Beelzebub—" He closes his eyes and his voice breaks. "Why didn't he come for me sooner?"

"You disappeared," I say apologetically. "He didn't know where you were. None of us knew how to find you."

But as soon as I say it, the words feel wrong, because Beelzebub strode into the church through the front door like a man on a mission, like he already knew exactly what he would find.

Obie blinks dazedly, glancing toward the door. "What's he doing now?"

"I think he wants to have a talk with Truman, just the two of them. I don't know if you knew, but he's Truman's father.

That's why he had you take him back when Truman showed up in Pandemonium."

Obie is holding Raymie tight against his chest, looking so disoriented, so tired. "He went out of his way to send Truman back to Earth, then just abandoned him again?"

"Not abandoned. He just returned Truman to his normal life."

Obie shakes his head. "There was nothing normal about it. Azrael's spent the last year breaking Truman down in some stupid attempt to redeem him. If Beelzebub cared about Truman so much, why would he let Azrael do that to him?"

At first, I don't even understand the question. The answer to it is apparent in the way that Obie is holding Raymie. The way he never told Azrael how to find her, even under torture. Even under penalty of death. "Well, I guess because Truman's his son. He just didn't want him to wind up in Hell."

"Oh, *no*." Obie reaches for my arm suddenly, fingers digging into my shoulder. "Run."

I stare up and he lets me go.

"Run, now. Stop him!"

And I twist away, bolting for the doors.

Outside, Beelzebub is walking beside Truman. They seem a long way off. As I leap down the steps, Beelzebub stops, resting his hand on Truman's arm. I can't hear what they're saying.

I'm closer now. But I won't reach them in time.

MARCH 11
0 DAYS 0 HOURS 0 MINUTES

"Just hold still," Beelzebub said. The barrel of the handgun looked nearly red in the glow of the sun. "In a moment, everything is going to be so much better."

RUIN
CHAPTER THIRTY-ONE

Beelzebub smiles.

Then, he levels the gun and shoots Truman Flynn, twice in the chest, once in the head. The sound is very loud.

From the steps of the church, I watch Truman fall and it's like watching through glass. I can only stand with my hands pressed to my mouth, thinking I am not seeing this, this is not how it's supposed to end. Truman was mine. He was finally free. We were supposed to be happy.

He's on his back, head tilted limply like he's staring up at the sky, and in the next moment, I'm on my knees beside him, touching him frantically, trying to find a heartbeat. In a movie, any movie, he would say something with his last breath, declare his love, his absolute devotion.

There is no breath. His ribcage is still, his mouth slightly open, and all I'm left with is a body.

I stare up at Beelzebub, waving my hands above the wreck of Truman's chest. "What did you do to him?" My palms are covered in blood.

Beelzebub looks down at me, smiling the kindest, saddest smile. "I sent him home."

"What?" My voice is so small.

"Home. He's gone to a better place."

"No . . . no, he can't." But even as I say it, I know that he's gone, has gotten out. He's gone someplace I can never go.

There's a feeling inside me like things are coming apart and it turns into a noise and the noise is coming out of my throat, breaking all the glass. My hands and face are sticky. On the pavement, spreading from underneath Truman, is a dark pool that grows and grows. When I look down into it, I see my own reflection.

A raw wail spills out my mouth like pieces of sharp metal. From far away, a car alarm goes off, then another, until the street is full of their steady throbbing. There's the dull popping noise of a street light exploding. The noise travels down the block, fainter and fainter, mixing with the shimmering sound of glass on the sidewalk.

Beelzebub takes me by the arm and pulls me to my feet. Truman's body goes sprawling out of my lap onto the pavement, and with it, there's a huge splash of blood.

"Get a hold of yourself." He gives me a shake and I don't do anything. Even as he holds me, my knees start to buckle.

"Daphne, listen to me. This is the best thing for him. It was the only way for him to receive grace, the only way to give him what he needed. "

I can feel the blood on my skin, trickling down my arms, dripping from my fingers. This can't be me shrieking. This is not me.

PART THREE

HEAVEN

GRAY
CHAPTER THIRTY-TWO

Home is colorless. Clean, and smaller than I remembered. It's peaceful and perfect like a snow globe, like a dream I had.

I'm still wearing Truman's sweater. It's the only thing I have left.

THE TRAITOR
CHAPTER THIRTY-THREE

When I cross the plaza with the mural of the giant snake coiled at the center, it's because there's a hollow in my chest, and because I can't think where else to go. Time feels like a never-ending loop, winding back on itself.

The doors to the museum look forbidding in the gray light. I step inside and he's there like always, my teacher, my friend. Truman's father. He hasn't even bothered to alter his routine. He just sits there at his desk, like everything is normal. He glances up, flies buzzing around him. From where I stand at the end of the gallery, I can't even tell if he looks sad.

"What have you done?" I say, letting the door slam shut behind me.

When he answers, it's with absolute courtesy. "I shot my son in the head. You don't have to ask—you were there."

"Why?"

I want to scream it, but it comes out thin and hoarse. I want to feel angry, but my crying is insistent, constant. It soaks everything.

Beelzebub just watches me walk up the aisle toward him,

looking so serene, so untroubled. I expect him to say *"c'est la vie,"* or something else in French, but he doesn't. He doesn't say anything. He spreads his hands in a gesture that reminds me so much of Truman that something aches in my chest.

"You gave my brother to Azrael," I say. My voice is louder now, echoing all around us in sharp, horrible fragments. "How could you do that? How could you just give someone away to be tortured and killed?"

Beelzebub shakes his head, smiling so gently. "We all have to make a few sacrifices to get what we want."

I step closer, holding my arms around myself. "What could you possibly want from Azrael?"

"Heaven," he says, and the word sounds wistful. The way he says it, he might as well be saying *oblivion*.

"That's ridiculous. It's not even possible. We don't *get* Heaven."

"It wasn't for me." Beelzebub sighs and leans back in his chair. "When I sent Truman home from the terminal, I knew if I didn't do something, he'd wind up right back here, so I went looking for a favor. I told Azrael that Obie was messing around on Earth. There may or may not have been talk of an address. All the arm-waving and the theatrics, though, that was pure Azrael."

I stand in the doorway to the office, shaking my head. "You used my brother as a bribe—to what? Buy Truman's way out of Hell?"

Beelzebub's face hardens. "I would have given Azrael Obie and your sisters and anything he wanted, rather than let that kid scream out his eternity in this house of horrors." He smiles and it's the most awful thing. "My heart may be black as rot, Daphne, but I'm not about to let my children suffer."

"You deceived me."

Beelzebub shakes his head. "I tried to keep you out of this, every step of the way. If you want to lay blame, blame your mother. You never should have been involved."

But it's absurd to blame any of this on my mother. Even if I'd been obedient, stayed here and waited for someone to fix things, I'd have lost Obie. I'd still be grief-stricken. The only difference is, I wouldn't be stuck crying.

"How could you expect to just get away with something like this?"

Beelzebub looks frankly shocked. "I *don't*. That's really the trade-off, isn't it? We all have to make sacrifices from time to time—if not our safety or our belongings, then our pride or our principles. I mean, look at Azrael. He's spent the last year trying to make Truman worthy of Heaven and losing the battle every step of the way. But despite everything, he never gave up. After all, we had an agreement."

"He terrorized Truman. He spent the last year telling him how bad he was."

"The method may have been a little lacking. Truman strikes me as the type who could have used a softer touch. Ironically, I think it was his love for *you* that finally made him worthy." He smiles easily. "I'd imagine that made Azrael absolutely furious, so good work there."

I cross the office and slam my hands down on Beelzebub's

desk. "Stop—stop acting like nothing happened! Truman is *dead*."

"Yes, he's dead—for the only reason that matters. He died for redemption. I gave him redemption, even if *I* will never be forgiven."

I turn and stare out into the gallery at all the miscellany, the trash. The museum, full of nothing but cheap, worthless clutter, artifacts that are only precious to him. Somewhere in the crowded shelves is a piece of every life he's ever lived, everyone he's ever lost. The museum is a constant reminder of all the things he cannot have.

"You sacrificed everything," I say, shaking my head and turning to look down at him. "Even the things you should have protected. You might have saved Truman, but you ruined *me*." I fold my arms across my chest, and even though the tears are running down my face, I feel my mouth turn ugly. "What's it like, not caring about anyone but yourself?"

His smile is gone as though I've slapped him. "I've *always* cared about you. I've loved you like my own blood."

And I laugh at that, at the sheer absurdity of it. He put a bullet through his own son's head to save him. His love means nothing. "I believed you once."

He smiles, reaching across the desk to touch my face. "Of course you did." Sighing, holding my face in his hands. "I remember the first time I saw your mother. She was distant and pale, standing on the surface of the ocean. There was a look on your father's face when he saw her, like he was already forgetting our war, seeing his next conquest. It seemed like I was bleeding from everywhere. I knew everything would be terrible from then on."

I want to start sobbing, but I'm stuck. The tears just keep dripping down my cheeks, running over Beelzebub's hands. "Why didn't you say something? Why didn't you tell him not to go to her, to walk away?"

"When it comes to your mother, nothing has ever been simple. She and your father are so alike. Can you imagine refusing them anything?" He looks at me, looks, looks, looks, and his face is so open and so full of sorrow. "The strong prevail. This is just the way of the world."

He kisses me on the forehead, then lets me go.

The cold is terrible. Worse than Chicago, or anything I've ever felt. My tears freeze before they have a chance to fall. The screaming in the pit is so loud suddenly that I think I'll go deaf from it. For a strange moment, I believe that Beelzebub has done this with his kiss. That he's frozen me, a reverse fairytale. I should be waking up now, but instead the world is grinding to a halt.

Then I see that the door to the museum is chocked open. My father is leaning in the entryway, hands in his pockets. His face is as calm and as sculpted as Greek statuary, but his eyes are dark and hot like coals.

"So, it's come to this," he says.

Beelzebub turns in his chair, turns his back on my father. He's staring off at the tidy rows of drawers and the filing cabinets. "Are you really here to punish me over a few dead

Lilim? They weren't even your daughters. He wasn't your son."

"Don't presume to tell me about family," my father says, removing his hands from his pockets and adjusting his shoulder against the door frame. He's holding something dark and narrow in one dangling hand. "What you've done is unforgivable. Now turn and face me."

Beelzebub only sits, facing away. "You'd have done the same thing for your children if you had a chance to save them." His voice is resigned and he still doesn't turn around.

I see through a trembling film that the thing in my father's hand is an onyx-handled straight razor. He looks at me a long time, face blurred. With his thumb, he caresses the razor, and the blade opens like it's unfurling its wings. He steps forward, moving around the desk to stand beside Beelzebub's chair.

Beelzebub remains motionless, and through the film of my tears, he could be anyone at all. "Get on with it," he says, voice like stone. "Don't waste your time."

My father holds the blade in his right hand. With his left, he reaches out. "Turn and look at me."

But Beelzebub doesn't. I'm not breathing. I never breathe, and Truman's sweater feels thin, almost insubstantial.

"You will turn and face me," my father says, in a voice that has made stars collide.

Beelzebub only keeps his back turned, his head bowed.

My father squares his shoulders. "Are you redeemable?"

"No. How can I be?"

337

My father rests his palm on top of Beelzebub's head. I've never seen him touch anyone but my mother. "There's never only one answer," he says, and slides the blade under Beelzebub's chin.

From outside comes the sound of the furnace door slamming open. The sky glows red again and my tears begin to thaw. When I blink, they slip solid from my eyelashes. The sound when they land is like pebbles scattered on the tile, but the floor of the museum is already growing hot, burning my feet through my slippers. The tears melt and sizzle where they fall. Beelzebub is jerking, sighing out.

Out in the gallery, the artifacts are going up in flames— all the remnants of the collected souls. The wooden shelves collapse and clatter to floor, blackening to ash. The metal ones only stand solid as they've always done, shining silver, while the flames lick brightly around the edges.

My father steps back and Beelzebub slides down in his chair. Above his slumped body, flies go off like match-heads, exploding to life as they burn, settling to the floor— ash, then nothing. A violin smolders peacefully, its strings snapping one by one. The front of my father's shirt is smoking as the blood begins to burn off.

He grabs my wrist, yanking me up. Around me, the burning wool of Truman's sweater crumbles off my body in the scorching heat, burning like all the other artifacts, because of course, now the sweater is just the lost property of a dead boy. Everything's unraveling now. Everything has become temporary.

I scrub my eyes with back of my hand, then with my fingertips, trying to scrape away the tears. They're sizzling on my cheeks now, steaming away into nothing. Everything is too hot, but not painful, never painful. I close my eyes, once, twice.

He crosses the gallery and shuts the door, but the damage has been done. There's nothing left of the collection but charred metal and ashes.

With the stasis of the museum restored, the screaming in the pit seems muted again, but harder to ignore. It sounds real. Temperature is gone, leaving my arms numb. I'm wearing my shift, my slippers, nothing else. Truman's sweater is long gone and the blood has burned away from my fingernails, just like it's burning off the desktop now, smelling vague and slippery. Beelzebub is slumped on the floor beside his chair, the gash in his neck open wide like a mouth. His skin is blistering, his hair smoking.

"But you closed the door. How can he be burning?"

"Because he's dead."

I look down at the body, someone's body. Beelzebub is nothing but a body. The flames are so hot they don't look like separate flames at all, but one burning pool of fire.

"Was it like he said?" I ask. "Did you really damn us all?"

"I must have, if this is what it's come to."

"Why would you do that?"

"Because I loved her," my father says.

The shape of Beelzebub is shrinking, getting blacker.

"When do you stop loving someone?"

He looks at me, shaking his head. His mouth is open, just a little. He makes the shape of the word *never* but no sound comes out.

I wait for him to say something aloud, all the things people are supposed to say upon the death of a comrade. "O Captain, my Captain." "Goodnight sweet prince." Even Yeats, "The center cannot hold. What rough beast." His mouth is a hard line.

"Say something," I whisper.

He slides his hand into mine. He says nothing and doesn't need to. His hand is everything. I lean against him, resting my head on his arm.

LOSS
CHAPTER THIRTY-FOUR

Truman dies again and again inside my head. It's a bright, wet death, and I sit on the floor of my room and watch it happen.

My father's answer was revenge—has *always* been revenge—and the outcome was just, but not better. Nothing is fixed.

Across the room, Petra is a dark shape, blurred around the edges. She's walking back and forth, touching the walls. I wish she would sit down. We've been here forever.

I'm dressed like I belong here, in one of the silver tunics I used to wear, glossy and reflective. My Freddy sweater is lost somewhere on Earth. Truman's is nothing but ash.

"Daphne."

I look up and Obie is standing in the doorway, just the way he did before, when he came to tell me he was leaving. Only now he's disheveled and bloody, holding Raymie in his arms like he'll never let her go. His departure seems like a lifetime ago.

He crosses the room and sits down beside me with Raymie in his lap. She waves shyly at me, but doesn't say anything.

"You have to stop crying," Obie tells me, as though he doesn't understand that I can't. "I know this hurts, but they're gone and we have to manage without them now."

His voice is steady, but I can see the devastation in his eyes. He's only pretending, saying the words he's supposed to say. He's ministering to me when he should be crying alongside me.

In his arms, Raymie is quiet. I barely remember the moments after Truman's death, but it was loud and bright and messy. She must have seen.

"Daphne," Obie says. "You have to find a way to live without him now. You have to carry on."

But he has someone to carry on for.

Out the window, everything is dim. Petra gets out the paint set, crouching on the floor beside us. Her first strokes are mysterious, but the picture quickly becomes a horse. Its tail is long and soft. Then, under her careful brush, the horse sprouts a single horn. The sky is as dim as it ever gets and the furnace will come on soon.

I watch Petra, with her wide eyes and silvery skin, her liquid-looking hair, and suddenly, I see that she's very beautiful bending over her unicorn. With the tip of her brush she shapes its flank as carefully as she once rendered my face in eyeliner and now I know, undeniably, that time passes. It was a different girl who sat on the hassock while her ugly sister drew pictures.

She touches the picture and the paint rubs off on her

fingers, leaving round depressions along the unicorn's body. Outside, the furnace hums and the sky glows red.

Obie is quiet, looking at us both with painful tenderness. I watch to see if the blood on his arms will catch fire and smolder to nothing, but it doesn't. Of course it doesn't. The cuts are his condition now. He brought it like Beelzebub brought his flies. Like the tears dripping slowly and constantly down my face.

The four of us sit quietly, staring down as Petra's painting begins to bubble and crack. Thin columns of smoke rise up from a unicorn glowing red. The brush in her hand becomes a torch.

She looks at me over her burning picture. "Unicorns can't last here."

On Earth, Alexa Harding, with her muddy-colored hair and skinned knees, is already forgetting about Truman Flynn. Putting on eye makeup, fumbling in someone's backseat. Truman was a boy she knew once when she was young. I want to scream suddenly, but when I open my mouth nothing comes out.

"There was a girl," Petra says, putting her hand in the fire. "A girl who fell asleep, and when she did, so did everyone around her. The whole kingdom just fell asleep."

I nod because it sounds real and possible. It sounds like a story I know.

Truman was like that once, motionless, diverting people from his pain, reassuring them and soothing them, sinking farther into the depths of his own grief.

But then one day, he woke up.

More than anything, I want to wake up from this.

❀   ❀   ❀

On the roof, my mother is sitting on her filigree bench like she's waiting for me. I want to climb into her lap. I want to lie against her shoulder and never get up again. This is what Earth has done to me. But I know that's not true. It's what I've always wanted, but never understood.

Instead, I sit next to her and stare blankly down at the sundial. My face stares back at me, red-eyed.

"Tell me what to do," I say, trying to keep my voice from shaking.

"What makes you think I know?"

I had almost forgotten how her voice has the power to cut through me. She looks over, looks right at me with grim, silvery eyes and I see a black hollow in her, like seeing the future. Like looking down the barrel of a gun.

"I'm not kind-hearted," she says. "If I had my way, I would tell you to stop loving that boy. I would tell you to stop being sad."

"I can't."

She watches her reflection in the sundial, combing her fingers through her hair. "Then you need to find him."

It's what I want to hear, but the very idea is impossible. I shake my head, just barely. "He's in Heaven. How can someone like me find him in Heaven?"

She shrugs. "Who am I to tell you what you are? You're half an angel, just the same as he is."

344

"I don't even know how to get there," I whisper. "I don't know the way in."

"What is it that ties you to him?"

I close my eyes and the shapes of the garden are still printed in negative on the inside of my eyelids. I want to keep my eyes closed forever, and everything reminds me of Truman. The tree, how it made him turn his face away and how he kissed me anyway.

"I have his sadness," I say with my eyes closed. "He gave it to me."

"Then take it back to him," my mother says. "Take it to the place where it was the strongest. The place that speaks to him."

I nod, thinking about love and sadness, and how they've started to feel the same. I remember kissing Truman on the balcony, and maybe he never said he loved me, but he meant it anyway.

And there's my mother, shrieking in pain when she thought something had happened to her son, and Myra with her sly smile and her dead eyes, grieving for Deirdre in the only way she knew how. My father, holding the razor to Beelzebub's throat, telling him that it would all be over in an instant.

I know about grief now. I know the complex weight of it, and more than that, I know where to take Truman's.

✳ ✳ ✳

In the terminal, I press my palm to the pass panel, speak my word, and the door gasps open, revealing the corridor. I follow it, keeping track of the turns, stepping out of the hallway and into Cicero.

SINKING
CHAPTER THIRTY-FIVE

The air under the bridge is cool, but not like it was when I first came to Earth. It's dusk, and the streets are windy and deserted, rattling with fallen leaves from the park down the block. Autumn, then.

For a long time, I just stand under the bridge, looking out at Cicero. Everything is the same, but incrementally different, just like I'm the same, but not. My eyes feel swollen and hot, but I've finally stopped crying.

I find the Avalon apartment complex by memory. The door is still broken, and inside, the air is stale with cigarette smoke and dusty carpet. I stand in the lobby, breathing it, then step into the stairwell and start up to the fourth floor.

Alexa is sitting on the landing with her feet pulled up and her back against the wall, reading a paperback. When she glances up, her expression registers confusion, and then shock. We just look at each other, and for a second, she doesn't say anything.

I climb the stairs and I stand over her, waiting for some sign that I'm in the right place. Some revelation. The silence echoes around us and time stretches out.

"You look the same," she says finally.

I don't know if I'm the same or not. It doesn't feel like it, but I suppose that if it's worth remarking on, I must be. She isn't. Her hair is shorter and in the bright florescent light of the stairwell, her face seems older, more cynical and more wary.

"You've been crying," she says, and her voice is gentler than before.

I nod, mildly surprised that it shows on my face. I should have known, though. Everything feels scalded.

Alexa nods. "Yeah, I did too for awhile. I wait for him," she says, staring down at the book. "But he never comes back."

"No," I say, surprised by how normal I sound. "He can't."

She nods. "I figured. It was almost kind of inevitable, I guess—like, meant to be. You just showed up one day, and then he was gone. I mean, I don't blame you or anything. He was on his way out anyway."

I want to tell her that it isn't like she thinks. Truman didn't swan-dive into oblivion. He wasn't carried away in a wash of carelessness or self-destruction. He was noble. At the end, he was good.

The stairwell is narrow, cold. I glance up and Alexa follows my gaze.

"Charlie still lives here, if you're looking for him. He should be home by now."

I thank her but don't start up the stairs. I feel like the moment is more significant than our strange, sad gazes and our silence. I should have something to say.

For a minute, I just stand there looking down at her. Then

347

she holds out her hand and I take it. The gesture is familiar and she smiles, a slow, sad smile that makes something ache inside me.

"You should go up," she says. "I think he'd like to see you."

On the fourth floor, I'm gripped by an even more crushing feeling of familiarity, of finality. In the hall, I hesitate at the door of 403, hand raised. I already know how this goes— Charlie shambling to the door in his undershirt, looking irritable and rumpled.

But when I knock, he answers almost at once. He stands in the doorway, looking worn-out, but perfectly alert.

For a long time, he doesn't say anything. Then he passes a hand over his face and shakes his head. "He isn't here."

"I know."

"Then why'd you come back?" His voice sounds defeated.

"I needed to see you." I don't know how to say what I really need, the thing that brought me to his door. I need to see the apartment, to find out if any vestige of Truman is still here.

Charlie closes his eyes for a moment. Then he opens the door wider and steps aside to let me in.

The apartment is different now, sparser and cleaner, if that were possible. Lonely. Charlie's wearing a blue mechanic's jacket, like he just got home, and I understand that he doesn't work nights anymore. It's impossible to think that his life has gone on without Truman, but it's true. Things have changed so much, even in a few months.

"Come on in and sit down." Charlie leads me into the kitchen.

I must look worse than I feel, because he takes a seat across from me and regards me kindly. "Why don't you tell me what happened."

"He died."

Charlie doesn't react immediately, but it's clear that those were not the words he was expecting. He sits at the table with his head in his hands. "What do you want, Daphne?"

"To bring him back."

"From the *dead*?" Charlie's voice is derisive, but his shoulders slump. He looks broken.

"It's happened before."

For a moment, he doesn't move. Then he raises his head and looks at me. He looks at me a long time, and his look tells me he knows that I am not the thing I pretend to be. Not some girl off the street. Not harmless, not human.

Jesus is still hanging patiently over the kitchen door, and Charlie believes in miracles and mysteries.

"I'd like to see the apartment," I say. "If that's all right."

We pass through the living room and down the hall, which feels unbearably like Truman. Even though there's no solid evidence of him, no belongings or photographs, the whole apartment breathes him. His feelings and his memories are here, and even the furniture and the walls are steeped in all the tiny, priceless moments of his life.

His bedroom is just as it was the last time I saw it, but

abandoned now, colder. The shades are down and the floor is dusty.

Behind me, Charlie breathes a heavy sigh, but doesn't say anything.

Across the hall, the bathroom is small and cramped, exactly as I remember. It's chilly and white, and every tile and fixture screams Truman.

I understand that Charlie has not let him go. Alexa still waits for him, holding vigil, and in their sorrow, they keep him alive. Truman might have died on a nameless street in a nameless city, but here in the Avalon, it's like he has never left the building. His memory is a palpable thing, more solid here than in any other place on earth. They carry him with them.

With my heart beating much too hard, I step into the bathroom and sit down in the bottom of the tub. When I turn on the faucet and lie back, the water rushes around me.

"What are you doing?" Charlie asks, but his voice is gentle. Not the tone one would normally use to speak to a strange girl in his bathroom, lying in the tub in all her clothes.

"Following him," I say, because there's no other way to say it. The fabric here is so thin. This is the place he lost everything.

Standing over me, Charlie looks dim and faceless, the overhead light making a blinding starburst behind him.

I close my eyes and remember pain and longing that are not mine. Truman's memories wash over me in a chaotic wave and I hold my breath and let the water cover me. Underwater, I feel suddenly free, like I'm falling down. I'm closer to him than I have ever been, in the one place he was sadder than any other, and still, I'm filled with a strange, unbridled joy.

Charlie let me into the apartment because he loved Truman. He's not dragging me out of the tub now for the same reason. He's ready, like I am, to go as far as it takes. Ready to try anything.

The breathlessness hits and when it does, the sensation is not grief, but a celebration of Truman's life—all the laughter and the longing and the tragedy. I'm taking it with me. It's taking me down through the cluttered museum of memory. Taking me to him.

HEAVEN
CHAPTER THIRTY-SIX

When I open my eyes, the light is soft. Under me, the floor is white and glossy, smooth like marble, and I lie on my back, staring up at a pale blue sky. Staring up at nothing.

After time passes and no one comes, I push myself up from the floor and get to my feet. My hair is soaking wet and water pours off my dress, dripping onto the glossy ground.

I look around, surprised to find that I'm surrounded by buildings, high-rises, shell-white and shimmering. The streets are wide and clean, and the sky is a pale, delicate blue.

"It's the same," I whisper to myself—to no one. My voice is shaking. "It's a city, it's just a city."

I thought Heaven would be better, more exalted. I thought the holy and the sanctified would look less like home. From the corner of my eye, I see a flutter of color like sunlight, someone moving, but then it's gone.

With cautious steps, I follow the parade of flickering lights across the empty plaza and into a vast, silent building.

The lobby is long and empty, with an atrium at the far end, full of pale light and delicate, translucent plants. A man is standing with his back to me, studying a pocket watch. As I cross the lobby, he turns and snaps the watch shut. It's Azrael.

I feel so tired. I feel like everything inside me has come undone and I just stand there, looking at him.

"You again," he says, and his voice sounds as tired as I feel.

Me again. I keep seeing movement from the corner of my eye, snatches of color and light, gone before I look.

He stands over me, arms folded against his chest. When he looks at me, his mouth twists in an odd sneer, showing perfect teeth. It's not a smile.

I stand looking up at him, dripping water all over the white floor. "I want to see Truman."

Around me, colors are squirming past in fits and pulses, but when I turn to look, there's nothing but white. I keep thinking I hear voices, low, impossible to decipher.

Azrael stares down at me, shaking his head. "Why in the name of goodness would I let you do that?"

"I love him," I say.

"*Love* him?" Azrael says, smiling for the first time. "I don't know if anyone's ever told you this, but you're a demon. You can't love."

"I can," I say breathlessly. "I can feel it, and it's wonderful and complicated and real. And he loves *me*."

Azrael's smile is bitter. "Let me tell you a little bit about demons. They love pain and other people's misery. They lie when it suits them and don't see anything wrong with it. They corrupt and kill and destroy, all without conscience. You just don't have the capacity for something as honorable as loving another person."

"That's not me, though. You're not talking about *me*. If you'd just listen—just believe me."

My throat aches and my vision has started to blur. Suddenly, tears are spilling down my face now, and they're hot. Not warm like over Truman's body in the street, but furnace-hot. They're the color of blood, trembling on my lashes and then they turn blue. White by the time they reach the ground. Where they fall, the floor smolders and starts to melt.

Smoke curls up from the floor, leaving charred pockmarks. Then the flames start, leaping around me, racing away in runners. "Please, I need to find Truman. I just need to *see* him."

Azrael steps closer, avoiding the guttering flames and blocking my view of the curtained window behind him. "Seeing him now would make no difference. He won't know you, and there's nothing you can do to make him know you now that he's forgotten."

I wipe my cheeks with my fingertips and the tears are scalding. "I think you're wrong."

The voices are hazy but insistent now, whispering all around me. My heart is beating very hard.

Behind Azrael, the window glows white behind its pale curtain and the voices are calling for me to go through it. With a dazed, heavy feeling, I push past him, toward the window. The curtain is thin, fine as gauze, obscuring what's beyond. I step through, pushing it away easily.

In a translucent garden, a boy is sitting on a bench under a crystal tree, holding the hand of a black-haired girl. Their heads are bent close together and they're talking in low voices.

As I step over the low windowsill and down into the courtyard, Truman turns to look at me. His eyes are a pale, transparent blue. His hair is dark blond, close-cropped and clean. He's different now, but I know him. I would know him with my eyes closed.

He stands, coming to meet me across the glass garden. He looks so long I want to hide my face in my hands. I fight the urge to turn away. It's so hard to look at him.

"You're wet," he says, reaching out to touch the water dripping down my face.

I'm holding onto myself, elbows cupped in my hands. "I had to be. I couldn't find you, otherwise."

He nods and smiles, like I'm actually making sense.

The girl has come up beside him, her hair long and shining, hanging in a sheet down her back.

I look at her, at the perfect lines of her face. "Why is she with you?"

He grins like the question is silly. "Well, I couldn't be happy without her."

Without me. She reaches for him and he takes her hand. He says, still looking at me, "I thought for a second that I knew you."

The black-haired girl smiles, so placid. "Who is she," we say, pointing to one another.

"That's Daphne," he tells us.

"Do you love her?" we ask.

"More than anything."

I'd thought that at those words I'd want to scream in triumph, to Heaven or Azrael or to God Himself. To shout *See? See, he loves me.* But Truman is holding the other girl's hand and she is not me.

Once, he told me that I was the thing in the world that made him happy, that I made him feel like he wasn't full of broken glass. Now, he's holding someone else's hand.

My eyes feel brittle and hot. The girl reaches out, smiling, patting my arm. But I know she's just a mockery of me, a doll made of how much I love. Of how much he loved me.

He keeps looking back and forth between us. "Don't I know you? I think I know you."

"Wouldn't you remember if we'd met before?" I reach out, taking his hand in mine, and he doesn't pull back. The three of us—Truman, the girl, and me—each holding someone's hand. He smiles as I turn over his wrist, then slide his shirtsleeve up, folding the cuff back carefully.

"What are you doing?" he says, like he might start laughing.

His wrist is smooth. There are no marks on his arms, not anywhere.

"What have they done to you?" I ask. Trace the pattern with my fingertip, like I could put it back on his skin. Close my eyes, imagine him sick, filthy, sobbing. When I look at him again, I see how healthy he looks. There is nothing broken in him now. "What have they done?"

"What do you mean?"

"Your wrists, they used to be . . . "

He laughs, sudden and bright. "See, I *do* know you. You look familiar, I just—I can't place it." Then his face clouds. "What about my wrists?"

"Nothing," I tell him, trying not to cry, afraid that if I burn heaven down, he will never love me. "They used to be— they used to be—"

"Hey," he says, reaching out. "It's okay. Why won't you just tell me what's wrong?"

Beside him, the ghost of me is standing with her chin lowered. They have always been so much braver, but now her eyes are filling with tears. They'll overflow and then I'll burn down the garden and it won't even be me doing it.

Truman reaches for me again, and this time he pulls me against his chest, cradling my head on his shoulder. It's like a physical hurt, being so close to him, like burning myself again and again.

I wrench myself from his arms. "Don't—you don't have to touch me."

He steps back, looking worried, and I want to grab him by the shoulders, smash my mouth against his, but I'm so, so afraid of how much it will hurt.

"Were you happy, on Earth?" I say.

He looks serious for the first time, and uncertain. "No," he says. "No, I wasn't happy."

"Why not?"

"A lot of things. I don't really remember all of them now. I was lonely. My mom—she died when I was sixteen. But even before that, I guess I wasn't very happy."

It makes my eyes sting to hear him talk easily about things he could barely say out loud when he was alive.

He says, "I don't remember a lot of it. I keep thinking I do, but then it gets mixed up." He stares at me so hard he must be looking past me. "There was this girl I knew. I think she saved my life."

"Yes, you were going to die. But she woke you back up."

"How do you know that?"

"It doesn't matter. She woke you up and you wished very hard that she hadn't. You wanted to stay asleep because it hurt too much."

"Hurt?" He's squinting down at me. "What are you talking about?"

I want to cover my own mouth so he can keep living in this white dream, but it scares me. "I love you," I say, and the ghost girl says it too.

He's looking at her, not at me, and his expression has turned cold. "You what?"

"Love you," I say again, watching her mouth move.

He steps back, even as she smiles up at him.

"Something's wrong." He's shaking his head. "Something's really wrong."

"What is it?" I ask, and now she's quiet.

"Her," he says, moving closer to me. "This isn't right. She wouldn't say something like that."

"How do you know?"

"I know her, I know what she's like. She just would never say that."

"Are you sure?" I say, hating that he would ever doubt it.

I have nothing to give Truman but the worst parts of himself. I can only give him back the fact that once, he cried upon realizing he wasn't dead. How can I ask him to choose that again?

"This is all wrong," he says. He's breathing too fast, a sharp, panicked sound. "How do I wake up? Please, you need to tell me how to wake up."

"Don't you want your perfect life?"

"I want *my* life."

"Then kiss me," I say, like someone is squeezing me by the throat. I know the fairy tales. "If you kiss me, you'll wake up."

He looks down into my face and his eyes are so blue. His mouth is open a little as he bends his head, and my cheeks feel hot and too shiny, like my tears have scalded everything. When he puts his hands on my shoulders, it burns, but in a way that barely even feels like anything once his mouth is on mine. I feel his tongue, warm and familiar, a flicker between my lips, then gone, and now I see the tree, stark and gouged and twisted, but alive.

He backs away, looking hurt, frightened. And now is not the time to be wondering if I've done the right thing. In front of me, he's gasping, taking long, hoarse breaths. My ghost is mute but trembling, reaching for my hand. We stand side by side as he begins to change.

At first, it isn't much. With his fingers pressed to his collarbone, he closes his eyes and now his face is thinner, gaunter. His sweater is turning dingy. Seconds ago, it seems, I sat on the floor while that same sweater burst into flames on my body. Now, it's unraveling at an alarming rate, new then old then nothing. I watch, holding the girl's hand so tightly, squeezing as Truman's hair turns lank and tangled. Why am I doing this? He could have been happy forever. How am I doing this?

When I open my mouth, the girl cries out beside me, a shrill, timid little cry, but I don't make a sound. I cover my mouth and his scars bloom pale and shining on his arms. I wrap my arms around her and we hide our faces in each other's hair.

"Daphne." His voice is husky, like the morning after I found him.

I expect us both to turn, but when I let go of the girl, she collapses at my feet, clattering in pieces where she lands. It's just me now, me and Truman Flynn, and surely this is the worst, most selfish thing I've ever done.

But when he looks into my face, his eyes are so pale they're almost like no color at all and he's already reaching, not looking anywhere but my face. And this time, the kiss is hard and hungry and laughing all at once. His hands slide over my shoulders and my waist, drifting to the back of my neck. He holds my face between his hands and presses his forehead to mine. I'm the real thing and he's smiling. He's smiling.

HEREAFTER

Truman Flynn woke up.

Life after death was beautiful and extraordinary. Sometimes, the world was so vibrant and true that it became overwhelming, and he had to close his eyes and wait for the vertigo to pass. In the mornings, the sun rose, low and red on the horizon. The sprawl of towns and cities was so huge, so filled with buses and taxis and people.

He saw himself in the people that he helped—every child of every demon—and it didn't disgust him. What he saw only supported the fact that the work was good and necessary.

He didn't have Obie's memory for novels and sermons, so he read aloud, carrying paperbacks and collections of poetry everywhere he went. He sat beside hospital beds in recovery rooms. Sometimes he put flowers on graves.

Daphne was earnest, full of energy. She liked the kids best, and would sit on the floor with them, brandishing dolls and puppets, wearing nurses' whites or colored scrubs, hair pulled back in a ponytail. She looked older now, more substantial, more definite. She still smiled, though—that clear, open smile.

And sometimes, she would spring at him, throwing her arms around his neck, and he would catch her.

And if he did get tired of the work from time to time, tired of the hopelessness, it was only because he'd been too close to it for too long, and then he left the shelters and the clinics and the sickrooms and went out into the world to see it.

※　　※　　※

On an afternoon in May, the two of them stood in the tropical fish exhibit at the aquarium, in front of the shark tank. On either side, the corridors stretched on, dim but clean. The building smelled damp and briny.

Daphne was fidgeting with her hair, looking thoughtful. "Obie used to tell me about the sea, how it was large and full of salt and angelfish."

Truman thought—for the first time in a long time—of his nights in the hospital, and the memory was clear, but not painful. Obie, standing over him, speaking kindly about stars and galaxies and all sorts of miracles.

"He was good at that. Describing things, I mean." He reached for her hand, warm, inarguable. On the other side of the glass, sharks were circling.

She stood with her nose against the glass as a sand tiger shark approached, its mouth bristling with teeth. It bumped its snout against the tank and she pressed her palm to the glass in return.

He squeezed her hand. "Do you want to go get something to eat?"

"Yes." She smiled at him. "Pie."

Outside the aquarium, the sun was bright and Truman squinted. As they started down the steps, Daphne stopped abruptly and leaned against him, throwing her arms around his waist and pressing her face into his shirt. Her weight against his chest was sudden and fierce, catching him off guard. In the street, cars rushed past like water and she let him go.

He touched her cheek. "Why did you do that?"

"Because this is us—right now—you and me. Because I can."

ACKNOWLEDGMENTS

My undying gratitude belongs to:

My agent Sarah Davies, who is a rockstar in the most elegant sense.

The editorial team at Razorbill—you guys are incredible (not to mention patient). Particular thanks go to Lexa Hillyer, who got me started; Jocelyn Davies, who saw me through to the end; and Ben Schrank, who made sure we did, in fact, have a middle.

Alex, Alex, and Allison at Rights People, who help my books find homes across the world.

The miracle workers at Penguin. Especially Gillian Levinson, whose magical abilities include—but are not limited to—encouraging notes, surprise packages, and answering all-my-questions-ever; Anna Jarzab, who tames the Internet and is extraordinary on all fronts; and Casey McIntyre, who provides me with wonderful places to be and then makes sure that I get there (even when it seemed like there would never be a taxi, you didn't give up).

My critique partners, Maggie and Tess. *The Space Between* would not exist without them. Seriously, you guys. No, *seriously*. It's been three incomparable years, and we are just getting started.

My family, for being vast and far-flung and interesting, but mostly for being amazing. They bear no resemblance to the people in this book, I promise.

My classmates and professors at Colorado State University, who taught me how to start and also how to finish things, but mostly how to revise. I owe a particular debt to Professor Milofsky and my fellow novel writers, Mia, Stacy, Dave, Tom, and Zach. They were kind enough to see merit in even my most frivolous ideas and have a very high tolerance for the bizarre.

Syl. After all these years, she still reads everything and is still up for anything.

And finally, my husband, David, who ordered Chinese food night after night, never said a word about the disreputable state of my hair, and reminded me that hard work makes anything possible. This book, most of all.

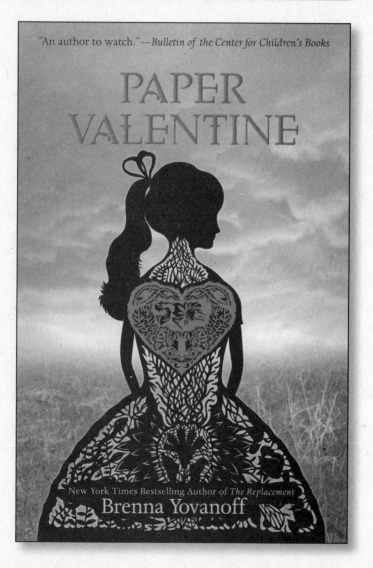